THE
ART
OF
GETTING
STARED
AT

Also by
Laura Langston

Laura Langston

THE
ART
OF
GETTING
STARED
AT

razor
bill

RAZORBILL
an imprint of Penguin Canada Books Inc., a Penguin Random House Company

Published by the Penguin Group
Penguin Canada Books Inc., 90 Eglinton Avenue East, Suite 700, Toronto, Ontario, Canada M4P 2Y3

Penguin Group (USA) LLC, 375 Hudson Street, New York, New York 10014, U.S.A.
Penguin Books Ltd, 80 Strand, London WC2R 0RL, England
Penguin Ireland, 25 St Stephen's Green, Dublin 2, Ireland (a division of Penguin Books Ltd)
Penguin Group (Australia), 707 Collins Street, Melbourne, Victoria 3008, Australia
(a division of Pearson Australia Group Pty Ltd)
Penguin Books India Pvt Ltd, 11 Community Centre, Panchsheel Park, New Delhi – 110 017, India
Penguin Group (NZ), 67 Apollo Drive, Rosedale, Auckland 0632, New Zealand
(a division of Pearson New Zealand Ltd)
Penguin Books (South Africa) (Pty) Ltd, 24 Sturdee Avenue, Rosebank, Johannesburg 2196,
South Africa

Penguin Books Ltd, Registered Offices: 80 Strand, London WC2R 0RL, England

First published 2014

1 2 3 4 5 6 7 8 9 10 (RRD)

LIBRARY AND ARCHIVES CANADA CATALOGUING IN PUBLICATION

Langston, Laura, 1958-, author
The art of getting stared at / Laura Langston.

ISBN 978-0-670-06750-3 (bound)

I. Title.

PS8573.A5832A77 2013   jC813'.54   C2014-901284-5

eBook ISBN 978-0-14-319298-5

Visit the Penguin Canada website at **www.penguin.ca**

Special and corporate bulk purchase rates available; please see
www.penguin.ca/corporatesales or call 1-800-810-3104.

For Tlell, with love

"We should not feel embarrassed by our difficulties,
only by our failure to grow anything beautiful from them."

ALAIN DE BOTTON

One

Big disasters can start small. A little hole can sink a big ship. A lone cell can grow to cancer. A single spark can burn a forest.

A video going public can burn people too.

"It's absolutely unreal!" Lexi says as we walk down the hall after school Thursday. Lockers are being slammed. People are laughing and making plans to hang out. The late September sun is warm; everybody wants to get outside and enjoy it. "It got six hundred thousand hits on YouTube in less than twenty-four hours."

It is the video I produced for a film class project.

"Six *hundred thousand* people," Lexi repeats.

My stomach flips and it's not the yogourt I had for lunch. Never, in a bazillion years, did I expect Breanne to upload our video project to YouTube. But there's a lot I didn't expect.

"That's over half a million bodies." Lexi's eyes are the size of small eggs. "And every single one of them saw your video."

Every single student at Barrington High apparently saw it too. The whispers and looks started when I got to school this morning. Six hours later, I'm still getting them.

"Think about it, Sloane."

I can't *stop* thinking about it. A piece-of-fluff video I produced with two people who betrayed and humiliated me is attracting way too much attention. And now Fisher wants to see us. No doubt he's pissed that the video went viral before we handed it in. He's probably going to dock us marks.

Thank you, Breanne.

"I can't believe you aren't more excited."

"It's a video about shoes, Lexi. *Shoes!*" Michael Moore would never do a video on shoes. I shouldn't have either. I'd let Breanne—and Matt—railroad me. In more ways than one.

We weave around a group of girls blocking our path; I hear one say, "I sent that top to the thrift store last month. Can you believe it?" They all laugh.

And then I see Mandee Lingworth crying by her locker. My stomach tightens. Those damned girls are at her again. As I march towards her, Lexi mutters, "I thought you had to see Fisher."

Fisher can wait. This can't. "Hey, Mandee. Remember what I told you last week. They're all bitches." I jerk my head to the girls behind us. "Every single one of them."

Tears wobble down her chubby cheeks. "You swore. That's bad."

I've known Mandee Lingworth since grade three. She's overweight, a little slow, and one of the kindest people I've ever met. But her easygoing nature sometimes makes her a target for bullying. "Sometimes a bad word is the best word."

"One of them said I was wearing her shirt." Her voice trembles. "It's not her shirt. It's mine."

"That's right. It is yours." Mandee has a classroom aide.

But outside of class, the aide disappears and that's when the trouble starts.

"They also said I'm too fat and it doesn't fit me right."

"Well, they're wrong." I force myself not to look down at the muffin top between her jeans and T-shirt. "All those stupid girls care about is clothes and hair and makeup. We're better than that, remember?"

Her face brightens. "Yeah, you and me don't care about that dumb stuff." She wipes away a tear and gazes at my cargo pants, my shit-kicker boots. "We both dress ugly."

Lexi snorts.

Not ugly. Practical. I can't be bothered worrying about things that don't matter. But Mandee wouldn't get it. "That's right."

"Wanna go get ice cream?"

"Another time, Mandee. I have to see Mr. Fisher."

Lexi and I start to walk. Within the space of three feet, two people give me thumbs-up signs. A third person yells, "Awesome video."

I acknowledge the recognition with a weak smile.

Lexi shakes her head. "I don't get it. This is what you've always wanted. To produce films that people watch!"

"Watch because they matter."

She wrinkles her nose. "Shoes matter. Think about how disgusting our feet would be without them. Cuts, calluses, all those germs floating around. I even read about this disease called Podoconiosis that people can absorb through the soles of their feet." She crosses her fingers. "Thank God it hasn't hit San Francisco yet."

"You are such a hypochondriac."

"It's true," she insists. "Some guy in Argentina discovered it and developed a line of shoes so all the poor peasants wouldn't get it."

I skid to a stop. "Why didn't you tell me this before? I could have used it in the video!"

"First, I didn't find out about it until I was googling symptoms on that blister that got infected. By then you were almost done. Second, why ruin a perfectly good piece of shoe porn with some depressing information about poor people and a disease only I care about?"

Shoe porn? My breath hitches in my throat. Is that what they're calling it?

"It's a good video," Lexi insists as we head through the school foyer and pass the open front doors. A warm breeze hits my face; I catch the scent of something sweet—camellias maybe. "Six hundred thousand people can't be wrong."

"The whole thing's a fluke."

"It's not a fluke, Sloane. You always do that."

The bells of Grace Cathedral ring out in the distance. The sound is soothing. For a minute, I imagine myself walking up its sweeping staircase, through the gilded bronze doors, and zoning out in front of its amazing stained glass ... or maybe sitting across the street on one of the benches in Huntington Park. Forgetting this day happened.

Lexi nudges me.

I snap back. "Do what?"

"Downplay your achievements. Underrate yourself. You have an incredible eye and great insights. The way you made those feet morph into a pair of yellow stilettos and kick the rest of the shoes off the screen ... it was amazing!"

"Yeah, amazing shoe porn."

Lexi gives me a little push. "Stop it. It wasn't all fluff. You managed to make that point about running shoes and Asian sweatshops, right?"

Two minutes worth of tape reduced to two lines. Two lines I had to fight for because Breanne and Matt both thought it didn't fit with the rest of the film. I should have known then something was going on between them. Matt has always been big on social justice. Or he had been until Breanne's boobs blinded him.

"Hey, Sloane! Sloane Kendrick!"

I turn. A tanned senior with dimples and shoulders the size of a small car comes up and high-fives me. "That was a freaking amazing video. Great job!"

A flush hits the back of my neck. Oh man, being noticed for something this stupid is ... stupid.

When he walks away, Lexi grabs my arm and squeezes. "OhmyGoddoyouknowwhothatwas?" She rattles off a name that sounds vaguely familiar followed by a pile of football statistics she clearly figures will impress me. And then she stands on her toes and peers down the hall. "I just hope Matt saw that and realizes what a tool he's been."

"Don't mention his name."

Lexi eyes me with a mix of pity and concern. "Honestly, if my guy was caught on somebody's cell doing it in a—"

My cheeks heat up again. "Don't!" I'm not ready to talk about it. When Matt and I started dating last spring, I figured it was perfect. *We* were perfect. How could it not be? We've known each other since grade six. We've been friends forever. We think alike. We care—and don't care—about the same things. Except, he's a computer geek and I'm a film nerd. He likes all-dressed chips; I like salt and pepper. Other than that, we're totally alike. Or we were.

"Revenge is sweet. Just saying."

I don't want revenge. Revenge is too good for someone who pretty much got naked in a library stall last Friday. I'm thinking murder. He crossed a line.

Nerves flutter in my stomach as we near Fisher's classroom. Matt is early for everything. He's probably already inside, most likely with Breanne. I'm so not looking forward to seeing them. My lips are stupid dry; I whip out my tube of balm.

"No, no." Lexi reaches into her purse. "You need lipstick."

"I'm good." But then I'm not. Because as we turn into the doorway, Breanne and Matt are coming out, walking arm in arm. They've obviously finished talking to Fisher. A beam of sunlight from the window frames their shoulders, making them look like a pair of live, golden Oscars. Nausea cramps my stomach.

Of all the girls in the entire school, my ex had to cheat with a member of the Bathroom Brigade, those shallow airheads who spend more time doing their makeup in the bathroom than doing their work. The same girls who bug Mandee.

Plus, he did it in public *and* got caught. I seriously thought he had more brains than that.

Obviously I was wrong.

He won't meet my gaze. But Breanne does. She tosses her two-hundred-dollar blonde streaks and gives me a triumphant smile as they saunter past. I grit my teeth. Mom has told me for years that beauty can hide a lot of ugly. She's right.

"I'll wait for you out here," Lexi says.

"It's okay. I'm heading to the hospital right after this. I'll call you later." We need volunteer hours as part of our graduation requirements so I read to sick kids once a week at the hospital where Mom works.

Fisher's at his desk, straightening a stack of DVDs. A few kids are hanging out at the back of the room arguing the merits of one director over another.

"Sloane. Thanks for coming." Fisher has the rangy build of a runner, thick grey hair that's a little too long, and an easy smile. This afternoon, however, his face is serious. "Your YouTube video is getting a lot of attention."

My scalp prickles. Damned blush is back. "Yes."

"And I'm getting calls."

Oh God, people are *complaining*?

"One call was from a friend of mine at Clear Eye."

"Clear Eye?" Clear Eye Productions is up there with DreamWorks. They're huge.

"Yes. They wanted to know who produced the video. I gave them your names."

My heart begins to thrum.

"They have a scholarship program, as you may know."

Oh, I know. Clear Eye is the Cadillac of film schools. Their scholarships are highly coveted and almost impossible to get. Just like acceptance into their film program.

"And they have invited you to apply."

Outside his window, a car horn beeps. Another car backfires. The student parking lot is emptying. "Pardon?"

Fisher smiles. "Clear Eye has invited all three of you to apply for their scholarship program."

A whooshing white sound fills my head. I can't believe

it. When I open my mouth, my vocal cords don't work. This is huge.

"Matt and Breanne aren't interested." Of course they aren't. They only took the class because they thought it would be easy. "But something tells me you might be."

Might? I've wanted to go to film school since I was twelve. My parents are against it. They're insisting I go to college and study for a career that'll be steady and reliable. That's what happens when one parent is a doctor and the other is a pilot. They're all about being practical. But my stepmother ... she's another story.

"To apply, you must submit two videos between five and ten minutes in length. The shoe video can stand as one."

Shoe porn as part of my scholarship application? I don't think so. "It's not my best work. It's too light." Clear Eye favours topics with substance.

"Apparently they want to get away from hard-hitting stuff. Something in your shoe video caught their eye." As I struggle to make sense of that, he adds, "Besides, you don't have time to produce two new pieces. The deadline is three weeks away—October sixteenth."

Three weeks to research, write, produce, and edit a video good enough to get a scholarship? "That's tight. Especially working alone. Plus, I'm only in grade eleven. It'd be eighteen months before I could enrol at Clear Eye." And only if my parents agree, which is questionable. All the reasons why I *can't* do it keep mounting. "Maybe I could apply next year? That would give me more time."

The truth is I'm scared. What if I try and fail? This is too important to screw up.

"Whoa." Fisher holds up his hand. "I understand this is overwhelming. But opportunities like this are extremely rare. I've been teaching for twenty years and this has happened only once before. Clear Eye sees something in you they like. Right now. Today. They'll hold the scholarship until you graduate next year. If it were me, I'd seize the opportunity." Fisher studies me for a minute and then adds, "I wouldn't encourage you if I didn't think you could do it. And if I didn't know how important film is to you."

I am so light-headed I could float up to the ceiling. It's the kind of opportunity people dream about. *I've* dreamed about. "But *three* weeks?"

"I'll act as an adviser, but strictly hands off, of course." He straightens the stack of DVDs on his desk. "I'll excuse you from class to do the necessary planning, scouting, and shooting, and I'll see if I can get you excused from your other classes too."

My mind is already racing through timing, topics, and treatment. "I need a second person. Someone to operate the camera." It's too much of a challenge to juggle everything myself. And the deadline leaves no time for screw-ups. "Can Matt be excused?" I'll swallow my pride and ask him to help. I have no choice. He's great with a camera.

"Matt isn't interested. But don't worry." He motions someone forward. "I have a camera operator for you."

I swivel around. When I meet a pair of laughing amber eyes, my heart flips like a dead turtle and sinks to my toes. Voice Man? a.k.a. Isaac Alexander? Fisher has to be kidding. Isaac saunters into the room from the doorway. What does he know about film?

"Hey." He grabs a chair, flips it backwards, and straddles it with his long, jean-clad legs. "How's it going, sunshine?" He gives me that lopsided smile I know so well.

Sunshine? That's what he called me last year when I figured—my thoughts skid to a stop. *Don't go there.* "I didn't think you were in this class." *You're hardly even in this school. Much. Not since you got picked up by that PR firm.*

"He is now," Mr. Fisher says dryly. "Mr. Alexander needs two arts credits and the counsellor decided this class fits with his other commitments."

Commitments like skipping school, charming girls, and doing voice-overs in his flirty baritone. I know exactly how that works. Isaac was in my socials class last winter and we teamed up for a project on Pearl Harbor. He promised to do his share of the work but all he did was flirt. At first I was charmed. I figured he liked me. I quickly realized Isaac likes all the girls. He flirted with every single one of them in that class and I ended up doing the socials project myself.

"I've agreed to take him on providing he works with you and does what you tell him to do."

What you tell him to do. Warmth creeps into my cheeks. Isaac's lower lip twitches. As we stare at each other, a weird kind of heat unfurls in my stomach. There's something about Isaac—something beyond the edginess of his wiry black dreads, smooth, brown skin, strange amber eyes. Something that draws me. Crazy but true.

He breaks the connection first, glancing down at the V of my white T-shirt. "No problem." His gaze travels lower, to my cargo pants, my "don't-mess-with-me" boots. "We've worked together before."

Not we. Me. My silly daydreaming skids to a stop. Guys

like him don't go for girls like me. I figured that out last year.

"We can start this afternoon." He flashes me another grin. "I'll buy you a coffee and we can talk about it."

And let him weave another flirt spell around me? I don't have time for that. Besides, I'd rather work with someone who knows how to run a camera. "I'm busy this afternoon."

"Tomorrow morning, then. I'll buy you breakfast. Over at the diner. Just the two of us."

Isaac Alexander flirts like he breathes—effortlessly and without thought. But I cannot be charmed by coffee or an egg wrap. Not today. I think of Matt. Possibly not ever. "I'd like Mr. Fisher to be there."

Isaac lifts his hands, an expression of mock horror on his face. "Whoa, man, as much as I like you, I'm not buying you breakfast. Sorry."

Mr. Fisher laughs. "Why don't the three of us meet before school tomorrow to discuss topics and treatments?"

Reluctantly, I agree. Isaac takes nothing seriously. I can't work with a guy like that. Or with someone who knows nothing about film. This opportunity is too big to mess up. That means I need to find another camera operator between now and tomorrow morning.

———

In order to get to UCSF Medical Center from school, I hop on a bus to downtown before transferring to the light-rail line. Traffic is heavy and I fight my impatience as the bus slowly chugs its way down Nob Hill towards the heart of the city. I'm forced to stand beside a couple of tourists— English, judging by the accent—and the man does a running commentary for his wife on what they see out the window: the Pacific-Union Club, one of the few surviving buildings from the famous 1906 earthquake; the pagodas of Chinatown; the distinctive spire of the Transamerica Pyramid. I get off near Saks Fifth Avenue, walk past people snapping pictures beside the palm trees in Union Square, and pop into a bakery to pick up sugar cookies for the kids.

Back outside, I walk quickly through the financial district, hardly noticing the throngs of business people pushing past me. I can't stop thinking about Clear Eye, or about Isaac. When I get to the Montgomery Street Station, I almost bump into a skinny saxophonist playing outside the entrance. But as soon as I see the escalators leading down to the platforms, I force myself to concentrate. Rapid transit in San Francisco is a beast of a thing with all sorts of different modes of transport and various lines—buses, streetcars, Muni Metro, and BART—and a pile of them converge at this particular station. Luckily I don't have to wait long for the line I need. As soon as we leave the tunnel on Church and come above ground at Duboce Park, I call Lexi.

She doesn't answer. Knowing we'll be heading into the Sunset Tunnel in a few minutes, I text her instead. *Invited to apply 4 Clear Eye scholarship. Need demo tape. Fisher's set me up with Voice Man.* When she doesn't respond, I'm left alone with my thoughts.

Isaac is something of a celebrity at Barrington High. Last year, a rep from a Bay Area PR firm was at the school picking up his son and he heard Isaac—aka Voice Man—doing his noon hour DJ gig. He was blown away by his voice. He got him a TV spot promoting dirt bikes and then some radio spots. Isaac's popularity soared. A local lifestyle magazine featured him on their cover as part of a story on teen talent, and just a few months ago, he started working as a DJ at a trendy local club, The Ledge. Needless to say, he has no time for noon hour DJ shifts at school anymore.

A vision of his crazy lopsided smile pops into my head as I get off on Carl Street and head towards the hospital. And he has no time for a video project either.

Besides, I can't count on him, I remind myself as I take the elevator up to the Children's Wing and walk into the nurses' lounge. Isaac Alexander is unreliable. He's a charmer. And he doesn't know the first thing about film. I'd be crazy to put a possible scholarship in his hands.

The low drone of rush hour traffic floats through the windows as I open the locker for my books and wig. The kids at the hospital know me as Miss Cookie. For those who can eat them, I provide cookies while I read. And I wear a special wig with fake plastic cookies glued onto the strands. I pull it out, give it a gentle shake, and twist my hair up under it.

Nurse Leslie Anders walks into the room. "Oh good, you're here." She looks about twelve with her freckles and ponytail. "The kids have been asking for you."

I grab my stack of books and whirl around. "You'll never believe what's happened!" Leslie is an old family friend. I tell her about Clear Eye, the demo tape, my need for a professional camera operator. "I'm going over to emerg to talk to Mom after I'm done here. Hopefully she'll pay for a freelancer."

"That would be great." Leslie fiddles with the round gold watch face pinned to her light blue uniform. "You deserve this opportunity, Sloane." But her smile is forced.

"What's wrong?"

She hesitates a second too long and my heart skips a beat. "Jade is back," she murmurs.

I stop breathing. Jade. My favourite five-year-old. Last time I saw her, we celebrated the fact that she was in remission and going home. "How bad?"

She's not supposed to tell me. Patient confidentiality and all that. But Leslie has known me since I was in diapers and this is *Jade* we're talking about.

"We don't know for sure."

I glare at her.

She glances over her shoulder to make sure nobody is nearby. "An infection," she whispers. "We're running tests."

The books I'm clutching jab my chest. That's all she needs to say. I'm a doctor's kid. I know the subtext. The cancer's back.

Leslie wishes me luck. I grab my bag of cookies and head down the hall to start multiple readings of *Don't Let the Pigeon Drive the Bus; You're Mean, Lily Jean;* and *What Do You Do With a Kangaroo?* With so many sick children, you'd expect the Children's Wing to be a sad place. But it's not usually. Sure, the parents are stressed, and if a child "leaves," the atmosphere gets heavy, but kids are generally more optimistic than the adults. Especially Jade. I save her for last.

She doesn't notice me when I reach her doorway, and that's a good thing because when I see her tiny body dwarfed by that white hospital bed and surrounded by beeping machines, my knees go weak. Her dad is beside her, his face tight with fear.

"Miss Jade!" I struggle to keep my voice upbeat as I move into the room. "How come you're back here?"

Her huge ebony eyes look droopy but she still giggles. That's my Jade. "I have a 'fection, that's how come."

My shoulder blades tighten. I cannot look at her father. "Well you know what the problem is, Miss Jade?"

"What's that?"

"We miss you around here, that's what." I manoeuvre around the thin IV trailing into her tiny hand, lean over, and scoop her into a hug. Her backbone is knife-sharp under my fingers. She's skinnier than ever. And there's another port in her chest.

Her father leaves us to get a coffee and somehow I manage to get through three stories and a pile of lame jokes that make Jade laugh. When I walk into the nurses' lounge fifteen minutes later, I'm completely wiped out. I decide to go straight home and talk to Mom about the video shoot after her shift.

Leslie appears in the doorway. "How did it go?"

I remove the wig and pick up my brush. "Fine, I guess." I point to the bag on the table. "There are a few cookies left. You can have them." Leslie's sweet tooth is notorious.

"Thanks." She picks up the bag; her eyes meet mine in the mirror. "You okay?"

"Yeah." Not really. I yank the brush through my hair. Life is so weird. Two hours ago, I was floating. Ecstatic. And now there's Jade. It's not fair.

Leslie reads my mind. "There's no point in worrying. There are treatment options."

"Right." I part my hair, move the brush to the other side. That's when I feel it. A tiny, smooth surface, slick against my finger. "What the hell?" I rub my scalp.

For a second, I think it's a chunk of conditioner I haven't rinsed out or something caught in my hair. But when I touch it a second time, my heart skips a beat. I have a bald spot. The size of a quarter. A little above my right ear.

"What's wrong?" Leslie asks.

This is too weird. I'm vaguely aware of the burble of traffic seven floors below. The ping of the hospital intercom. A muted voice calling for a radiologist.

But mostly I'm focused on *it*. The bald spot. My finger is stuck to it like one of the cookies I hot glued onto my wig. People don't get bald spots on their heads. Not unless they're old and going bald. Or sick.

"Are you okay?"

I'm not sick. Jade ... the other kids ... they're the sick ones. I'm healthy. Although right now my body is trembling like I have the flu. "I'm fine." I lower my hand. I want her to leave so I can check the rest of my head. I'm probably just reacting to the new wig. Or I caught my hair somewhere, pulled out a chunk, and didn't notice.

"I banged my head on the bathroom door at school and I have a little cut, that's all." I'm not sure why I lie. Perhaps because telling her will make this into Something and I want it to be small-n nothing. Or possibly because I feel like a baby complaining about a bald spot when there are ten cancer kids down the hall. "My scalp's a little sore, that's all."

She studies me with her "nurse look," face tilted slightly to one side, grey eyes intent and questioning. "I should get back to work then."

"Sure," I say. "Go ahead."

But she doesn't move. "I'm really sorry about Jade, Sloane. I know you have a bond."

I want her to leave. Talking about Jade makes me want to cry. Plus, I want to check my head. "Yeah, it sucks. But like you said, there are treatment options."

"Right." But she still doesn't move.

"So," I say. "See you next week."

Finally she moves to the door. "See you next week."

As soon as her pale blue nurse's uniform disappears around the corner, I spin to the mirror, yank my hair back, and stare.

Whoa. It's a bald spot all right. Pink and shiny. I touch it. It's as smooth as a baby's scalp. How bizarre is that?

Hands shaking, I separate my dark, thick hair into sections. My fingers comb through the strands, rubbing and searching. Nothing. My trembling eases. I'm fine. My hair's fine. I'm being silly. There's a logical explanation for that spot. There has to be.

And then I feel another one. It's so small that I missed it the first time. An inch above my left ear, almost directly opposite the other one.

"Shit!" Fear knifes through me, sharp and unexpected. This isn't normal. I need to see Mom. Right now.

Two

The hospital complex is huge and it takes me almost five minutes to reach street level. As I walk along the sidewalk to the emergency entrance, the low rumble of rush hour traffic and honking horns is familiar and reassuring. The spots are nothing. *Nothing.* Then an ambulance whines and my heart picks up speed.

What if they are something? What if?

I weave around a weary-looking doctor in green scrubs, a man on a scooter. When I pass a trio of laughing women, the tallest one pushes a clump of red hair off her forehead. Involuntarily, I reach up to touch my own shoulder-length dark hair. It's coarse, slightly unruly, and it needs to be trimmed every six or eight weeks just to keep it in check.

Somewhere around my ninth birthday, I'd gone through a phase where I'd wanted to be blonde. And pretty. Every once in a while, I still get that twinge—like when Matt ditched me for bimbette Breanne—but then I remember that study Mom showed me last year: half of all women think their appearance is more important than their intelligence. That's not me. That's not who I am.

Except, that doesn't mean I want to lose my hair.

By the time I reach the emergency entrance, I've convinced myself I'm overreacting, that I don't need to bother Mom with this. At least not this second. I'm not like Lexi who has a panic attack over a hangnail. She even admitted once that getting free medical advice from Mom is one of the benefits of our friendship.

As I stand there thinking about Lexi, the doors whoosh open and a gust of wind blasts me. My hair flies back. I see my reflection in the glass. I see the spot. Right here.

And my stomach does a nauseous flip. This *isn't* normal. I do need to talk to Mom. I pull my hair forward, cover the spot, and walk inside.

Emergency is always busy so I'm surprised to see empty seats in the waiting room. Only six people are sitting in the orange pleather chairs and nobody's moaning or anything.

That's pretty amazing.

It's also a sign. I head for the admitting cubicles. A sign I'm supposed to be here.

Sara, one of my favourite nurses, is on duty but she's doing an intake on a mother holding a crying baby. Take-no-shit Nancy is in the cubicle beside her and she's alone.

"Hey, Nancy."

"Sloane." She doesn't look up from the chart she's studying.

The butterflies in my stomach roll and dance as I speak to the top of her head. Nancy is a sharp, angular woman. Even her head seems to be all angles and planes. "Can you tell Mom I'm here? That I'd like to talk to her for a minute?"

She looks up then. Her flinty grey eyes narrow; her skinny lips almost disappear. "She doesn't have a minute. A flatbed truck crashed into three cars over on Third. It's ugly." She inclines her head to the waiting room. "Those guys out there are going to be waiting two hours at least."

I resist the urge to squirm. "Tell her it's important."

"Is it an emergency?"

Yes. No. Maybe?

Nancy taps her barely-there nails against the desk, arches a measly eyebrow. "Well? Is it?"

"It's not an emergency but it—" I pause. "It could be ... significant."

"Significant." She snorts. "That's a new one."

Underneath her crusty exterior, Nancy is a good nurse. And fair. I lean close and lower my voice. "Something's going on. With me. I think." There's a shift in her eyes. A softening. Just a little. Just enough. "It's private and it's important and I need to talk to Mom."

Her sigh is long and dramatic. "Give me a sec." She stands. "I'll go tell her."

She's back two minutes later. "She takes her break in half an hour. She'll meet you in the cafeteria."

In the cafeteria? I want to see her in private. And I want to see her *now*. I open my mouth to protest but Nancy speaks before I can. "That's the best I can do, Sloane. You're not dying here. Lots of young women have been in your position before. It's not the end of the world."

I flush. She thinks I'm pregnant. "I'm not—"

"Go. Go." She shoos me away with her hand. "She'll see you there in thirty."

Forty-five minutes later I'm sitting at a table in the corner, surfing WebMD on my iPhone when Mom walks in and scans the crowd. She's tall and brown eyed with a too-wide mouth that a patient once said reminded him of Julia Roberts. I stand up and wave. She waves back and heads for the food stations.

I watch her check the pasta offerings before moving on. She'll have soup. She always does. We have the same taste in food and the same sense of humour. Physically, though, I'm more like my dad—not too tall, round face, small nose. But I have Mom's hands. I stare at her head. And the same thick, dark hair. Only hers is flecked with grey, twisted into a knot, and not falling out.

"I've only got a few minutes," she warns when she finally joins me. I catch a whiff of garlic and tomato as she unloads a bowl of minestrone soup, a roll, and a cup of black coffee. "There was a messy accident over on Third and I can't be gone long." She puts her tray aside and sits down. "What's up, babe?"

A couple of interns are walking by, their trays loaded with meatloaf and salad. I wait until they pass and then I pull back my hair. "Look."

She adds pepper to her soup, gives it a stir. "What am I looking at?"

"My hair."

Disbelief blankets her face. She raises her eyebrows. "You asked me here so I could look at your *hair*?"

"Not my *hair* hair. The spot."

She scoops up some soup. "What spot?"

For an ER doctor, sometimes she can be thick. "*My* spot." I lean across the table and point. "Look. Right here."

21

I can tell the second she sees it because she goes very still. "Oh." Her spoon tilts; she lowers it to the bowl. "I see." Her index finger is cool when she touches me. "Are there more?"

"There's one on the other side." I turn my head to show her. "But it's so small I almost missed it."

She touches me a second time and she's so gentle I want to cry. "Any other symptoms? Rashes or anything like that?"

"No. Why?" She drops her hand and I stare into her eyes, trying to read what she's thinking, but her face is a careful blank. The "doctor look" I call it. "What do you think it is?"

"I don't know."

"Maybe I'm reacting to that new shampoo I bought?"

"Could be."

"You think? It's possible, right?"

"Anything's possible." She pushes her soup aside. "Your skin's sensitive; you know that."

Relief makes me giddy. Mom's right. Last year I broke out in hives when I ate too many strawberries.

"In the meantime, we need to rule everything out."

Rule everything out is not a reassuring phrase.

"We need to find you a dermatologist. So they can take some blood and run some tests."

"Blood tests?" My fear returns, dark and heavy. "This is serious then?"

"I don't think so. You've lost some hair, that's all."

"That's *all*? That's huge."

"It's all relative, Sloane. There's a guy down in ER about to lose his leg because he was in the wrong place at the wrong time." Most people wouldn't notice the wobble in Mom's voice but I do. "*That's* huge."

Ashamed, I glance at a tiny spill of pepper on the table.

And there's Jade, in the hospital again. That's huge too. "I'm sorry for him. I really am. But this is weird. Almost scary. What if I have some kind of disease? What if I'm dying?"

She smiles. "You aren't dying, *Lexi*."

I manage a weak giggle.

Mom reaches across the table and squeezes my hand. "I know you're scared but you're fine." She winks. "I'm a doctor, remember?"

"Then what is this? What's *wrong* with me?"

She squeezes my hand a second time before releasing it. "It's probably nothing but I'll make some calls and see who can fit you in."

"Soon, right?"

"It has to be soon because—" She averts her gaze, reaches for her cup. "There's been a change in my travel plans."

"What do you mean?"

She sips her coffee. "I'm flying out sooner than expected."

Mom has been volunteering in Sudan every other year since I was twelve. She usually goes for two weeks, often over Thanksgiving. She's supposed to fly out a month from now, at the end of October.

"How much sooner?"

"I'm leaving next week."

A cold chill prickles my spine. "Next week? But you know how busy specialists are. There's no way I'll get in to see one before you go." This isn't something I want to face alone. This isn't something I want to face at all.

"I'll pull some strings. I'll do my best. And if I can't go with you, your dad will."

"No!" If Dad knows, he'll tell Kim and I don't want my stepmother involved. *No* way. "I don't want him to know."

"That might be tough. I'd like you to stay with him while I'm gone."

"But you *promised* I could stay at our house. That Lexi could come and stay with me for the two weeks you're away!"

"That's the other thing." Her coffee cup clatters when she lowers it to the saucer. "Admin has extended my leave." Finally she looks at me. "I'm going for eight weeks."

"*Eight* weeks?"

Her eyes plead with me to understand. "They need me, Sloane. You know what it's like there."

I do. I know all about the village in Sudan and the poverty and the terrible medical conditions and how they rely on doctors like Mom to come in and devote their time. I'm proud of what Mom does. I am. But I need her too, especially right now. "I can't spend eight weeks with Dad." That's two months. With *Kimberly*. I'll never survive. "I ... I can't stay there. I have this—"

"I'll get you in to someone," she interrupts. "Before I go."

This demo tape to do. A possible scholarship to try for.

"We'll talk more when I get home." She stands, picks up her soup. "I need to get back. I'll wrap this to go."

I follow her to the stack of Styrofoam containers by the cashier. I don't want to wait. I want everything settled now. But that's not going to happen. "I'll see you later then."

Mom snaps the lid on her take-out container. "Promise me something, Sloane."

"What?"

"Promise me that you won't pull a Lexi."

I frown. "What do you mean?"

She steers me out the door towards the elevator. "Promise

me you won't google symptoms. Nothing good comes of that."

In spite of everything, I smile. Lexi's hypochondria is equal parts entertainment and annoyance. "I promise," I lie. WebMD was a bitch to navigate; I don't know how Lexi does it. I'll have to find an easier site when I get home.

━━

The sun is setting in streaks of coppery orange forty minutes later when I stop in front of our three-storey Edwardian and dig for my house key.

Unlike Dad, who lives in the suburbs, Mom and I live in Nob Hill, one of the best neighbourhoods in San Francisco. Our house on Jackson, which originally belonged to my grandparents, is in a coveted location just off the Hyde Street cable car line. If I feel up to tackling the hills, I can walk to a pile of places: school or downtown, the beach, and even the more touristy destinations like Chinatown or Fisherman's Wharf.

Letting myself in, I drop my knapsack on the floor and head for the kitchen, carefully avoiding my reflection in the hall mirror. Button meows at my heels. As I scoop some seafood supreme into her dish, I notice the light flashing on our answering machine.

I lunge for the play button. Maybe Mom has found a specialist. But in that second before the voice spools out, I realize I'm being stupid. Mom deals with emergencies; the spot on my head doesn't qualify. At least not to her.

Lexi's voice fills the kitchen. "*Sloane, it's me. I called your cell but you didn't pick up. Call me back STAT.*" Lexi loves to use medical terms. "*I need deets.*"

Details. Clear Eye. Mom. My hair.

I catch my reflection in the microwave and immediately turn away. Then I'm staring into the small pink hand mirror Mom has propped on the shelf above the sink. In the dining room, I come face to face with the rectangular mirror over the sideboard. We have too many mirrors in this house. I go into the hall for my knapsack.

And I am pulled to the mirror like an addict to a fix.

My blue eyes have a marblelike sheen; my skin is pasty white. But it's my hair that draws me. I separate the dark strands, looking for more spots. What if I've lost more since I took the bus home? Crazy maybe, but this whole thing is crazy; nothing makes sense.

I search twice. Just to be sure. There are still only two.

I'm relieved, but faintly disgusted by my paranoia. As I dig for my cell, I promise myself I won't look in another mirror today. And I won't google symptoms either. Not until I see a doctor and have some answers. It's too easy to become obsessed. Lexi does it all the time. Quickly I tap out her number.

"Hello?"

There's a ton of noise in the background. "Where are you?"

"At the mall with Harper and a few of the others." In the background, Harper yells out a hi. I hear a couple of other familiar voices too. Tannis, I think. Chloe maybe. The usual crowd. "We're getting some food and then catching a movie. Why don't you come down?"

"I've got stuff to do. I told you about the scholarship and—"

"I know! I can't believe it. A scholarship to Clear Eye. *Isaac A*? Really?"

"Really." I grab a handful of crackers from the cupboard and a cheese string from the fridge. "It's the opportunity of a lifetime." I repeat what Fisher told me. "But I can't work with Isaac. He knows nothing about film."

"So?" Lexi says. I hear a nasally masculine voice in the background ordering a large pepperoni with double cheese. "He's hot, Sloane. Majorly."

I almost choke on a piece of cracker. Yeah, smokin' hot. "Hot doesn't produce good videos. Besides, he's a flirt. I know his type."

Lexi groans. "Like you knew Matt's type?"

"So Matt had hidden layers I didn't know about." Ugly hidden layers. Besides, Lexi's in no position to offer me relationship advice. She and her boyfriend, Miles, have been on-again, off-again for over a year. The only way to keep up with their relationship is to watch Lexi's Facebook status, which sometimes changes three times in a day. "I can't work with Isaac. He might be cute, but he's a total slacker."

"Judgments can bite you in the ass," she adds. "I've told you that before."

Yeah, yeah. Whatever. "I have other news. Mom's going to Sudan for eight weeks."

"*Eight* weeks? That's terrible."

I wedge off a chunk of cheese. "And she wants me to stay with Dad."

"Oh no!"

"I know, right?"

"What'll I do with your mom in Sudan for two *months*?" Lexi wails. "I went to the doctor today and he thinks the only thing wrong with me is panic attacks, which is totally bogus because I have this lump on my knee!"

And I have a bald spot on my head. Two if you want to get specific. But I'm not ready to tell her yet. "Lexi! Think about *me*. Living with Dad and *Kimberly*. In Sebastian Heights. For *eight* weeks. When I have this demo to do for *Clear Eye*."

"Oh God, you're right. I'm so sorry. What can I do?"

"Help me convince Mom you and I can stay here alone for two months."

There's a long, pregnant silence. "Your mom isn't the problem," Lexi finally says. "Mine is."

She's right. Lexi's mom is uber-protective. Disappointment weighs me down. "I hadn't thought of that."

"Why don't you stay with us?" Lexi suggests.

"Could I?"

"I'll ask."

I hear the clatter of cutlery on a tray, someone yelling, "Large Hawaiian with mushrooms."

"Our food's up," Lexi says. "I'll call you in a few minutes."

And she is gone.

My vow not to google symptoms mocks me when I go upstairs and see my laptop sitting on the desk. Ignoring it, I go into the bathroom to check my hair care products. It occurs to me the spots might be an allergic reaction to my new Moroccan oil shampoo. My scalp has tingled in an itchy-burny way since I started using it.

The front of the bottle proclaims it sulfate-phosphate-paraben-free. Turning it around, I read the ingredients list. For a so-called natural product, there's nothing natural about the long list of chemicals.

I've been using this stuff for about a month. Lexi and I had been out shopping and she'd dragged me into the Sephora on Powell. Bored, I'd found myself in the hair care section where a pretty turquoise bottle had called to me. It smelled like summer in the tropics and claimed to cure frizz. I was less concerned about my hair than shutting Lexi up. I wasn't about to buy makeup to appease her, but the shampoo appealed to me. I'd even picked up the matching conditioner.

I'm reading the ingredients list on the conditioner when Lexi calls back.

"Good news and bad news," she says as I perch on the edge of the bathtub.

"You're cutting out."

"... walking ... through ... mall."

I toe the edge of our black bathmat. "What did your mom say?"

"Stay ... us ... second month ... not ... first. She needs ... guestroom."

Lexi's mom is an agent who reps writers from the Philippines. She often has authors staying with her when they tour the US.

"And I can stay with you ... the first month."

I jump up so fast I bang my arm on the shower surround. "Really? You can stay with me the whole first month?

"On the weekends," Lexi says. "Not during ... week."

My excitement fizzles. "Oh."

"Ask," Lexi orders. "Maybe your mom will go for it."

———

She doesn't.

"We've gone over this three times, Sloane. You're not staying here alone during the week." Mom is sprawled in her favourite leather armchair cradling a mug of Lemon Zinger tea. "Lexi coming on weekends isn't enough. You'll go to your father's for the first month."

"But this is an old house. Anything could happen." Button's claws are digging into my jeans. I shift her sideways; she meows in displeasure. "Remember when we went away and the pipe in the basement blew? It's safer with someone living here."

"Mrs. Abernathy is next door. She'll look after Button and watch the place." Her eyes look tired over the rim of her mug. "I don't understand, Sloane. You've stayed with Dad and Kimberly before."

"When they lived in the city." Until a year ago, Dad and Kim lived in Cow Hollow but the commute south to the airport had been too much for Dad. They've moved to a new suburb in San Mateo County. Better schools, Kim says, and much easier for Dad to get to work.

"Sebastian Heights is only twenty minutes from town."

"*If* there's no traffic. And I need to be here. You won't believe what's happened. That crazy shoe video we did got six hundred thousand hits on YouTube!"

"Sloane, that's amazing!"

"I know!" As Mom drinks her tea, I fill her in on the Clear Eye invitation and explain how Fisher is excusing me from class to work on the video. "Can you believe it? *Inviting* me to apply? It's a huge compliment."

"You're right. It is."

Mom doesn't seem all that excited. Maybe because she's tired. "Wouldn't it be amazing if I got in?"

She grimaces. "You know how your dad and I feel about this, Sloane. We're not sure film school is the place for you.

Besides, you're only a junior. You have another year of high school, and then college. You need to explore your options."

I bite my lip. I don't need to explore my options. I know what I want to do with my life, but arguing with Mom, especially when she's tired, won't get me anywhere. "I don't have to enrol right away," I placate her. "But if my video is good enough and I get a scholarship, Mr. Fisher says they might hold a place for me. It doesn't hurt to try, Mom, but it means extra work. And I can't be out in Sebastian Heights. I need to be in the city to do it."

"Oh come on, Sloane, there are lots of options for transiting in."

She's right. I can take BART, the bus, a streetcar even. But it's slower and less convenient than living at home. "I guess, but you know how weird Dad gets about me taking rapid transit at night."

She nods. "Then he can drive you in. Or Kim can."

"I'd rather eat spiders than share a car with Kim," I mutter.

Mom rolls her eyes. "Oh, for heaven's sake. I know you and Kim clash sometimes but she's your father's partner and we need to be tolerant. Besides, it's only a month. Not a life sentence."

Easy for her to say. She's never lived with Kim. The woman is so critical. And so obsessed with looks. "I need to be closer, Mom."

Sighing, she puts her tea on the coffee table. "Sloane, this is not negotiable. You're staying with your father. I'm not making alternate arrangements based on an offer I'm not crazy about."

Laura Langston

My stomach sinks. With that attitude, there's no point in asking her to finance a freelance camera operator. Maybe Dad will advance my allowance. And give me a little extra.

"Make the video if you want. But you're staying at your father's. We'll talk more about it Saturday at Ella's birthday breakfast."

Startled, I jerk upright. Button jumps from my knee in disgust. "At the breakfast?" Mom's not supposed to be going to Ella's birthday celebration. Her and Kim together? Disastrous. "But I didn't think ..." My voice trails away.

Mom pins me with a look. "That I was going?"

I flush. Crap.

"Ella called and invited me." She shakes her head. "Frankly, Sloane, I'm disappointed that you tried to orchestrate things so I was out of the loop. I expect more from you."

The heat spreads down my neck. "Sorry."

"If Ella wants me, I'm happy to go. You should know that."

"Yeah, I know." It's true. Mom will do whatever it takes to make my half-sister happy. We all will. "Don't say anything to Dad about me staying there yet okay? Maybe I can stay with someone else for the first month."

"I've already talked to your father." Mom unfolds her legs to the floor. "And I'm sure he's already discussed it with Kimberly."

"This is not a done deal," I tell Mom. "I'll stay with Lexi the second month and find someone else to stay with the first month. Harper maybe."

"Ella won't be happy."

"Ella doesn't need to know." I stand. "Did you—?"

"Call on the specialist?" Mom interjects.

I nod.

"Not yet." She stifles a yawn. "I'll call tomorrow. First thing."

Three

Mom is gone before I get up Friday morning. There's a note by the toaster: *Called in early, short staffed. See you tonight.*

Worried that someone at school will notice my spots, I root around the bathroom for hairspray or gel. All I find is an orange aerosol can of mousse that's about a thousand years old; half the writing has been rubbed off the label. Still, it pumps out a wad of white foam so I work a handful through my hair, ignoring a stab of alarm when a pile of strands comes off in my fingers. It's normal to lose hair after showering. *Normal.* I spend half an hour drying my long hair into place, making sure both spots are covered by the hair around them, and praying the mousse still has some holding power.

"Hey, Sloane," Mr. Fisher says when I walk into his classroom well before our eight o'clock meeting. He's clearly just arrived. "You're early." He stashes his blue cycling helmet under his desk and shrugs out of his windbreaker.

"I need to talk to you about Isaac."

He drinks from his stainless steel water bottle. "Sure, what's up?"

I take a breath. "I worked with Isaac last year for a socials project and, well ... I'd rather have someone who knows film. Who knows how to work a camera."

Mr. Fisher puts his water bottle down. "Isaac did an extensive project for Urban Planning last year. He used a camera for that."

Isaac took Urban Planning? I'm surprised. That class is restricted to academic students with a high GPA. I never pegged him for that type.

"Was there a problem in social studies?" His gaze is shrewd, a little too piercing. "Is there something you need to tell me?"

I flush. He thinks Isaac put a move on me. Or worse. "No, nothing like that. He was—" I hesitate. *An outrageous flirt who made me laugh. A flirt who took my number and promised to meet for coffee, but never showed up.* "He was fine, but I want to hire a freelance camera operator. This is a huge opportunity. The video is important. I want to make sure it's done right."

"I'm afraid that's not allowed."

My heart skips a beat. "What do you mean?"

"The demo tapes must be done by amateurs who are still in school. Hiring a crew or even a camera operator would automatically disqualify you."

My shoulders slump. I hadn't realized.

"However, after you left yesterday, Breanne came in and said she'd changed her mind. She'd be happy to work with you and Isaac on a second video."

Of course. Isaac being the operative word.

"She isn't interested in the scholarship," Fisher adds. "She was clear on that. She said she wanted to help you out."

Right. Like she "helped out" with Matt. "Having another person would be great but, to be honest, Breanne and I had issues on the shoe video"—*understatement of the millennium*—"and working with her is not my first choice." I must sound like a bitch—first Isaac and now Breanne—but there are limits. I can't let Breanne hijack another video. This is too big an opportunity to blow.

Fisher frowns. "You can't do this alone. Not with the time constraints."

"I'll work with Isaac then."

"Good!" His frown dissolves. "And I'd urge you to reconsider Breanne's offer. If you do accept, I'll excuse her from class as well."

I thank him, and then explain how I'd like to do the second video on Jade. "She's an amazing kid. A lot of them are, you know? They seem to take their illnesses in stride. Especially Jade. She's always laughing."

"Who's always laughing?" says a familiar voice from the doorway.

Isaac? I look at the clock. Five minutes early? What's up with that?

He pulls up a chair as Fisher fills him in. His dreads are damp from the shower; he smells of fresh air and citrus. A small silver earring flashes in the sun when he turns his head. Suddenly self-conscious, I fiddle with my hair, making sure the spot facing him is covered.

"I remember you talking about her last spring," Isaac says. "When you started the gig at the hospital."

My breath hitches. He remembers?

"She sounds cool," he adds.

I find myself softening, falling under the Isaac spell. "She is."

Mr. Fisher brings me back to earth. "A topic like that demands time, Sloane. You'd need to show progression. Jade getting and dealing with treatment. You'd need to show some kind of outcome."

"I could leave the ending nebulous."

"You could." He tents his fingers together. "But it wouldn't have the impact of something more specific. As I said yesterday, Clear Eye is moving to lighter topics. You may want to consider that."

Isaac shifts, sending his long legs sprawling across the floor with an easy grace. "What about laughter itself?"

"Laughter?"

"Jade is always laughing, right?"

I nod.

"And you want to film her." It's not a question; he knows.

I nod again.

"So we could do it on laughter and incorporate Jade and the other kids into it."

It might work. As if to underscore Isaac's suggestion, a burst of laughter erupts in the hall; someone slams a locker. The school is starting to fill up.

"Laughter as a topic has a lot of scope," Fisher says. "You could look at it from a physiological and psychological perspective." I'm not surprised Fisher has made that leap; he teaches psychology. "You could also explore funny movie outtakes or whatever else you decide on."

Isaac snaps his fingers. "We could tape people laughing at the monkeys at the zoo. A laughter yoga class."

Laughter yoga? Monkeys at the zoo? I'm not feeling it. But laughter as part of human behaviour has potential. "Where would Jade fit in?"

"Laughter as part of the healing process," Isaac says. "Because that's what it's all about for Jade, right? Healing?"

Is he feeding me a line? Saying what he thinks I want to hear? But sincerity shines from his face. I can't help myself. I am charmed. "That's right."

Fisher pushes away from his desk, a spiral-bound daybook in his hand. "I need to see the secretary about a scheduling issue. You two work out the details. We'll talk more on Monday."

I stand; Isaac does too. As we walk into the hall, I'm suddenly tongue-tied. Part of me is already preoccupied with the subject of laughter and what I might do with it, but mostly I'm consumed by the zap of electricity that races up my arm when Isaac accidentally brushes my elbow.

"We should get together this weekend," he says.

It's a logical suggestion. Yet for some stupid reason, his comment makes me think "date" and that makes my nerves jangle. Besides, he did this to me last year, suggesting more than once we get together outside of school but he never followed through. "It's kind of a busy weekend. It's my half-sister's birthday." I babble like a freakish fool and he just listens, smiling his crazy half smile and making me feel even more awkward and dumb.

"How 'bout at night? I'm DJing at The Ledge. Come down and we can talk on the break."

I shrug. As night spots go, The Ledge has a great reputation, but I'm not crazy about clubs. Too much noise. Too many distractions. "I'll see. Maybe."

"I'll leave you a couple of tickets at the door."

Half a dozen members of the Bathroom Brigade turn the corner towards us. When they spot Isaac, they all slow. In sequence. Like they've rehearsed. It's a perfect movie shot; all that's missing is the music. One straightens her sweater; another smoothes her hair. Collectively, they smile at Isaac. He smiles back. "Hey."

In terms of being attractive, I'm about average, right down the middle. It's not a bad place to be. People form opinions of me for things that matter, like how I behave or what I say—I glance at a girl flaunting her summer boob job in a low-cut pink tank—not for how I look.

"You can always call my cell," Isaac says after they pass.

I pull my gaze back to him. "Pardon?"

"My cell. If you can't make it to The Ledge, call me. My number hasn't changed from last year."

How does he know I kept it?

Behind me, a familiar voice calls out. "Isaac!" My guts turn to cement. *Oh crap. Breanne.*

"I'm glad I caught you," she says. I may as well be invisible; she doesn't even look at me. Instead she stares at Isaac like he's some kind of god. "I heard about the video we're working on." She touches his arm. Her black and grey nails look like bugs. "I can't wait to get started."

Isaac shoots me a look. "We're working in a group?"

"No." I stare at Breanne until she has no choice but to acknowledge me. Her lips are frozen in a fake smile. She is so much like Kim, pretending to like me when I know she doesn't. I cannot believe Matt dumped me for someone this shallow. "Isaac and I are working alone. Not in a group."

She drops her hand from Isaac's arm. "But—"

"I just talked to Fisher. We're clear on that." Breanne can play games and so can I. Impulsively I step closer to Isaac and lower my voice enough to imply intimacy. "I'll call you this weekend."

Isaac says something as I spin on my heel but it doesn't register. I'm too busy gloating at the look of fury on Breanne's face.

━━

I wake up Saturday morning tired from a brutal nightmare.

I was on a plane with Ella. We were flying to Sudan and Dad was piloting. Mom and Kim were flight attendants. Isaac was there and so was Breanne. Then Breanne yanked Isaac's dreads out and they floated through the plane like chunks of brown twine. Ella screamed and screamed and I tried to hide her eyes, but then Ella turned into Jade who laughed and laughed. Until the tiger came and lunged at both of us. That's when I woke up.

I hadn't fallen back to sleep until almost dawn.

Eventually, I stumble out of bed and head for the shower, a small knot of unease lodged behind my breastbone. I'm worried about Ella's birthday breakfast. About my hair. About Breanne. The video.

The hot water is soothing as it sluices down my back. I lather and rinse, letting the heat and steam and smell of lavender soap erase my nighttime fears. When it's time to do my hair, I use Mom's shampoo, pouring a dime-sized circle of the clear gold liquid into my palm. I work it in gently before rinsing and applying conditioner. But when I wash out the conditioner, I'm left with *a lot* of hair in my hand.

A tangle of the stuff. I stare at it. More of a clump than yesterday.

I lean against the cold tiles and try to make sense of things. But I can't. I can hardly breathe, never mind think. After a minute, I slip into autopilot: stand up, rinse, dry off.

I dress quickly, wrap my hair in a towel, and hurry to the bedroom. Kicking my door shut, I race to the vanity, sit down, and stare at myself in the mirror. Fear twists my stomach. I want to take the towel off but I'm scared to. Something tells me this won't be good.

Holding my breath, I pull the towel from my head. I lean into the mirror. My hair looks like it did yesterday. Exactly. I start to breathe again. "The average person loses about a hundred hairs a day," I say out loud.

It's something like that, I know it is. But then I wonder, *How many were in that clump?* It's in the bathroom trash. I could go back and dig it out. I could count.

Don't be stupid. Don't pull a Lexi.

Gently, I finger comb my hair into place, taking special care on the right to arrange more strands than usual over the bald spot. Then I start on the left side.

And freeze.

The spot feels bigger. A *lot* bigger.

I twist sideways to see my reflection. "Oh my God." The knot of unease behind my breastbone morphs into flat-out panic. The spot is twice as big as it was yesterday. As noticeable as the spot on the right. Maybe even more.

I fly down the hall and burst into Mom's room. She's

tucked and rolled into her blankets like a human sausage. "Mom!" I shake her shoulder. "Wake up!"

She bolts to a sitting position; the covers go flying. "What?" Her eyes are wide with terror. "What's wrong?"

"The other spot. It's way bigger. Probably bigger than the first one. And a pile of hair came out when I showered. I'm guessing a hundred hairs at least and I'm pretty sure that's what you're supposed to lose in an entire day, only I lost that much in *one shower*. It's in the trash if you want to see it and—"

"Slow down, babe, slow down." Mom wiggles onto her elbows. She's wearing a psychedelic orange and green Grateful Dead T-shirt. The left side of her face has a creased-road-map-going-nowhere look. "Now give this to me again."

I sink onto the edge of her bed and repeat myself, ending with, "You have to call somebody else. Today." Mom called three specialists yesterday. Two were booked solid for three months; the third hasn't called back.

She glances at the clock on her nightstand. "It's not even eight o'clock, Sloane. And it's Saturday. I doubt if I'll be able to find a specialist on the weekend."

Sweat blooms on my palms. I wipe them on my pants. "You have to find somebody. You leave in a week!"

"I will, darling, I will. Right after we see Ella."

I freeze. Ella's birthday breakfast. "I can't go out like *this*." My vision blurs; I'm about to lose it. "I can't let anybody see me." I can't let *Kim* see me. She thinks the entire world and all the people in it should be as perfect as a magazine spread.

"You have to go." Mom tosses back the covers and reaches for her robe. "Nobody will see. Not if you wear a hat."

I own three hats. A raspberry-coloured toque my grand-mother knit for me when I was five, a frayed straw hat with holes in it, and an oversized sage green vintage cap Dad found for me in New York last year. *Oversized is good,* I tell myself two hours later as I sit at the Harvest Moon Café sucking down a mango-lime smoothie. It means everything is covered.

All I have to do now is get through this birthday break-fast and then I can go home and surf the web.

Outside, a red and brown cable car clangs its way down the hill, a faint boxy outline in the morning fog. Inside, a harried server sprints past our table bearing a tray loaded with waffles and eggs. The gold and green tiffany lamp hanging over our table sways in her wake.

Ella leans towards me. "I told you it would be okay." Her blue eyes flick to the three adults who sit beside us.

Mom, casual in jeans and a cream sweater, and Dad, preppy in beige chinos and a navy polo, are discussing Bay Area development. My stepmother, Kim, with her flawless makeup and smooth, blonde hair, sits quietly beside them. She's wearing a metallic bronze cami, a faux fur vest, and leggings with thigh-high boots that lace up the back. She looks like she's ready for a photo shoot.

Ella gazes back at me. "You worry too much."

I squish a piece of icy mango between my teeth and resist the urge to scratch. Damn hat is making me itch. "You may be right."

Ella's braces glint like pink tinsel when she grins. "Of course I'm right."

When Ella had suggested me and Mom come for her birthday breakfast, I'd discouraged her. I couldn't take all three parents first thing in the morning. The negative undercurrents make me nuts. Mom and Kim tolerate each other because of me and Ella, but with only barely concealed hostility. So I told Ella I'd come but Mom wouldn't. I reminded her that the two moms didn't get along and it was probably better if my mom stayed home.

I should have known better. Ella had told them both what I'd said and, predictably, both had discounted my concerns. Coming from a broken family is a pain in the ass when the people in question adopt an air of strained civility. I envy my friends whose divorced parents don't talk. It's a lot simpler.

Ella's grin widens. "I'm always right," she adds.

Exasperation is quickly followed by the complicated devotion I feel for my nine-year-old half-sister. Correction. Ten-year-old. This morning. "Except when you're not," I tease.

She giggles and sips her pineapple juice. Ella thinks she's right about most things, most days. I can't fault her for it. We share an unfailing sense of self. I scratch my head. Along with blue eyes and the same father.

Kim leans towards me. "Must you wear a hat at the table?" she asks quietly. "It's rude."

Kim is all about appearances and always has been. The first time I had a sleepover after she and Dad were married, I came downstairs for a glass of water and overheard her telling a friend, *Sloane is so plain I'm embarrassed to be seen with her sometimes. I tried, but the fallout from her mother wasn't worth it.* So plain. She'd said it years ago, but it still hurts. "I'm fine," I say now.

"Maybe, but the hat isn't." She openly appraises me. "And painter's pants to a celebratory breakfast? Honestly, Sloane, I expect more from you."

Which is why I can't stay with her and Dad.

She leans back in her chair. "If you ever decide to make more of an effort with your appearance, I have some magazines you might want to look at."

Mom comes to my defence. "Sloane is fine. Some of us weren't born with your sense of style, *Kimberly*."

Oh man. Breakfast isn't even here and already the first Kimberly has been volleyed. How long will it be before Kim fires back with *Barbie*? Determined to avoid any more conversational icebergs, I turn the attention back to my sister. "Wasn't it great for Ella to invite us all for her birthday breakfast?"

Mom picks up my cue. "It was!" She beams at Ella. "Thanks for inviting me, darling."

A flash of displeasure darkens Kim's green eyes. She gives Mom a frosty smile. "We wouldn't dream of leaving you out, *Barbie*."

Whoa, that was fast! But instead of reacting, Mom looks at Ella and says, "Why don't you open your presents while we wait for breakfast?"

"Yes, yes!" Ella launches herself across the table and grabs a pale pink gift bag.

Who would have guessed a child from Dad's second marriage would pull us all together? It still amazes me.

I was six when Ella was born. Back then, I spent every other weekend with Dad and Kim. By the time I was eleven, they'd leave her with me for a few hours while they went to a movie or out to dinner. One memorable Saturday night,

Ella started throwing up and wouldn't stop. When Dad didn't answer his cell, I called Mom, who rushed over to help.

She'd seen Ella before, during pickups and drop-offs, but only at arm's length. That night Ella was a sick little girl. It turned out she'd eaten some tainted meat. Mom diagnosed and treated her, not leaving her side for the rest of the night.

Dad and Kim were deeply grateful. But underneath Kim's gratitude was a trickle of jealousy that rivered into something bigger. Not only was Kim jealous of the bond that formed between Ella and Mom, she was jealous of my mother's career as a doctor, though she'd never admit it. *Makeup artists save lives too,* Kim has told me more than once.

And that pretty much sums up the difference between the two women. One is substance and the other is style.

I watch Ella open a gift certificate for a facial (from Kim, naturally), some CDs from Dad, and a quilted Vera Bradley purse in a garish fuchsia and turquoise paisley (also from Kim). "Like yours!" Ella squeals. "Now we can be twins!"

Not likely. The purse Kim gave me for my birthday is way too flashy. I prefer the vintage leather satchel I found at the thrift shop last year.

I hand Ella the navy blue gift bag with sparkly gold stars. "This is from me and Barbara." I'd had to do a *lot* of wrangling to get Mom on board.

Ella paws through the yellow tissue paper to the small box inside, a sliver of pink tongue poking out between her teeth. A fierce rush of love pierces me. She is beyond beautiful, this half-sister of mine. It used to bother me the way people stared. Not anymore. Better her than me.

The box is upside down. Ella flips it over and sounds out the red letters. "V. I. R. G. I. N." Giggling, she glances from me to Mom. "Virgin?" Her voice is high-pitched and loud. "What kind of gift is a *virgin*?"

Snickers break out at the table beside us. "Lower your voice!" Kim snaps.

"You got me a *virgin* for my birthday?" Ella shrieks. "I thought a virgin was—you know—a person. Or is there another kind of virgin I don't know about?"

Mom is practically snorting with laughter. "Just open the box, Ella."

Ella removes the lid and gasps. "*A phone!* My very own phone!" She shoves the orange rectangle into Dad's face. "Look, Dad! My very, very, very *own* phone!"

All around us, people are smiling. I hear a boy two tables over ask why he can't get a phone.

Ella waves it under my nose. "Look, Sloane, it's *orange*. My favourite colour!"

"I know, goofball. I picked it out."

Kim frowns. "Not smart, Sloane. Ella is too young for a phone."

Too young for a phone but old enough for a facial? Geez Louise.

Mom tries to pacify her. "I hear you, Kim. Sloane had to work hard to convince me."

"Lots of kids Ella's age have phones," I say before sipping my smoothie. Mom was right. This has disaster written all over it. If Kim takes the damn phone back, Ella will never forgive me. But if Ella keeps it, Kim'll punish me for the next year. My head prickles. I resist the urge to scratch again.

Kim leans across the table. "Cell phones contain radiation," she whispers to Mom. "They're dangerous." My stepmother is obsessed with health. One of the cornerstones of her makeup artistry business is that she uses only natural products, and insists her clients do too (although I happen to know she makes an exception when it comes to the heavy duty hair dye she hides in her bathroom vanity).

"The jury's still out on that," Mom says. "I wouldn't worry."

Kim plays her trump card. "We can't afford it."

Dad makes good money as a pilot but Kim's income as a freelance makeup artist is only modest. And they have a large mortgage, fees for Ella's private school, and my child support to pay. As Kim often reminds me.

"Mom and I added Ella to our plan." I rustle through the box and pull out the paperwork.

"Kids under sixteen are half price," Mom adds.

Dad ignores the fury tightening Kim's face. "That's very nice. Thank you."

"Yes, thank you, thank you, thank you!" Ella is already dialing. "Look, I'm going to phone home and leave a message. Won't that be cool!"

"You can call me too," I tell her. "I programmed my number in."

Kim opens her mouth to comment but her own cell emits its familiar ring tone. Radiation danger clearly forgotten, she quickly digs through her purse and views the screen.

"Who was it?" Dad asks after she tucks the phone away.

"No one important." But her colour is up and she won't meet his gaze. Kim gets a "no one important" phone call just about every time I'm with her. Plus, when Dad's away, she sometimes goes on these mysterious "errands." I've wondered a few times if she's having an affair.

She turns to me. "I understand you'll be staying with us while your Mom's away."

"It's not for sure," I say.

"Your father told me eight weeks," Kim says. "I'd like to know. I might need you to babysit."

Big surprise.

Ella finally clues in to the conversation. "You're staying with us for *eight* weeks?" She claps her hands.

Shit, shit, *shit*. "Don't get excited, Ella. I'm staying with Lexi for part of the time. I might stay with another friend for the rest."

"You'll stay with us," Dad says firmly. "Your mother and I have already discussed it."

"I have that video to make, remember? And I have to work with this guy at school."

"But I'm giving you money to hire a freelancer."

Mom's lips form an O. "You are?"

Kim's lips tighten. "How much?"

"Turns out I'm not allowed to use one so I have to work with a classmate instead," I tell Dad. "But it'll be easier if I'm closer to the school."

"Stay with us!" Ella bounces up and down in her seat. "That would be the best birthday present ever. Please Sloane!"

I'm so furious I can't speak. Which is just as well. It's impossible to say no to Ella. Impossible.

"You *have* to stay, Sloane." Ella's blue eyes plead with me. "Promise?"

"I'll think about it, Ella Bella Boo. No promises."

"But—"

The server materializes as if I've summoned her to my

rescue, plopping down plates of eggs and bacon and waffles. "There's a guy out front who asked if he could join your table." She gestures with her head to the gift bags on the extra chair. "You might want to make room."

Ella cranes her neck. "What guy?"

Four

I t's Matt.

As he slides into the seat beside me, he avoids my gaze, though there's a touch of pink underneath his freckles. "I can't stay," he says, turning to Ella. "But I wanted to wish you happy birthday." He hands her the wrapped Clarice Bean books we picked out together a few weeks ago. The mango smoothie flips in my stomach. *Books. The library. Breanne.*

Ella goes nuts as I knew she would and Dad insists Matt have a coffee. I'm forced to push my waffle around my plate for thirty minutes while Matt and Dad talk computers and gaming and cars. Matt and I became friends during a school fundraiser when our dads volunteered at a weekend car wash. We shared a deep and mutual embarrassment over the antics of our fathers as they tried to entice drivers in from the street to get their cars cleaned. Our friendship grew out of that. The evolution from friend to boyfriend six months ago seemed natural. But now everything about it, including his presence here at breakfast, feels awkward. So when he turns to me and asks, "What's with the hat anyway?" and Kim laughs and says, "Unfortunate, isn't it?" I know it's time for him to leave.

I say my goodbyes to everybody and push back my chair. "I'll walk you out," I say to Matt.

We weave through the crowd to the front door where only a few people still wait in line. A seagull wheels overhead when we reach the sidewalk, its shrill cry piercing the morning air. I stare across the street, waiting for Matt to speak first. I can just make out the low-rise brick buildings and windswept trees in the fog, and a couple of runners heading for Aquatic Park. Out on the water, a foghorn bellows, low and mournful.

"That's great news about the Clear Eye invite," Matt finally says. "I always said you'd make it as a filmmaker."

Matt said a lot of things.

"I know that wasn't the easiest video given the circumstances and it says a lot about your skills that you turned it into something so great."

He's sucking up and I don't like it. "What's this about, Matt? Why are you here anyway?" All the fury I've stuffed down for the last few days boils to the surface. A couple of tourists look up from the oversized map they're studying. I turn my back and lower my voice. "We are *not* going out anymore. In case you missed it." I'm hurt and confused. I can't believe he did what he did. I can't believe he had the nerve to show up today.

"Just because you and I had issues doesn't mean Ella should suffer."

Issues. As in Matt wanted to take our relationship horizontal and I wasn't ready for that yet. In spite of the fact that I cared about him, something always made me hold back. Matt could be cold sometimes, and distant too. Sleeping with him just didn't feel right to me ...

"I didn't have anybody else to give the books to." He waits while a cable car clangs past. "Besides, we need to talk."

"There's nothing to talk about."

He won't meet my gaze. "Yeah, there is."

My heart lurches. Matt feels bad. He's going to apologize. He's going to admit he did a stupid thing and ask for another chance.

"Isaac is bad news."

And I will give him one because everyone d—"Pardon?"

"Isaac. You need to be careful. The guy's a player."

The two tourists brush past us; I move so we're not blocking the sidewalk. "You came here to *warn* me?"

"Mostly, yeah. We've been friends for a long time. I don't want you to be hurt." A muscle twitches in the back of his jaw. "Plus, I think you should let Breanne work with you on the video. Just because you don't like her doesn't mean she should be penalized."

"Are you *kidding?*"

Matt's mouth falls open. "No." And it hangs there.

I realize that Matt hangs his mouth open a lot. Like he's catching flies. Clearly we are less alike than I thought. My mouth never hangs open.

"She was the one who posted the shoe video to YouTube. If it wasn't for Breanne, Clear Eye wouldn't have seen it and you wouldn't have been invited to apply for a scholarship."

The fog is starting to roll in. The air is cold; I feel the chill to my bones. "That's bullshit. Fisher has contacts there. He could have sent it in."

Matt ignores me. "If Breanne could get on-camera this time, instead of just her feet, it would mean a lot. She needs another credit for her acting portfolio."

"So why didn't she say yes when Fisher asked if she wanted to help out?"

He shifts awkwardly from one foot to the other. "It didn't occur to her until later."

Until she heard Isaac was involved. "I thought you guys had hooked up. Aren't you worried about her and Isaac hanging out? Him being a player?" I taunt.

His flush deepens. "I figured she could, you know, help you keep an eye on him."

Fury dances through me. "Like she kept an eye on you?"

"That's different."

"Right. And here I thought you were going to apologize." I turn to go.

Matt frowns. "For what?"

For what? Is he really this dumb? I turn back. "Maybe for cheating on me?"

"That was unfortunate."

I am so angry I can barely form words. "*Unfortunate?*"

"Yeah, but things happen." He spreads his hands. "I like you, Sloane. I hope we can still be friends. But you're kinda intense with the whole 'film is my life' thing. Breanne, she's—"

"Easy?"

His eyes narrow. "Not easy, *easy*. Easy as in easygoing."

My throat is tighter than a closed fist. "Easygoing enough to do it in the library where everybody could see? You're just lucky the librarian didn't catch you." One of the science nerds had caught them instead, taking a picture on his cell and uploading it to Facebook while Matt and Breanne were still groping each other.

"We weren't doing *it* but I guess we could've been more discreet."

"You're an asshole, Matthew. You and Breanne deserve each other."

I turn on my heel, head for the corner. When I reach the light, Matt shouts, "FYI. That hat makes you look like a freak."

—

Matt's comments leave me feeling unhinged. I text Harper to see if she wants to hang out. I need the distraction, plus I want to see if I can stay with her when Mom is away. When she doesn't answer, I head up the hill on Columbus past the San Francisco Art Institute, in the general direction of home. My thighs burn with the effort but it gives me something else to focus on. As I walk, the fog starts to lift and eventually my mood does too. I walk through North Beach, San Francisco's answer to Little Italy, with its funky mix of apartments, cafés, and Victorian homes. When I reach Jackson Street, I decide to keep going. I head past the shops near Portsmouth Square, skirting the edges of Chinatown where the smell of shrimp dumplings and pork buns makes my mouth water, to Anthropologie downtown where Lexi works.

Since it's Saturday, the store is packed. It's no surprise, but it's not exactly conducive to a long talk. I find Lexi, grab a royal blue criss-cross T-shirt, and pretend I want to try it on. While Lexi escorts me to a change room, I tell her about Matt.

"Forget him." She knocks on one of the doors. "You've got more important things to think about." When no one answers, she opens the door and we slip inside.

Like change rooms everywhere, the place is a wall of

mirrors. I won't look; I won't. "He called me a freak." Tears prickle behind my eyes. I thought the walk had helped, but obviously not enough. Matt's words were harsh and they still sting.

Lexi hangs the T-shirt, crosses her arms, and comes to my defence. "Matt is an asshole. He's just pissed because you wouldn't sleep with him." Lexi's loyalty, which is always there when I need it, is comforting. "You're a million lifetimes from freakdom, Sloane, though I have to admit that green hat does make you look jaundiced." She sighs. "I don't know why you pretend not to care about your looks. We both know you do."

Wrong. Lexi just *wants* me to care about my looks. The familiar argument is a welcome reprieve from thoughts of Matt. "I've told you. I should have been born Muslim. The veil is liberating. It frees you from worrying about clothes and makeup and hair."

She rolls her eyes. "Yeah, yeah, blah, blah."

"Seriously! Who wanted to be a mummy for Halloween when she was nine so both of her hands would be covered in bandages?"

"There are germs on doors," she says primly.

"Yeah, and I had to knock on every single one of those doors for both of us."

Her cheeks grow pink. "I gave you extra candy, remember?"

"Forget the candy," I tease. "How's that mummy suit thing working for you these days?"

She snickers. "Do we have to talk about this?"

"Of course we have to talk about this! I'm telling you, Lexi, the burka is the answer for both of us. You'll never have to worry about another germ and it won't matter what I look like. We'll both be happy."

"Yeah, until some guy wants to kiss us."

"Trust you to get to the heart of what really matters." We both start to laugh. After a minute my gaze is drawn to the mirror. To my lips. To the hat. Covering up isn't liberating at all today.

Lexi glances at the T-shirt I chose. "Blue isn't your colour either. Why don't I bring you something else to try?"

"No thanks."

"Go home and work on your video," Lexi orders. "It'll take your mind off stuff."

It doesn't. Not really. Once I'm home, I spend some time researching laughter on my laptop, and I text Harper again. When she doesn't answer, I call her cell and leave a message asking if I can stay with her the first month Mom's away. I call a few other friends too but nobody can commit. A few minutes later I'm back on the laptop surfing. And I can't help myself: I google "hair loss." Over sixty-three million results pop up. Whoa!

I click on the top link. The first two paragraphs detail the normal cycle of hair loss and growth but paragraph three— what causes excessive hair loss—is the one that interests me the most.

Surgery can cause hair loss, I read. So can hormonal problems, having a baby, and thyroid disease. There's a section on infections; I click on it and scan the entries. Ringworm. Folliculitis. Something called Demodex. It's a wormlike creature that lives in hair follicles. I stop breathing.

Oh. My. God.

Mom taps on my door. "Sloane?"

Worms? My stomach does a queasy flip.

Mom pokes her head inside my room. "Sloane?" Her gaze lands on the laptop resting on my knees. Her lips turn down. "Oh, Sloane."

Heat hits my cheeks.

"You said you wouldn't."

"That was before I lost more hair." But I slam it shut. I could seriously throw up. *Worms?*

Her eyebrows fold into a frown. "Please don't."

"Fine. Whatever."

"I found a specialist who'll see us Monday afternoon at one."

I have film after lunch Monday and Isaac and I need to get going on the video. But I need to see the doctor too. "Can't I go Monday morning?"

"It's the best I can do, baby. He's squeezing us in right after lunch."

I should be grateful. It can take weeks, months even, to get into specialists. Maybe Isaac and I can get some planning time in at lunch. "Thanks."

"I'll write you a note for school." Mom gestures to the laptop. "And please stay off the Internet. Don't be like Lexi."

—

To avoid temptation, I stash my laptop in the dining room. Mom's prying eyes, coupled with my worry that I could go into cardiac arrest if I find any more disgusting diseases, are enough to stop me from googling symptoms.

While thoughts of my hair are never far from my mind, I spend the rest of Saturday working on the video. When I find out that men and women view laughter differently—women want someone to make them laugh while men prefer to make people laugh—I consider a gender approach. I brainstorm shoot possibilities, do a list of potential locations, a rough storyboard, and then I compose a couple of emails: one to a local professor who may be able to address gender differences and another to the hospital asking for permission to film some of the sick kids.

Sunday Mom and I go to the store to buy supplies for Sudan and I pick up the biggest can of hairspray I can find. Mom gives me a look and I know why—I need to stop obsessing. So that afternoon, I veg out in front of the TV, first watching *Pina*, a German documentary I haven't seen that focuses on the contemporary dance choreographer Pina Bausch, and then losing myself in an old favourite: *Religulous* by the crazy Bill Maher.

Monday morning, I contribute to the hole in the ozone by using a third of the can to spray my hair in place. The two spots are covered by my surrounding hair but what if I turn suddenly and my hair swings out ... or if the wind comes up? I can't take a chance that someone will see. But to be honest, I'm feeling pretty good about things. I've lost no hair since Saturday, *and* the itching on my scalp is practically gone. I'm positive it's not worms. It's probably that new shampoo. I had a reaction to it. That's all.

Isaac stops me as I'm walking to the library before first bell. "Hey, sunshine, I didn't see you at The Ledge this weekend." He's wearing a distressed black jacket that gives him a tough edge. *Isaac is bad news.* Maybe, but bad news never looked so good. "I watched for you."

I know it's a line, but my stomach still does a little tap

dance. What would it be like to have Isaac *really* looking for me? "I was busy with the video. I've got a possible shot list, a few locations we might want to scout, and a very rough storyboard." I slide my overdue library book through the slot and dig through my knapsack. "I was hoping you could look at everything."

"A storyboard?" He whistles low and deep; I almost drop my bag. "That's, like, intense. I figured we'd just wing it."

Intense. I'm beginning to hate that word. "I don't wing anything. The key to success is planning." And not succumbing to flirty guys who make whistles sound like mating calls.

His amber eyes twinkle. "I'd say the key to success is having fun and going with the flow."

Of course he'd think that. And maybe, under different circumstances ... "I've got some kind of flow going here. Though it's pretty rough because I won't know what form this thing will take until we get footage." I hand him the papers. "But it's a starting point."

He sticks them into his back pocket. "No problem. We can talk about it in film class."

"I, ah, won't be in class today. I have to leave." A telltale blush starts behind my ears. "I, ah, have a toothache." The heat creeps into my face. "I need to see the dentist."

He levels me a look. For a second I think he'll call me on the lie but then he says, "Sure. Let's meet in the library."

Does he know? I stare into his crazy gold-brown eyes, but all I see is flirty charm. "The cafeteria would be better." Without giving him a chance to respond, I turn and walk away.

Before meeting Isaac, I ditch into the bathroom to check my hair. Reassured the hairspray is still working, I head for the cafeteria where I spot Isaac immediately. He is surrounded by the Bathroom Brigade.

Of course.

I get in line for food, make small talk with Mandee, and try to figure out how I'll get Isaac alone. But, by the time I finish paying, he's sitting at an empty table by the window, and the girls—Breanne included—are two tables away watching him. They look like a pack of coyotes eying a baby bunny.

"I thought you had a toothache?" he says when I set my burger and fries down.

Shit, shit, *shit*. "I'm okay on my left side. And if it hurts too much, I've got the yogourt." And thank God for that. My storyboard and notes are on the table. I see red ink on the possible locations list. He's scribbled comments. "What did you think?"

"Pretty drawings," he drawls.

"Ouch!" I'm a lousy artist; my storyboard figures are barely stick people. "Hey, it's meant to be rough, okay?"

"Chill. I'm teasing." He dips his burrito into a container of hot sauce.

"Let me tell you how this video thing works." I point to the storyboard, explaining how the visuals and accompanying text is a rough guide only, giving me a sense of the major areas and images to be conveyed. Isaac asks a couple of questions about his role taking primary footage, how I'll handle backup audio. He says he's made arrangements to get a small extension arm that will help with shot balance and allow him to pan and tilt more easily. I'm relieved and more than a little impressed that he's done his homework and already seems to know his way around a camera.

"So as you can see from the storyboard, I have the basic video direction down but nothing definitive for the ending." Resisting the urge to shove the entire burger into my mouth, I tear off a chunk of bun and nibble at it. "A lot depends on what we get during the shoots but overall it's still lacking punch."

"What about a flash mob?"

"A flash mob?"

He swallows his last bite of burrito. "Yeah, a laughter flash mob."

It might work. In that documentary on Pina, they had an amazing segment showing a dance routine performed by different generations—teens, adults, grandparents. It wasn't a flash mob but the way they blended the visuals was impressive. Maybe we could create the same look. "We'd have to do it somewhere with lots of foot traffic."

"Somewhere like the ferry building at the Embarcadero." He gulps his chocolate milk, wipes his mouth with the back of his hand. It's a great location, down on the waterfront. The historic ferry building is gorgeous too with its Spanish-style clock tower and arched arcade look. "We'd have to promote the shit out of it," he adds, "so people would show up. Plus, we'd only be able to film it once so it's a bit of a risk, but you could weave the footage into whatever else we get. It would be powerful."

"Powerful would be great! *If* people laugh."

"They'd laugh." He tips back in his chair. "You'd have to work it, that's all."

"I'd need an A camera and a B camera for sure. One for

close-ups and the other for crowd shots. Lexi could help. She and I could each run one."

"I'm the camera operator," Isaac says. "I'll run one. Lexi can run the second one. You'll have to start the flash mob."

I almost choke on a sliver of meat. "*I'm* not going on-camera."

"Why not?"

Because I'm more comfortable behind the scenes. Because I'm not an on-camera kind of person. "I just … can't."

He rocks forward; his chair hits the floor with a soft thud. "Well, I can't. I have this agreement with the PR firm about where I can and cannot appear. Getting permission from them could take weeks. You have to do it."

Go on-camera? Not my idea of fun. But. Images spool out in my mind. How I could juxtapose the flash mob with more serious bits from the professor, from the kids at the hospital. The flash mob is fresh, light, fun. Just what Fisher said Clear Eye wanted.

"I'd still need a second camera."

He raises a brow. "You just said Lexi."

"I'm not going on-camera alone. I'll need her with me."

"What about Breanne?"

Oh man. I wish Breanne would crawl under a rock somewhere. Preferably one that weighs about a thousand pounds. "Not her."

He glances towards their table. Three girls give him a little wave. I want to gag. "She has some great ideas. And she's willing to help."

No doubt. I lean forward and lower my voice. "FYI. There was a little incident in a library stall last week. You may have heard? Breanne making out with my ex." My voice is starting to climb. I force it back down. "Only he wasn't my ex at the time."

He eyes me like I've turned into a fire hydrant or something. "*You* dated Matthew Squires? He's a total loser."

Maybe. Maybe not. But he's no longer my friend.

He shakes his head; his dreads bounce. "You're too smart for him."

I wrap up my burger with more force than necessary. "Smart has nothing to do with it." *Because obviously my brain cells were on holiday at the time.*

"Just calling it like I see it."

"Do you have no filters?"

He grins. "Filters are for coffee machines."

Why does he have to be so cute? "So, anyway, that's why I'm not working with Breanne." I pile everything back on my tray. "I need to go. But I think the flash mob is a good idea. Let's figure out the logistics tomorrow."

"Sure thing."

As I stand, he looks up at me and says, "And FYI, you're way hotter than Breanne."

My stomach does a backflip. "Nice try, Voice Man, but I don't fall for one-liners."

He just laughs.

Hotter than Breanne. I almost wish it were true.

Five

Dr. Thibodeau's office is a spacious corner suite with plush carpet, a wood-panelled wall displaying his degrees, and a bank of windows overlooking the downtown office towers.

He gestures to two chairs in front of his desk. "Have a seat. Please." He's a tall, dignified man with a shock of salt and pepper hair, piercing eyes, and a slight accent.

As Mom and I sit, he takes the leather wingback behind the desk, reaches for a pair of gold-rimmed glasses, and quickly skims the open file in front of him.

Dr. Thibodeau wasn't Mom's first choice—he's a good doctor but rather cold, she'd said Saturday—but he's the only one who could fit me in on short notice.

"Yes, right." After a minute, he removes his glasses and glances at Mom. "You gave me a brief rundown when we talked earlier." His smile is carefully neutral when he looks at me. "I understand you have some spots on your head?"

"Yes."

"When did you notice them?"

"Last Thursday."

"And what were you doing? Shampooing your hair or—"

"I was brushing my hair. By Saturday the smaller one seemed bigger." Beside me, Mom shifts in her chair. I've overreacted, I know I have, and I'm suddenly embarrassed. "But I'm sure it's an allergic reaction."

He reaches for a black pen and begins to write. "What makes you think that?"

I tell him about my new shampoo. The new wig I made to wear at the hospital. The clump of hair in the shower. The itching and burning that's basically gone now. When I'm finished, he asks if I've had a sudden weight gain or weight loss, if I've noticed any change in my energy levels.

"No," I say.

He inclines his head to a small doorway I hadn't noticed before. "Let's have a look, shall we?"

His examining room is tiny. There's a narrow bed, a built-in cupboard with a series of shallow drawers, and a couple of huge spotlights. Mom stands in the doorway while I sit on the bed. When Dr. Thibodeau switches on one of the spots, the temperature in the room shoots up about twenty degrees, making me hot and uneasy.

"Any rash?" Gently he runs his fingers over my scalp.

My chest constricts as though I can't get enough air. I force myself to take deep, even breaths. "No." He's so close I smell the coffee on his breath. I see that the gold specs on his burgundy tie are actually tiny stars.

He presses on one of the spots. "Does this hurt?"

"No." Perspiration is pooling under my arms, a combination of heat and nerves. I want this to be over.

"Any sensitivity here?" He runs his finger over a small area on the crown of my head before moving to a spot near my neck. "Or here?"

"No."

He looks behind my ears, examines my neck, presses on my lymph nodes. He even looks at my fingernails. But the fact that he asks no other questions reassures me. This is an allergy. It *has* to be.

Back at the desk, he writes a few things in my file and then he asks, "Any family history of diabetes?"

Diabetes? I didn't see diabetes mentioned on any of the sites I checked. To be fair, though, I didn't get that far after the worm scare.

Mom shakes her head. "No."

"What about arthritis?" he asks.

I sit on my hands and resist the urge to squirm. What's up with the family history?

"My mother had osteoarthritis," Mom says. "And my uncle—her brother—had rheumatoid arthritis."

He jots that down. "What about allergies, skin rashes, eczema, that kind of thing?"

"I have sensitive skin," I tell him. "I get a rash if I eat too much citrus."

He nods and then looks at Mom.

"My grandmother had severe eczema," Mom adds.

"On your mother's side?"

She hesitates. "Yes."

His eyebrow goes up just a fraction. I might have missed it if I hadn't been staring at him. The two adults share a look. My heart picks up speed. Something isn't right.

"We'll run some blood tests right away." He's still looking at Mom, not at me.

"Of course," Mom says.

"But I doubt they'll show anything."

"So it is an allergy then?" I ask.

They both turn to me. Mom's eyes are bright. Too bright, I think. Before I can process that, the doctor says, "I don't believe this is an allergy, Miss Kendrick."

My mouth is suddenly dry. "Then what is it?"

The doctor spins his pen between his fingers. "Though the blood work may say otherwise, I believe you have alopecia areata."

"Alopecia what?" I hadn't seen that when I'd searched online.

"Alopecia areata," he repeats matter-of-factly. "It's an autoimmune disease in which the immune system mistakenly attacks the hair follicles and causes hair loss."

Blood rushes to my temples. "A disease?"

"It's not life threatening," Mom quickly adds.

I'm suddenly light-headed. "But I have this new shampoo," I tell him again. "I'm sure it's an allergy. And it's just two small spots—"

"Three," he interrupts.

"I have *another one?*"

"A third one above the neck," he says. "Small but noticeable. And a possible fourth on your crown. It's a little early to tell."

My hand shakes as I touch my head. The doctor watches with vague curiosity. It's as if I'm a specimen to him, nothing more. I'm instantly and inexplicably furious. This can't be happening. I put my hand back down.

"Like your mother said, this is not a life-threatening condition, Miss Kendrick." He could be talking about the weather he's so unemotional. "You will be fine."

"Fine?" My voice comes out in a squeak. I have a disease but I'll be *fine*?

"Alopecia causes no pain, although there can be some irritation when the hair falls out. You've already experienced that with the tingling you've described."

I cannot believe this. "So you're saying I'm sick?"

"Not sick in the classic sense of the word," he says. "Patients with alopecia are generally quite healthy. Other than the disease, of course."

It doesn't make sense. None of this does. "So how do we treat it? How can I get my hair to grow back?"

A weighty silence hangs in the air. The doctor clears his throat. "That's a difficult question to answer."

My heart skips a beat. "What do you mean, difficult?"

"There are things you can try," Mom interjects. "Drugs. Injections. Ointments." She looks at the doctor for confirmation. "Am I right?"

"Yes." Dr. Thibodeau flashes her a brief smile before turning back to me. "My nurse will give you some literature. But I must be honest with you, Miss Kendrick. We don't know what causes alopecia, we don't know how to treat it, and we never know how the disease will progress."

"What do you mean how it will progress?"

"Some sufferers have minimal hair loss, but in other cases, it's more severe. Your spots could grow over next week or you could lose all of your hair. We just don't know."

Six

The closest medical lab is six blocks away; we go there right from the doctor's office. The long, skinny room smells like coffee and rubbing alcohol, and it's full of people.

"I want another opinion," I tell Mom after pulling a number from the dispenser and taking the last seat near the door. We're number fifty-two. The automated number counter on the wall is at forty-seven.

Mom stands beside me checking her BlackBerry; she doesn't answer.

"That guy's old," I mutter. The woman across from me—a wrinkled, grandmotherly type wearing support hose and a pink sweater—scowls. She can scowl all she wants; this is my life we're talking about. "He hasn't been to medical school in, like, forever," I add.

Mom is still preoccupied with her email.

The doctor said I have another spot, but as we took the elevator up to the lab, I checked my head and I couldn't find it. Plus, I haven't even had the blood work yet.

I flip through the papers his nurse gave me. There are several fact sheets on alopecia, information on alopecia support groups, a page on recent progress in hair diseases. And there are ads. Ads for Rogaine and bandanas and wigs. As I skim them, my fury grows. How *bogus*.

I nudge Mom. "That doctor said he *believes* I have alopecia." The lady across from us is staring; I lower my voice. "Believing isn't a diagnosis. What kind of doctor says *believe*? Either I have it or I don't. Plus, I'll bet the guy hasn't read a medical journal this *century*."

Mom slips her BlackBerry into her purse before looking at me. "Age has nothing to do with it, Sloane. Dr. Thibodeau is a respected and skilled dermatologist even though he is a little cool. But I warned you about that."

Cool? The guy's colder than a block of dry ice.

"I'm not taking one guy's word for this. Not when it's obvious he's not a hundred percent sure. There must be a test I can take?"

"As far as I know, there's nothing definitive." She glances at my hair and then back at my face. "Although we can get a scalp biopsy to rule out anything fungal."

"Fine. Let's do it."

"Dr. Thibodeau is requesting one," Mom says. "We talked about it when you were getting the material from his nurse. He's sending you to another dermatologist who handles scalp biopsies. You'll get the second opinion you want, and the woman specializes in alopecia."

"That's a waste of time because I don't *have* alopecia." If I had a disease, I'd know. Somewhere in my core there'd be a click, a kind of knowing, and I'm not feeling it. "I still think it's that new shampoo."

Mom slides down the wall until she's crouched beside me. "Oh, Sloanie, if this was an allergy, you'd have itching or swelling. You'd see pimples or a rash," she whispers. "But you have none of those things."

"I have itching."

"But it's mostly gone now, right?"

I don't answer.

"Let's get the blood work done and go from there." She stands back up and digs for her BlackBerry.

—

Forty minutes and four vials of blood later, we're back in the car and fighting downtown traffic. "You hungry?" Mom asks. The light ahead flashes amber; she coasts to a stop. "We could stop at Nick's for tacos."

"No, thanks. I'm fine."

Mom adjusts the rear-view mirror. "I'll order Vietnamese for later."

She's trying to be nice. Vietnamese is my favourite. "Don't bother. I'll have soup."

A cluster of people steps off the curb and heads for the other side of the street. "I don't want soup for dinner," she says. I'm so mired in my own personal hell that I don't get what she's saying until she adds, "I'm not working tonight."

"You aren't?"

She flashes me a smile that doesn't quite reach her eyes. "I thought you might want to talk."

There's nothing to talk about. On the sidewalk, a little girl wearing a bright yellow windbreaker laughs when a leaf flies off a nearby tree and lands at her feet. That shot, framed by the blue sky and the swell of people in the crosswalk, would have been perfect for our video on laughter. "You said this wasn't serious."

"It's not serious, Sloane. But I'm leaving at the end of the week and I feel bad that I'll be gone for eight weeks now instead of two. It would be nice to ..." She pauses. "To sort things out before I go."

"There's nothing to sort out," I say as the light changes. "That doctor is wrong."

Mom steps on the gas. Silence stretches out between us, taut and uncomfortable. Finally, Mom says in a too casual voice, "I borrowed some books this morning. From the Health Sciences Library over at the medical centre. They're waiting for you at home."

"Books on alopecia?"

"Yes."

My shoulders tighten as the truth dawns with startling clarity. "You agree with him. You think I have alopecia too."

Her hesitation tells me everything I need to know. "I'm not a specialist," she finally says. "But no matter what you think of Dr. Thibodeau personally, his credentials are impeccable."

"Credentials don't stop people from making mistakes!" I slump down in my seat and stare out the window. "Even doctors screw up sometimes."

And this one has.

—

After an hour at home sprawled on my bed reading the books Mom got from the medical library, it happens. I get that click deep inside, that terrible inner knowing that I can't ignore. The doctor was right. My symptoms are classic alopecia.

I fall back on my pillow and stare up at the ceiling. Nothing's changed. Yet everything has.

How am I supposed to live like this? What will people say? The questions tumble through my mind, a series of dominoes falling one on top of another. But I have no answers, and one question only raises three more, so I force myself to focus on the facts.

Most people develop two or three small coin-shaped patches of hair loss, and that's all. Most cases are mild. Suddenly cold, I reach for the spare blanket at the end of the bed and pull it to my shoulders. I do have a third spot. The doctor was right about that. It's just above my neck and the size of a garbanzo bean. And maybe a fourth on the top of my head too.

My teeth start to chatter. I'm lying right on it. What if it gets bigger because I accidentally rub it? I flip onto my side, pulling the blanket along with me. But I have spots on both sides of my head. Bigger ones. And I don't want to make them worse or stop the hair there from growing back. Except, the books say those spots probably won't produce hair for a while. Maybe even forever. There's no way of knowing. Just as there's no way of knowing how much hair I'll lose.

An image from the last book I looked at flashes through my mind. The woman was completely bald. Shivering, I tug the blanket to the tip of my nose. She was thin and unsmiling too. She looked like a concentration camp survivor.

After a while I sit up and start googling. It's a good thing Lexi isn't around to read some of the horror stories I find in one of the chat rooms. She'd be disgusted. Eventually, I smell garlic and meat and noodles. My appetite is shaky, but I'm desperate for a distraction, so I go downstairs.

"I hope you're hungry," Mom says when I walk into the kitchen. She's opening a takeout box of BBQ pork and rice vermicelli. Four more takeout cartons march along the breakfast bar like boxy white ants: eggplant with shrimp, scallion pancakes, lemongrass beef, crab spring rolls. My favourites.

"Not really."

She licks a smear of sauce from her thumb and looks up. When her eyes lock with mine, her mouth softens. "You read the books."

"Yeah." Tears ball in the back of my throat. "He was right."

Mom opens her arms. I launch myself across the room. "I could lose every single hair on my body." I sob into her shoulder, making so much noise Button comes to investigate, curling and mewling around my ankles.

"You're getting ahead of yourself," Mom murmurs as she strokes my back. "You don't know that."

When my crying slows, she hands me a box of tissues from the top of the fridge. I blow my nose and wipe my eyes while she pulls plates from the cupboard and sets them on the breakfast bar.

"You okay now?" she asks after a minute.

How can she ask that? "No, I'm not *okay*." More tears well up behind my lids. I slide onto a stool. "I take care of myself. I'm a good person. This isn't fair."

"You think you'll have a totally fair life? That you'll never be challenged?" She looks up from the cutlery she's setting out. "Come on, Sloane. A life without challenges doesn't exist."

She's right. Inexplicably I think of Jessica Cox, the star of the inspirational film *Rightfooted* who was born without arms but went on to become the world's first armless licensed pilot. Shame unfurls in my belly. I have it easy. But still ... "Losing my hair sucks."

"Yes, it sucks." She shakes a spring roll onto each of our plates and opens the small round container of sweet chili sauce. "But you haven't lost a limb. You don't have a degenerative disease. You aren't going to be confined to a bed, locked in your house, or forced to learn to walk again. You can still function in the world. Completely and fully." She dips her roll into the sauce, bites into it. "It's hair, Sloane. That's all."

That's all. My gaze travels to her hair—thick and long and out of her normal twist. It spills down her back ... a river of black flecked with silver.

"There are worse things in life than alopecia." She glances at the boxes in the corner. They're stacked three deep with books, shoes, and clothes destined for Sudan. "I know it doesn't feel that way, but trust me on that."

At Mom's urging, I manage to eat a full plate of food, even having seconds of scallion pancakes. When we're finished, she brews a pot of chai tea and pours us each a mug.

"You aren't in this alone," she reminds me. "The specialist will help you."

It's like I'm out of control, on a raft rushing down a river and there's no way to stop it. "How soon can I get in?"

"I don't know. Dr. Thibodeau's office is making the referral. We need to wait for a phone call."

"I can't wait!" I clutch the spicy tea like it's a lifeline. "I need to get treated!"

"Relax, Sloane. Stress could make things worse."

The jury's still out on that. According to the books, some studies say stress can cause alopecia but others point to auto-immune or genetic factors.

"Right now you have three spots and they're easily hidden," Mom adds. "No one can see them unless you point them out."

"Or if my hair flies up. Besides, I don't want them getting bigger. I was reading about treatments. Cortisone injections could make me gain weight or give me a rash or high blood pressure. And there are creams but one of them stains every-thing it touches brown and—"

"Dr. Paxton will help you figure out treatments," Mom interjects. "She'll outline a course of action for you."

"Soon."

"As soon as the referral goes through." Mom leans over and squeezes my knee. "You're scared and confused, babe. That's understandable. It's a lot to take in. I wish I could be here to help. But you have a good head on your shoulders. You know you're more than your looks." She pauses. "Good thing it's not Lexi dealing with this. She'd be a basket case. So would Kim and she's twenty years older."

"I *am* a basket case." My lower lip starts to tremble. "I don't want to go to school with bald patches on my head, except I have to do the video."

With Isaac. A shiver of dread snakes down my spine. I have to interview people too. And do the flash mob. Oh my *God*. "At least Mr. Fisher said he'd get me excused from classes if I needed it." And I really need it now.

"Running away is never a solution," Mom says.

Tell that to somebody caught in the crossfire of war. She puts her tea down. "You've faced challenges before and overcome them."

True. I broke my leg in three places when I was ten. I survived my parents' divorce too.

"You're strong and sensible. Stronger and more sensible than most other young women. You know that, right?"

Maybe, but am I strong enough and sensible enough to handle something this big? My throat constricts. "I know you've always told me looks aren't everything, but I don't want to look like a freak."

"You are *not* a freak," Mom says fiercely. "You're normal."

"Normal people don't lose their hair!"

"You're the same person you were last week. You're smart and caring and funny and wise. And you're going to make this family proud the way you always have by holding your head high and moving forward."

A single, hot tear rails down my cheek. Mom's right. As problems go, this isn't the worst thing in the world. It just feels like it.

"You'll use the hairspray. You'll get a hat. You'll style your hair differently—"

"A comb over? Don't be ridiculous."

"You can handle this, Sloane. I *know* you can. And you have good friends who will support you. Friends like Lexi and Harper and Chloe."

"They can't know. No one can. We don't know if this ..." I can't say the word *alopecia*. "If this *thing* is going to get worse or if this is as bad as it'll be. We don't know why I have it or how we'll treat it. People will ask questions that I won't be able to answer. I don't even want to try." I need to focus on hiding it. And getting well.

Mom frowns. "It's your choice, of course, but friends can be a support."

They'd all be grossed out. Especially Lexi. She'd probably think I had some kind of contagious disease. "Nobody else finds out," I repeat. "Not Lexi, not Harper, not Chloe. Not Dad. Not Kim. Not Ella."

"But—"

"No," I interrupt. "This is my disease and my issue and I'm going to deal with it my way."

I'm determined to show Mom that I can handle this. I'm determined to live what I've always known: that I'm more than my looks. And I'm determined, at all costs, to keep this a secret.

Seven

Before I leave for school Tuesday, I spray my hair into a helmet of steel and stuff the ugly green ball cap on my head. It's not ideal but it's all I've got. And to be honest, I'd rather people think I'm ugly than bald.

Although, really, the two go hand in hand.

I'm at my locker grabbing books for morning classes when Harper comes up. "My parents said yes! You can stay with us all month. We'll have to share a bathroom but you can have my sister's room and I told them you'd be okay with that, right?" She digs into her pocket, retrieves a key, babbling the whole time. "Here. It's for the front door. You'll need it because I'll be at volleyball practice three afternoons a week."

The diagnosis changes everything. I don't want to be in a strange house now, or even at Lexi's. I need to tell them both no.

"Uh, Harper—"

But Harper races on about how much fun it'll be to have company with her sister off at college, how she can drive us to school when her mom doesn't need the car. And I can't think of a single reason why two days after I first asked—okay, practically begged—I don't want to stay with her. So I nod and smile and stick the key into my pocket as I walk to math class.

Aside from a smirk from Breanne when the teacher asks me to remove my hat (and my escalating heart rate as I take it off), math passes in an uneventful blur of equations and formulas. Film studies is next.

"I need as much time as I can get to work on the video," I tell Fisher when I get to film studies. "So if you could get me excused from classes for the next couple of weeks that would be great." I am so grateful to Clear Eye. Not only is the scholarship the opportunity of a lifetime, but it gives me the perfect excuse to avoid everybody at school.

"I've already talked to your teachers. Other than math, that won't be a problem." Fisher nods to a couple of students who wander in and take their seats. "However it could be more difficult for Isaac to get permission."

"Did I hear my name?"

A ripple of awareness flutters down my spine. I turn, acknowledge his presence with a lift of my chin, and ignore the posse of girls behind him. He gives me a lazy, deliberate once-over. My stomach flips. *You're way hotter than Breanne.* He didn't mean it. Isaac would flirt with a chair.

"Sloane will be excused from everything but math class for the next few weeks," Fisher tells him. "However, I've spoken to your teachers and most have issues with you missing class time."

He flicks his dreads off his face, smiles that crazy half smile. "I'll talk to them. It won't be a problem."

Of course it won't be a problem. Isaac could charm the whiskers off a cat.

"Okay. Good." Fisher nods. "We're watching a series of outtakes in class today but you two don't need to be here. I suggest you go to study hall and work on the video."

Study hall is almost empty. As we sign in, I quietly tell the teacher in charge we need to discuss a project and I ask her if we can push two seats together.

"That's fine as long as you go to the back of the room." She gestures to my head. My breath slams to a halt. "No hats allowed. Please remove it."

I consider arguing but this particular teacher is a hard-ass. She'd stand her ground. And I'd look like a fool. I take my hat off. Isaac looks up from the sign-in sheet. His gaze lingers on my hair. "Ready?"

Fear turns my legs to rubber. What did he see? I used a ton of spray. It can't be wearing off already? As he leads the way to our seats, I quickly check my hair.

All there. Helmet head in place.

"You still feeling rotten?" he asks as we sit down.

Our knees accidentally brush. When I shift sideways, he lifts a brow and grins.

"I'm fine, thanks." But my words are too loud and a girl at a nearby carousel glares.

"Your tooth is better?"

"Tooth?"

"Didn't you go to the dentist yesterday?"

Crap. "Oh that. Yeah." Scared that he'll know I lied, I lay it on thick. "I had a huge cavity to fill. It's mostly better but still tender." Avoiding his gaze, I retrieve my notebook and dig through my bag for a pen.

"I think we should shoot the laughter flash mob a week Sunday," Isaac says. "It's the Columbus Day weekend and

Fleet Week. People will be in holiday mode. There'll be a ton of people at the Embarcadero."

Fleet Week is insane. The annual celebration of sailors, marines, and the coast guard draws thousands of people to the harbour to see the active military ships. The Embarcadero will be even more crowded than usual. "That's the thirteenth. The video is due in at Clear Eye by five o'clock on the sixteenth. That only leaves three days to do my final cut and write the narrative. That's tight."

"It's the best choice."

"I don't know."

"What's the issue?"

Me going on-camera. "Timing, like I said. It's way too close. Plus, I'm rethinking the whole laughter flash mob thing."

He looks at me. I stare back, resisting the childish urge to squirm. Just when I'm about to say something, anything, to break the awkwardness, he says, "Better to try and fail than not try at all."

I grin. "Nice one, Dr. Drew."

"I'm serious. You loved the flash mob idea yesterday."

Yesterday was a different life. "It's too risky. If it doesn't work, we can't reshoot." And I am *not* going in front of that camera.

"So what? Life's a giant risk. And besides, I've already texted people."

My heart starts to thrum. "You have?"

He nods. "Tons of them. The rugby guys. The stoners. A friend in drama class. Breanne and her crowd."

Oh no.

"They're psyched, Sloane. Really. You can't back out now."

Not without looking like a total tool. And raising too many questions.

"I figured we could drive over to the Embarcadero today and scout the location."

"I can't. I need to go to the hospital and talk to someone about filming the kids." It's an excuse. I could easily follow up by phone, but the less time I spend at school, the better.

"Tomorrow then?"

"I want to do the zoo tomorrow, during film class block."

"That's after lunch. What about before?"

"Don't you have a class?"

He grins. "I'll get out of it."

"I'm not sure—"

"Trust me. I'll drive us to the Embarcadero, we can scout locations and do the zoo in the afternoon. We'll stop for pizza in between. I know this great place."

Blood rushes into my head. I hate this. Everything's out of my control. My hair, the flash mob, now Isaac pushing me to go for pizza. It sounds too much like a date and that reminds me of how I got my hopes up last year when he flirted with me. I am so not Isaac Alexander's type. *So* not.

"Don't worry. I'll brown bag it."

"I'm not worrying and I'm not brown bagging it. But I need to eat."

I shrug. "Sure. Okay."

The next hour flies by as we refine the storyboard, discuss a line of questions for the psychology professor, and talk about what we'll do if the hospital turns down our permission to shoot Jade and the others.

When the bell goes, I stand. "So I'll see you tomorrow then."

Isaac stands too, only he's way too close and I step back too fast and the chair behind me goes crashing to the ground. The study hall teacher frowns.

We both bend to grab the chair, bumping heads in the process.

"Sorry, sorry." I want to sink through the floor.

But Isaac is laughing. "You're screwed now," he whispers. "Rule is when two people bump heads, they have to eat pizza together the next day."

I roll my eyes. "That is *so* lame."

"But true." He grins down at me. "I'll meet you at the front entrance after first block tomorrow."

—

While I'm at my locker getting my jacket, I text Lexi. *Won't be in planning. U around after school?*

Seconds later, I get her reply. *Whaaaaaa???????? Why?*

Lexi hates planning class, although I don't know why. She's actively planning to go to college, so the prep we do there benefits her. Me, I don't want to talk about SATs or hear about the pros and cons of one college over another. If they spent some time talking about film schools, it would be a different thing. I text her back: *Doing video stuff.*

Can't u do it at lunch?

No. I could, but I won't. *C U aftr school?*

Going 2 pick up pay check.

Perfect. *I'll go with U. Need new hat.*

Lexi's reply is a long time coming. I'm halfway to the bus stop before it hits my cell. *U need more than new hat 2 impress Isaac.*

Isaac has nothing to do with it. At all. Much. But I do need a better hat. And more hairspray.

—

The bus ride to and from the hospital takes longer than my meeting with Nurse Jeffries, which is over in five minutes. "I spoke briefly with administration after you emailed." She's a plump, British woman with springy grey curls and owlish glasses. "And they were open to your proposal."

"Excellent!" Her office door is open. I hear the *clack clack* sound of a cart being rolled down the hall. I smell soup; tomato maybe.

"But only if you focus on the clowns and avoid close-ups of the children."

My heart sinks. That would totally defeat the purpose. "I need shots of children laughing. I was hoping to show the resiliency of kids even in the face of illness."

"We would have to get permission from every single patient guardian for that. And you would also have to provide us with detailed information—where the video would be shown and in what context, that kind of thing."

That'll take time I don't have. The video has to be finished and ready to go in just over two weeks. "What if I were to take brief crowd shots and then focus on one child only?"

Nurse Jeffries frowns. "Just one?"

"I have a good relationship with Jade and her family. I wonder if I could arrange to shoot them?" It's not exploitation if Jade wants to do it. It might even give her a much-needed psychological boost.

"You need to approach them directly. If they agree, then I'll take it to administration. You'd still have to sign papers releasing the hospital from any responsibility for the final product but it certainly would be a simpler solution."

Simple is good. "I'll talk to Jade and her parents and get back to you later this week." I stand. "I assume Jade's in the same room?"

"Yes. 307."

In the hall, I weave around the lunch cart and wave to Leslie at the nurses' station but I don't stop. I'm too busy thinking about what I'll say to Jade and her parents.

As I near her room, I hear Jade's familiar voice. Smiling, I stop in the doorway. Jade rests in a nest of pillows. Her eyes and lips are downcast. My smile dissolves. She's picking absently at the white hospital blanket. She looks pale and lost and defeated. Her parents, Denver and Latanna, sit on either side of her bed.

I'm about to say hi when Jade looks over. I give her a tiny wave and force myself to smile again but she doesn't smile back. She stares right through me like I'm not there. That's when I realize: she knows me in my wig and costume as Miss Cookie, not in my jeans and green hat as Sloane.

Feeling foolish, sad, and uncertain, I drop my hand and walk quickly to the elevator. It's not the right time. I'm scheduled to read to the kids next Monday. I'll ask her then. But as I get on the elevator and the door closes behind me, I can't help wondering if the time will ever be right? If Jade's laughing days are over?

—

"I *have* to see your mom before she leaves," Lexi says a few hours later when we get off the cable car at the turnaround and head for Market Street. We weave around a group of Spanish-speaking tourists, and then pass a flower stand overflowing with buckets of colourful autumn blooms. "I need her to look at my thumb."

A woman carrying a Neiman Marcus bag cuts between us. The downtown streets are crowded with shoppers and it's another minute before I can answer. "Good luck. She's working in emerg for the next couple of days. And she's leaving early Saturday morning."

"Then I'm coming over tomorrow. Look at this." She sticks her thumb under my nose.

"Yeah, so?" I sidestep a busker blocking part of the sidewalk with his open guitar case.

"Seriously. Look." She thrusts her hand under my nose again. "The cut won't heal. And isn't that a red streak? Heading up my wrist?"

The cut on Lexi's thumb looks like a perfectly normal, three-day-old cut on its way to healing, but worrying about someone else's problem, even an imaginary one, is a welcome distraction from thinking about Jade or my hair. "Yeah. You probably shouldn't wait. You should go to the clinic right away and get it checked."

I've been checking out my own treatment options lately too, reading up on cortisone, PUVA treatments, drugs with names I can't pronounce. I want to be informed when I see the specialist.

"It's *that* bad?" Lexi jerks to a stop and stares at her thumb. "Really?"

"It could be staph." I keep walking. "You could lose your thumb. Your whole hand even."

"I knew it!" She moans. "Oh my *God*!"

I start to laugh.

She runs to catch up. "You're jerking me around."

"Only a little."

"I don't know why people won't take me seriously."

"Maybe because you're a hypochondriac?" I'm still laughing. Lexi is so fun to tease. "Isn't Miles always saying so?"

She sniffs. "Don't bring up his name. We broke up an hour ago."

And an hour from now, they'll be back together.

"My health isn't funny," she adds. "You shouldn't be laughing."

"Think of it as research," I say as we push through the doors at Anthropologie. "For our laughter video."

While Lexi heads off to collect her check, I wander through the clothes until I find the hats. When she returns a few minutes later, I'm trying on a brown pageboy with a fine weave of yellow and rust silk around the brim.

Lexi meets my gaze in the mirror. "What is up with you and hats all of a sudden?"

Alopecia is what's up. I stare at my reflection. It actually looks okay. And it comes down far enough on both sides of my head to cover the spots. "Since I have to do this laughter flash mob thing, I think it's time for a new look." I struggle to keep my tone casual. "I'm getting another hat."

"You can't." Lexi plucks the pageboy off my head and puts it back on the shelf.

I'm so stunned it takes me a few seconds to realize a chunk of spray-encrusted hair is out of place and one of my spots is showing. Quickly I cover it up. "What do you mean, I can't?"

"You aren't a hat person." Lexi grabs a newsboy cap in a pale blue houndstooth and wiggles it onto her head. She twists from side to side, studying her image in the mirror. "They don't really suit your face."

My nerves jangle. I hadn't expected resistance. At least not from Lexi. "A good salesperson could find the right hat to suit my face." I survey the store. "I'll go talk to Tannis."

Lexi whirls around. "Tannis has terrible taste. You know that."

I also know Tannis racks up the most sales of any part-timer and Lexi is trying desperately to catch up. I shrug. "Yeah. Well. I'm getting a hat. Either I pick it out or I have help. And if you won't help me ..." I let my voice trail away.

"A hat isn't enough." She eyes my baggy jeans and beige hoodie. "You need a do-over, Sloane. New clothes, proper makeup."

"Now you sound like Kim."

"Kim's right."

Heat hits the back of my neck. "I don't *think* so."

Her eyes widen. "Whoa! Don't take my head off." She puts the cap down and picks up a white beret.

I study the hats in front of me, wondering which one will do the magical trick of hiding my secret. "Then don't turn me into a statistic."

She stares at me like I just beamed in from Mars. "What are you talking about?"

"Statistics show most women under twenty-five spend

more time worrying about makeup and clothes than watching the news."

"So?"

"I have way more depth than that." I don't have time for makeup and clothes. I don't have time for my hair either. At least I didn't until I started losing it.

Lexi tilts her head to the left, examining the fit of the beret. "That's just stupid."

"No, it's not." I pick up a leopard print cloche and turn it from side to side. It's kind of out there. Especially with the bright pink ribbon. I put it back down. "We all have one bit of weirdness." When she doesn't answer, I lean close and whisper, "Some of us would walk around in mummy bandages all year if they could."

She giggles. But after a minute, she says, "Come on, Sloane. You said yourself you've got the laughter flash mob to lead and everybody will be staring at you. It only makes sense to make the best of what you've got. I don't see what the big deal is about wearing a bit of makeup."

"I wear lip gloss. I even put on mascara this morning." At least I tried to. It's not my fault the stuff in the tube had hardened into a lump. "Just because I don't bathe in makeup like Kim."

"That's what this is about, isn't it? You don't want to turn into your stepmother."

For a second I can't speak. I finally manage to say, "No, that's *not* what this is about. I'm nothing like Kim and I never will be." And thank God for that.

She puts the beret back. "That's why you dress like a slob."

Her words suck the oxygen out of me. "I *don't* dress like

a slob. My clothes are never ripped. They're always clean. I shave my pits. I wear deodor—"

She shakes her head. "I can't believe it's taken me this long to figure it out. You go out of your way to be plain because Kim goes out of her way to primp."

My palms are suddenly sweaty. I rub them against my jeans. "Don't be stupid. It has nothing to do with Kim. I refuse to obsess about my looks. I never have and I never will." Losing my hair is different. Anybody would freak over that. No girl wants to be bald.

"Right." She laughs. "You obsess just like the rest of us. Only you obsess about being different."

If she only knew.

"I'm telling you, Sloane, if you buy a hat and the rest of you looks like shit, people will stare for all the wrong reasons. You need to look halfway decent for the video."

She's right. I hadn't thought of it because I hadn't wanted to think about being in front of the camera. "So help me find a hat and I'll look at jeans."

"*Buy* jeans. And some blush."

"Look."

Lexi crosses her arms and glares at me.

"Okay, *fine*. Buy." I reach for a tweedy plum fedora with a tiny froth of feathers tucked into a wide black ribbon. "What about this one?"

Eight

Mandee is standing by the water fountain when I walk into school Wednesday morning. "You look different," she says.

My heart plummets. The only new thing I'm wearing is the hat. Everything else Lexi insisted I buy is on my bedroom floor. What looked good in the store mirror looked terrible in mine.

"It's the new hat." I tilt my head. "You like it?"

Mandee straightens and wipes her mouth with the back of her hand. "It's not just the hat. It's something else."

My stomach muscles clench. I lost a crap ton more hair in the shower this morning. The spot above my neck is bigger. And the "maybe it is, maybe it isn't" spot on my crown is more noticeable too. But you can't tell while I'm wearing the hat. I checked. "No other changes," I lie. "I'm still me."

"I dunno, Sloane." She peers into my face. "It's like you're trying to be pretty or something."

I laugh. "No." I don't do pretty. That was obvious half an hour ago when I tried on the new super skinny jeans Lexi picked out. I looked like a try-hard. A wannabe member of the Bathroom Brigade. "I just bought a new hat, that's all."

Plus two pairs of jeans, four tops, a pair of leather shoes, and some designer hairspray that's supposed to work for sensitive, damaged hair. At the price I paid, it better keep the rest of my hair on my head too.

Mandee looks at my feet and smiles. "At least you're still wearing those ugly black boots."

I smile back. "Yep." My feet aren't the problem here. Or so I think until Lexi confronts me at my locker a few minutes later.

"Why are you *still* wearing those ugly black boots? What happened to the turquoise ballerina flats we picked out?" She eyes my old jeans like they're radioactive. "And I thought you were going to wear the new jeans and that pretty tulip cardigan today?"

I spin my combination. "I have a busy day remember? Isaac and I are scouting at the Embarcadero and then shooting at the zoo. I wanted to be comfortable."

"You're not even wearing that blush I bought for you. You need to try harder."

That's harsh. I whirl to face her. "And you need to drop it."

Hurt flashes in her dark eyes. "Fine." She crosses her arms. "I'm only trying to help."

My breath hitches. I know she is. "I'm sorry, Lexi, really. It's just ..." I gesture to my head. "I'm wearing the new hat, okay? Maybe I'll wear the shoes tomorrow. We'll see." I grab my math book and slam my locker shut. "Have you seen Harper?"

"We both have socials next. Why?"

"I need to talk to her." I start walking.

Lexi runs to catch up. "Slow down!"

But I keep up the pace. I need to get to math early and get a seat in the far left corner so when the teacher insists I take off my hat, the worst spot faces the window and not the rest of the class.

"What is *up* with you? First you take my head off and now you're practically sprinting down the hall. Are you PMSing or what?"

I have to tell her. I take a deep breath. "Kim and I had a huge fight last night about me not staying with them." I'm turning into such a liar. What's scary is how easy it is. "I can't stay with Harper this month. I can't stay with you next month either."

"That's bogus."

I shrug. "Family peace and all that."

"I'll get my mom to call Kim. I'm sure she can—"

A frisson of alarm ripples down my spine. "No, no, don't do that. I'll talk to Kim and Dad again in a few days."

"If you're sure," Lexi says.

"I'm sure." What I'm sure of is that a week will give me time to come up with another excuse. Because I can't stay with Lexi or Harper or anyone else. Not when my hair is such a mess.

<hr>

San Francisco's Embarcadero area stretches for blocks along the city's waterfront, all the way from Fisherman's Wharf past the ferry building at the foot of Market towards AT&T Park. The funky mix of working piers, restaurants, and stores always draws a crowd.

"I guess we could shoot on the street here," Isaac says after he parks his van and we wait at the corner for one of the antique green trolley cars to pass. We're surrounded by people speaking English, Spanish, and a few languages I don't recognize. They all seem to be heading for the same place we are: the historic ferry building, a hub for both tourists and commuters catching one of the ferries to Sausalito or Oakland. "But shooting out back would probably be quieter," he adds.

Quieter is good. "I'm okay with that."

"Then let's cut through the terminal."

Palm trees rustle in the breeze as we cross the street and head for the white clock tower above the long, graceful building. As we get close, I see our reflection in the glass doors. My heart trampolines. I tell myself I'm checking my hair, making sure my spots are covered, but really, I am staring at us, walking side by side. Walking together.

We are a study in contrasts. Isaac in jeans and a T-shirt, tall and smiling with the camcorder hoisted on his shoulder, his dreads a dark frame to his dark skin. Me: shorter, paler, serious. A shadow of a person beside him, my hair pulled back and hidden under my new hat. So not his type.

Especially not now.

"Cool hat," he says when he catches me looking.

Is that sincerity, flattery, or Voice Man fakeness? Who knows? This *is* Isaac and I *am* female. "Thanks." I quickly change the subject. "By the way, Lexi says her boyfriend, Miles, can shoot B roll for the laughter flash mob. I confirmed it with him last night. And the prof at the University of San Francisco agreed to talk to us too."

"Excellent."

Inside the marketplace, we walk past stores, kiosks, and restaurants, weaving around people gawking at the beautiful marble archways and stunning arched ceiling. Near the back door, a little girl carrying a pink ice cream almost plows into my legs. "Watch out!" Isaac grabs my shoulder and steers me out of the way just in time.

But he doesn't drop his arm, and I want him to only I don't want him to, so I pretend the fluttery feeling in my head is normal and the press of his hip against mine is a regular thing.

Because I want it to be. Which is stupid weird ridiculous.

The salty tang of sea air is cool against my cheeks when we walk outside behind the building. Here, on the water side, a large, paved plaza overlooks the Bay. I spot a couple of sailboats in the distance. Somewhere in the water below us, sea lions bellow. Isaac grins. "Well, except for the wildlife, it'll be quieter." He stares across the plaza. "But there's lots of room and the market won't be here when we shoot."

It is today. People are lined up at stalls selling produce and sweets and savoury snacks. We make our way past a fruit stand loaded with apples and pears to a bench overlooking the water. I wait for him to drop his arm from my shoulder but he doesn't. Instead he looks at me and asks, "What do you think?"

That God gave you too much charm. That for the first time in a long time, I want to be pretty and that's just not who I am.

I ease away from him. "It could work." My hat hits his shoulder and goes sideways. I quickly straighten it. "As long as we avoid the loading areas for the ferries, we should be okay."

We wander around for the next fifteen minutes, looking

at shooting angles, camera locations, and traffic flow. My tension ramps up with each decision. I cannot believe I've gotten myself into this. By the time we decide on a spot where Lexi and I will stand, and the spots where Isaac and Miles will shoot, I am mute.

He notices. "It'll be okay." He gives my arm a casual squeeze. My heart does a not-so-casual flip. "You'll do great."

For a minute I almost believe him. But when he pulls the camcorder from its case, I snap back to reality. He's not filming me now is he? "What are you doing?"

"Taking some crowd shots for practice." He pans a group of tourists being led by a man holding a massive orange umbrella. "So I can get a handle on how the camera feels before we get to the zoo."

"We have to be discreet when we're shooting people, remember."

"As long as we limit the footage to twenty seconds or less, Fisher says we're fine."

I wander away and let him do his thing. Five minutes later, I'm back. "Let's go."

"One sec. I'm getting some good stuff."

I look past his shoulder to see what he's filming and I am horrified. "Stop!" I jab him with my elbow. "You can't shoot *them*."

He's filming a group of deaf students. Their hands are flying; their lips silently form words no one can hear. One of the girls, a petite, black-haired beauty, is almost doubled over with laughter.

Silent laughter.

"Why? Because there's no sound?"

"Not that," I hiss. "Sound can be dubbed. Just stop, okay? It's not fair."

He lowers the camera. "What's not fair?"

Why is he looking at me like that? "I dunno. For one thing, you haven't asked them. And it seems ... invasive almost."

"So it's okay to get random laughter shots from hearing people but not deaf ones?"

"I guess." His scrutiny is making me uncomfortable. "Something like that."

He switches the camera off. "They don't want special treatment. Trust me."

"How can you be so sure?"

"My brother's deaf."

I want the ground to crack open and swallow me whole. "I'm sorry."

He raises an eyebrow. "For what?"

When I don't answer, he picks up the camcorder case. "Come on, let's go for lunch."

Wild Wedge is a small, hole-in-the-wall place six blocks from the zoo. It has four tables, a counter with half a dozen stools, and a takeout window. Isaac says they make the best pizza in the Lake Merced area and pretty good cappuccino too. Judging by the line at the takeout window and the barista going crazy at the milk steamer in the corner, I believe him.

We get the last two stools at the counter. After the server takes our order, I unwrap my sandwich. "Is that roast beef on sourdough?" Isaac asks.

"Yeah." I'm not sure whether red meat is good or bad right now but we were out of peanut butter and it was my only choice.

Isaac is practically drooling.

I start to laugh. "What? Can't you wait for the pizza?"

"When there's roast beef in front of me?"

"Here." I push my untouched half towards him. "Take it."

"You sure?" But he has already picked it up.

"Yeah. If I'm still hungry, I'll have a slice of your pizza." The savoury smell of cheese and tomato sauce is killing me, except he ordered the carnivore special with double cheese, extra meat, and no veggies and that just *might* kill me. Not to mention that greasy junk food is a definite no-no. Sufferers and experts alike are unanimous on that.

"My mom and my two sisters turned vegetarian two years ago and our house has been a meat-free zone ever since." He stuffs the sandwich into his mouth. One bite and it's half gone.

"What about your dad?"

"He's a jazz musician and only home sporadically. Me and Jonas go out for steak at least once a week."

"Jonas?"

"My little brother."

Surprise flutters through me. Not that he likes steak or has two sisters, although both are news to me. But that he takes his brother out. Somehow that doesn't jive with the irresponsible, flirtatious guy I know.

"How old is he?"

"Twelve." He wipes a trace of mustard from his lips. "He's the baby of the family. With the girls in the middle and my dad on the road, we have to stick together." He smiles.

"It must be hard with him—" I hesitate.

"Being deaf?"

I nod and bite into my sandwich.

He shrugs. "It is what it is. Deaf people don't consider themselves disabled. They say they're having a different human experience."

A memory surfaces. "That was the theme of *See What I'm Saying*. You've seen that film, right?"

He shakes his head. "No."

"Oh my God!" I almost choke on a piece of roast beef. I swallow and say, "It was a *New York Times* critics pick. It won a pile of awards. It's about four deaf entertainers and one of them is a drummer with this band called Beethoven's Nightmare." I fill him in on a few of the highlights, getting more and more excited as I recall the inspirational film.

"I can't believe you were upset about me filming those deaf kids when you know all about deaf culture."

Awkward. I shift on the stool. "I don't, really. I saw one film, that's all. And I probably watch a dozen films a month, more for the production values than anything. But *See What I'm Saying* was special. Seriously!" I grab his arm. "You have to watch it. It was amazing!"

"You're amazing."

I drop his arm like it's radioactive. "Right, that's me." I giggle. "Sloane Kendrick, Ms. Amazing." I stuff my sandwich into my mouth.

"It's true. You know a pile of cool trivia. You don't follow the crowd. You're passionate about film. I like that."

At least he didn't say he liked my mind. "And you like my roast beef sandwich," I tease.

He wipes the crumbs from his fingers. "Yeah, that too."

"Excuse me." A voice from behind interrupts. "Aren't you The Voice?"

We swivel on our stools at the same time and I end up pinned between Isaac's long legs. I wiggle to try and free myself but he doesn't notice. He doesn't move either. He's too busy smiling *that* smile at the girl in front of us.

"That's me," he says.

"I thought so. I recognized you from that commercial you did for those dirt bikes." The bangles on her wrist jangle as she digs through her straw bag. She is wearing a mint green halter dress and black flip-flops. Tiny yellow daisies are painted on her toenails. "Could you give me your autograph? My little brother loves that commercial."

Isaac's smile deepens. "Glad to hear it. I'd be happy to."

He sounds so smooth. Practiced. And old. Like he's thirty-five or something. Part of me wants to look away but the other part of me is entranced. The guy who was chowing down on my roast beef sandwich and talking about his siblings is gone. The Voice is back. And in major flirt mode.

She produces a creased piece of paper and pen. "Sorry, but it's all I've got." She is angelically pretty with large, blue eyes, delicate features and Rapunzel-length blonde hair. Lucky, lucky her.

"No. This is good." Isaac leans over to take the pen and paper and breaks our leg tango. "What's your name?"

"Savannah," she says. "And my brother's name is Ben."

"Savannah." The name trips from his tongue like drops of liquid gold. I almost laugh but the tremble in the girl's lower lip stops me.

Isaac turns around and begins to write.

"Thanks." She gives me an apologetic smile. "If I'd

known I was going to see him, I would've brought something nicer." She's sweet. And nervous. Clearly overwhelmed by The Voice.

"That's okay." I want to tell her he's just an ordinary guy who drives a beat-up old van and right now has garlic-laced roast beef breath, but why burst her bubble? A little hero worship never hurt anybody. "He doesn't mind."

She visibly relaxes.

"Here you go." He hands over his autograph and digs in his pocket. "Listen, I'm hosting a gig at The Ledge this weekend. For an up-and-coming garage band called Jagged Five. Do you know where The Ledge is?"

She nods so fast I'm worried her neck will snap.

"It's by invitation only." He hands her four tickets. "It would mean a lot to me if you'd come out and support them."

Her face turns pink, then red, then a shade of purple I didn't know existed. "Thanks so much. I-um—" She looks down at the tickets in her hand, then up at him again. "Just ... thanks."

"You're welcome, Savannah. I hope you enjoy the show."

I expect him to check her out as she walks away—for sure she's his type—but there's nothing remotely predatory in his eyes as he watches her go. Mild curiosity, maybe. He doesn't even look at her ass.

"Pizza." The waitress slaps a bubbling, meat-saturated pie in front of us and hurries away.

"I hope that's the last interruption today," he says.

"No kidding." He has surprised me again. First his brother. Then Savannah. And now the video. "We'll get nothing done if we get interrupted." We need candid shots of people laughing; we'll never get them if we're being followed.

"I'm not worried about that." Cheese oozes in a long, fine string as he lifts a slice of pizza. "I'm almost out of tickets."

—

A cool wind kicks up as we walk through the gate at the San Francisco Zoo. The morning sun has given way to cloud. "I wish it was brighter," I say after we check the directory and head for the Primate Discovery Center. Although I'd look stupid wearing a wool fedora in bright sun. And I'd be too hot.

"High cloud is easier to work with," Isaac says. "Less glare and fewer shadows."

We pass the zebra enclosure. "You're right." He's done his homework. In spite of myself, I'm impressed.

We stop by the African savannah and I wait for him to adjust the settings on the camcorder. "Check out the bench to the right," I murmur. Three girls are looking at an iPhone and giggling. I study them objectively, watching their body language, reading their lips, thinking about how I might use the footage. When Isaac continues filming long after their laughter stops, I say, "Only twenty seconds, remember?"

He grins. "And not just girls, right?" He is not fooled.

When we get to the primate centre, most of the monkeys are inside. There's one outside, grooming itself in the corner. A family of five is waiting for it to do something more exciting, but people waiting doesn't make for good video.

"We could go inside and shoot," Isaac says, "but I doubt we'd have enough light."

We head for the chimpanzees. Luckily, two chimps are

out and there's a crowd, including some loud, active school kids. We discuss the pros and cons of various camera angles while surreptitiously studying people.

"Try for those kids there." I gesture discreetly with my head. "They're the most energetic."

An hour and a half later, we're done. "We got some great shots," Isaac says as we sit at the Leaping Lemur Café. After shooting people at the monkey enclosure, we wandered over to Penguin Island and got some wicked good stuff there too.

We watch the playback. The monkeys, the penguins. Lots of laughter. At one point, Isaac pans the group and catches a toddler who drops his hot dog and starts to cry. His older sister laughs.

"Laughter at someone's misfortune," Isaac says, glancing at me. "You going to use that?"

"It's real."

"Mean though."

"But honest. And that counts for something, right?"

I'm staring at the footage, watching the mother comfort her son, when suddenly I'm onscreen. Isaac has panned the crowd, and there I am.

I'm beside a woman with red hair. She's animated, fresh, vibrant. I'm all hat and washed-out face. I look like a shadow beside her. "We'll have to delete that."

"Why? You look fine."

Fine. A four-letter word that begins with *f*. Truthfully, I look like shit. I look fugly. "I'm not laughing."

"You just don't want to be on-camera."

"It doesn't matter anyway." And it doesn't. So why the sick, sinking feeling in the pit of my stomach? "Let's go."

"Sure, okay." He packs up the camera, stands, and digs into his pocket. "For you." He waves some tickets at me. The same tickets he gave to Savannah. "I hope you'll come."

I don't know if it's the sexy smoothness of his voice or the memory of how I looked on-camera, but I don't even pretend to consider it. "I'm moving my stuff to my dad's this weekend. I'll be busy."

"It would mean a lot to me if you were there." For a second I think he means it but then I remember Savannah and how he said the exact same thing, right down to the inflection in his voice, to her. "They should call you The Flirt instead of The Voice, you know that?" I tease.

"What?" His eyes widen in mock indignation. "You think I'm flirting with you?"

"Of course you are." The blush hits me like a tsunami, racing into my cheeks and down my throat. "I see right through you, Isaac Alexander."

"You do?" The corner of his lip quirks up. "Cool."

Not going there. I pluck the tickets from his fingers and stick them in my pocket. "I'll see what I can do." There's no way I'm going anywhere near The Ledge. All I can think about is how rotten I look. Even with the new hat. My stomach tightens. I can't worry about it. I can't afford to be so stupid. I have a video to produce. A scholarship to try for. That's way more important.

Or it should be.

—

Saturday morning, I'm floating in an uneasy slumber when a distant *thud, thud* trickles into my consciousness. I bury under the covers, grapple to hold onto my dream. It was something about a Ferris wheel.

"Sloane!"

The wind is howling. Sounding out my name.

"Sloane. Wake up!"

I bolt upright. Heart racing, I stare blankly at the picture of an olive grove hanging on the wall. Then I remember. I'm at Dad's. We moved my stuff last night.

"You have a phone call," Kim hollers. "It's your mother."

I toss aside the pale green duvet, jump out of bed, and grab a sweatshirt from the nearby chair. Why didn't Mom call my cell?

Kim bangs again.

"I'm coming!" I shuffle to the door, stepping over my laptop, my duffle, the file I started on the video. That's when I remember. I left my purse, with my cell, in the other room last night.

I open the door and hold out my hand, peering at Kim through slits that in another hour will become eyes. "Thanks."

Even half blind, I cannot miss her look of complete derision. "I don't deliver," she says, holding up empty hands. "And our phone stays in the kitchen. Unless it's an emergency. Which this isn't." A ghost of a smile flits across her face, or maybe that's the eye slits playing tricks on me. "Unless you count the obvious need for caffeine an emergency."

Grunting, I follow the smell of dark roast down the hall. Dad's kitchen is like something you'd see on HGTV. Dark cherry cabinets, granite counters, stainless-steel appliances. And the fancy white phone that Never Leaves The Room.

I lift up the receiver. "Hey, Mom." I'm almost afraid to put it near my face in case it picks up skin sheen. I spot a tub of pink baby wipes in the corner. Maybe I'm supposed to disinfect the thing when I'm done.

"I've just gone through security," Mom is saying, "but I couldn't leave without a final goodbye."

"You're already through security? It can't be that late?" Mom flies out at twelve twenty. I check the clock on the microwave: 11:02! I slept in.

"Clearing security can take forever. I decided to go through early. Kim says you were still sleeping. You must have had a good time last night."

I take a midnight blue mug from the cupboard and help myself to coffee. "Ella and I watched a movie. And I had trouble sleeping after."

"Huh." I hear a faint, metallic voice in the background making a final boarding announcement. "I love you, Sloanie. You know that right?"

"Of course, I know that." But her words make me feel little-girl weepy so I slug back a mouthful of coffee. And then choke. Damn, the stuff is hot. Fresh though. Gotta love that.

"Are you all right?"

"Yeah. Coffee went down the wrong way, that's all." I open the fridge and root around for coffee cream. I see skim, one percent, almond, rice, and soy milk but no cream.

"I know you have a problem with me leaving but I've made a commitment to the people in Sudan and I need to see it through."

Her going to Sudan isn't the problem. It's that she's going at the same time my hair is taking a trip too.

"I want you to know that I'm on your side," Mom says. "That I believe in you. That you're strong enough to handle whatever happens over the next couple of months."

An irrational rush of fury swamps me. Hot, vicious, and ugly. I stare into the bowels of the fridge and pretend my anger is over the lack of cream, but of course it's not. I'm jealous that Mom has her hair. I'm pissed that her life hasn't changed. I'm scared because mine has. And worried that it could change more. But I can't say that. I don't want to be childish. I don't want her to feel bad. "Sure. I know."

"Don't forget you see Dr. Paxton in three and a half weeks."

Almost four weeks but whatever. They called to confirm Thursday. "Yeah, I know." Four weeks is good as specialists go. But when your hair is falling out, it's four weeks too long.

"I have that stopover in London, but as soon as I get settled, I'll check out email and Skype possibilities, okay?"

After one more "I love you," we disconnect. I top off my coffee, go into the living room to retrieve my purse, and head back down the hall.

The house is quiet; the thick, white carpet squishes between my toes. I check Ella's room as I go past, but it's empty. She has dance on Saturday, I remember. Dad was taking her this morning. That leaves me alone with Kim.

Sounds like a good time to unpack my stuff and lay low.

When I walk into the guest room, Kim is standing beside the bed, her back to me.

I clear my throat. I'm about to ask, "What are you doing in here?" when she whirls to face me.

"What is this?" The soft voice and nostril flare are dead giveaways. She is seconds from a meltdown. Clearly furious with the stuff I've piled all over the floor.

My question dies in the back of my throat. I lick my lips. "I know. I should have cleaned up last night." I put my mug and purse on the desk and retrieve my bra and dirty socks. The laundry basket she provided for me sits empty and waiting.

Kim stares at me like I'm some kind of ghost that's taken form in front of her. A sloppy ghost. She's preppy perfect and wearing the same colours as her living room: brown denim, a V-necked white cashmere sweater, and a chunky beaded necklace in shades of green and blue. I wonder if she's expecting company and wants to be colour coordinated? I squelch a bubble of nervous laughter.

"I'll get right on it." Stepping over a suitcase, I pitch my underwear into the basket and retrieve my duffle from the floor. "Everything will be cleaned up by dinner." If it kills me.

"That's not what I'm talking about." She gestures to my pillow. "I'm talking about that."

I look past her shoulder and my blood stops. The sea foam pillow with the pretty lace trim is littered with hair.

Nine

The dark pit of panic, the one lodged permanently behind my breastbone, thumps good morning against my rib cage.

Remember? it mocks. *Remember, remember?*

As if I could forget. The duffle slides from my fingers and hits the floor with a soft plop.

The pale pillowslip is covered with curls and swirls of hair. It reminds me of a song Mom used to sing. Something about bows and flows of angel hair. And ice cream castles in the air. But this isn't a song. That's not angel hair. And I'm not a little girl dreaming of ice cream castles.

Don't look. Tears well up behind my eyes. I avert my gaze. I'm not dreaming at all. Unfortunately.

Kim is studying me. Or, more specifically, she's staring at my hair. That's when I realize: I haven't brushed it. What if she sees a spot? My gaze bounces from my duffle to my suitcase to my overnight bag. Where's my brush?

"It's nothing." I'm amazed I can speak around the lump in my throat. "Everybody loses hair, right?" I have a comb in my bag. I need to pull it out. I need Kim to leave.

And I need to call Mom. Her flight doesn't leave for over an hour. I'm sure she's still on the ground. I don't know what I'll tell her: Stay? Help? But I need to hear her voice again.

Kim steps towards me. She's so close I see the faint wrinkles radiating out from her eyes, a thin line of foundation that she didn't blend along her jaw. "My God, Sloane." Before I can move away, she reaches out and touches the spot just above my ear. "Why are you pulling out your hair?"

"I'm not!" My voice sounds strange, like I'm speaking through a tin can. "It's not what you think, okay. It's *not*."

"Then what is it?"

Is that concern in her green eyes? For a second I think so, and I'm tempted to tell her everything, but when she adds a sharp, "What's going on?" I snap back to reality. Kim is horrified and disgusted. As I expected.

Embarrassed, I turn away, only to come face to face with the pillow and all that hair. I squeeze my eyes shut. "I don't want to talk about it!"

"But—"

"Leave." Hot tears snake down my cheeks. Furious, I wipe them away. "Please. Just leave me alone."

I feel her staring at my back. I know she wants an answer but I'm not prepared to give it. Not now. Not to her.

"Fine. I'll leave. You can have a little time. Your dad and Ella will be out for most of the afternoon. But we're going to talk, Sloane. You and I. Before they come home."

＝

Forty minutes later, I'm in the middle of cleaning up when Kim knocks. "I made us some brunch," she says through the closed door. Unlike my mother, Kim is a surprisingly good cook.

I slide a blue shirt onto a hanger and put it in the closet. "I'm not hungry." So what if Kim saw something? I don't owe her an explanation. I don't need to tell her anything.

And I won't.

She opens the door and steps into the room.

I whirl around. "Excuse me! That door was *shut*. In my house, we respect that."

"And in future, I will." Her gaze is as steady as her words. I scan her face for some kind of judgment but all I see is bland indifference under a pile of makeup. "Come and eat."

"I'm not hungry," I repeat.

I've showered, dressed, combed and sprayed my hair, even put on the new jeans and a pale blue sweater Lexi swore did wonderful things for my complexion. I still feel like a slob beside Kim. What else is new? I pick up another shirt and turn back to the cupboard. At least my room is partway under control.

"Fine. You don't have to eat. But I do. And I'd like you to join me."

The last thing I want to do is sit across the table from Kim. I hang up the shirt.

"We need to talk," she says. "If you're not in the kitchen in five minutes, I'll bring my meal in here."

My stomach knots. If she does, I'll walk out. I'll leave the house if I have to. I'm not talking to Kim about my alopecia.

"I've spoken to your mother," she adds as she turns on her heel and walks out the door. "I know everything."

No freakin' way! Mom knew I wanted to keep this secret.

Like a madwoman, I dig through my purse for my cell

and punch out Mom's number. It goes straight to voice mail. Fingers shaking, I text her: *HOW COULD YOU?????*

I wait two minutes, three minutes, four minutes. She doesn't answer. No doubt she's on board by now. She's probably turned her phone off. There's a dull ache in my chest. Mom has betrayed me. Twice. Once by leaving and now by telling Kim.

I hear her out in the kitchen. She must be deliberately banging pots because this new house is solid and well built; noise doesn't travel. If I don't join her, I know she will join me in here. I can leave the house but I can't run forever. If I don't talk to Kim now, she's likely to corner me in front of Dad and Ella. And that would be disastrous.

"I made a spinach and artichoke frittata," she says when I walk into the kitchen. She's standing by the counter tossing salad with walnut oil and she's wearing a red apron shaped like a stick of lipstick. Across the top in white cursive are the words: "kiss and makeup."

"Make sure you eat the greens," she adds. "I've loaded them with nuts and goat cheese. The combo's great for your skin and hair."

Does she think she's going to *cure me*? I stare at the back of her head. I want her to glance over so I can give her the withering look she deserves but she keeps on tossing the salad. Eventually, she puts the rustic pottery bowl on the table and gestures to the counter. "There's fresh coffee too." She sits down, shakes out a teal napkin, and lays it in her lap.

I dump my cold coffee and help myself to fresh. "What's the point of coffee without cream?" I know I sound like a petulant child but I can't help myself.

"We don't drink cream."

"*I* do."

Normally Kim would lecture me on the dangers of high-fat dairy but today she is silent. She helps herself to salad before slicing into the frittata. I take the chair beside her. When she picks up her fork and begins to eat, she gazes mutely out the window at the cluster of teak loungers on the deck. My face fills with colour. Nice. She won't even look at me.

I'm dying to know what she and Mom talked about but I don't want to speak first. Childish maybe, but this whole situation is awkward with a capital *A*. Plus, the coffee is too strong without cream to temper it, and I lied when I said I wasn't hungry, so after a minute I dish out some food and begin to eat.

The frittata is rich with cheese, the way I like it, and even the salad greens aren't bad with the walnut oil. At home, I'd already be eying a second portion but I want to get this over with. *How long,* I wonder as I chew a chunk of artichoke, *will this take?*

Finally Kim looks at me. And it's not disgust I see in her eyes but pity. "We need a plan."

We? I inhale so quickly a chunk of egg sticks in my throat. I don't want her pity and I don't need her kind of help. "I don't think so. This is my issue, not yours."

She continues like I haven't spoken. "I know a good naturopath. We'll go Monday. He'll know what supplements you'll need. I'm thinking essential fatty acids and probably Vitamin D. There's a lot of research being done on D these days." She is pushing the same piece of frittata around and around the plate with her fork. "And he'll want to discuss your diet too. Obviously you'll need to avoid sweets but he may tell you to lay off wheat and dairy and maybe even meat. We'll wait until we talk to him and—"

"No, we won't."

Kim recoils like I've slapped her. "But—"

"I don't need a naturopath or anything else. I'm seeing a specialist in a month."

Her fork clatters as she drops it to the plate. "Yes, your mom told me. But that doesn't preclude you seeing someone else."

"I don't want to see anyone else. Besides, I'm reading at the hospital after school Monday."

"I'll make the appointment for Tuesday then."

"No."

"But—"

"I'm not Ella. I'm not ten. I don't need your help!"

"Stay calm." She glances nervously at my hair. "Stress will only aggravate things."

Her pseudo-soothing voice and fake concern infuriate me. "Don't tell *me* what will aggravate things. You've only known about this for five minutes. I've been dealing with it for a week. And this is a secret. Didn't Mom tell you? I'm not telling anybody. I can handle this myself."

"Your mom thinks you need support."

I need *Mom's* support, not Kim's. Kim is the last person on earth I'd choose to share this with. The tears are back, pushing against my lids. My whole damn body is beyond my control. I'm losing my hair. I can't stop crying.

I bolt for the sink. "This coffee sucks without cream." I pour it down the drain, blinking furiously to stop the tears from falling. I will not cry in front of Kim. I will *not*. I take a glass from the cupboard, help myself to water, take a few deep breaths, and sit back down.

"People are going to stare. They'll think you're sick." A tiny frown puckers the bridge of her nose. "I have clients coming to the house all the time." She worries the corner of her lip. "They don't always use the outside entrance to my studio. Sometimes they come through the house."

With Kim, it's always about appearances. "Don't worry. Your studio's in the back of the house. I'll stay out of your way."

"There are things you can get. Hair extensions. Wigs. I know someone who can help us."

This isn't about *us*. "I'm *not* getting a wig. I have a new hat."

"You'll need more than one. And something lighter than that fedora you wore yesterday. Your hair needs to breathe."

My hair doesn't need to breathe. It just needs to stay on my head. "I only have four spots. I may not get any more." An image of that pillow and all that hair flashes through my mind. The average person loses between one and two hundred hairs a day. I was right about that. This morning's hair loss was less than one hundred. I counted.

Kim's critical gaze sweeps my hair before settling on my face. "This is a chance to do something with your appearance, Sloane."

She's told me this before. *You have every opportunity to do something with your appearance and yet you don't. I just don't get it.* I brace myself for the rest of it but instead she says, "I can help with makeup. Get you in to see that naturopath," she says again. "My wig person."

I jump up from my chair so suddenly the cutlery rattles with my movement. "I don't need makeup or a wig or an appointment with a naturopath." I head for the door. "All I need is coffee cream."

And my hair.

—

The fridge is still a cream-free zone when I head into the kitchen Sunday morning. Through the glass door, I see Dad lounging on the deck wearing grey sweats and unlaced Nikes. He catches my eye and raises his mug in that universal "I need more" gesture.

I pour myself a mug, add two heaping spoons of sugar, and carry the carafe out to the deck. The sun is shining but the air is cool with a slight, salty kick. I'm glad I threw on jeans and a sweater.

After rearranging the pillow on the lounger beside him, I sit down. "Where is everybody?"

"Grocery shopping." He tops up his mug.

"This early?"

"Kim wanted to get it over with."

Fingers crossed she buys cream. And something that resembles real food. Last night for dinner she cooked a disastrous combo of spelt noodles, tofu, and chard. When Ella complained, Kim responded by saying that a vegetarian entrée was a good thing to have. But after five minutes of Ella's whining, Kim gave up and threw a dozen prefab chicken fingers in the convection oven. When I took two, she stared at me and shook her head.

"Kim left a smoothie for you in the fridge," Dad says. A red-winged blackbird swoops down to the pond, disturbing a cluster of starlings. "With raspberries and a bunch of other stuff."

A bunch of other stuff does not sound promising. Still. She didn't have to do it. "That was nice of her." I sip my coffee. Scientists have found no connection between alopecia and diet or vitamin therapy. I spent a pile of time googling last night. But anecdotal information seems to suggest cutting out junk and adding healthy food may help. It wouldn't hurt to cut back on my sugar intake.

"She told me what's going on. I've emailed your mother asking for more information."

I'm not surprised—Kim tells Dad everything—but I'm still angry. And determined. Even Mom's response to my text—*Sorry, babe, Kim needed to know*—hasn't swayed me. "I don't want *anyone* to know. You have to promise me, Dad. Promise me Kim won't say anything to anyone else."

"I can't make promises for Kim."

I clutch my coffee. "But you can talk to her. She won't listen to me. I told her this was a secret. And look. She told you."

Pain flashes in his blue eyes. "I'm your father. I have a right to know."

Heat hits my cheeks. I didn't mean to hurt him.

"Kim and I parent together. There was no way she'd keep this from me."

"It's not you specifically. I just—" He wouldn't understand.

"I get it." He gives me a half smile. His hair is early-morning messy, sticking up at all angles, making him look like a mad scientist. Mine is picture perfect, sprayed to within an inch of its life. "It's one of the few things you can control right now."

"What do you mean?"

"Life as you know it has changed and the only thing you can control is who you tell."

My mouth drops open. "How did you know?"

He winks. "Damned therapy couldn't save my marriage to your mother but it comes in handy sometimes."

The starlings lift off with a flap of wings. Dad and I watch the blackbird dive for fish.

"So you get it then? That I don't want anyone to know?"

"I get it. And I'll talk to Kim. But you need to cut her some slack. She really does try."

Tears feather the back of my throat. Kim tries all right. She tries to fix me. She's been doing it since her first date with Dad. Once she put my hair in ringlets and made me up with blush, shadow, and mascara. She even spritzed me with some great-smelling perfume. I felt so pretty, thrilled at the obvious joy she took in my appearance. When Dad dropped me at home a few hours later, I was still floating in a sweet girly-girl haze.

Mom took one look at my face and had a meltdown. She called Dad, screaming that I was not broken, that I did not need to be fixed, that I was perfectly fine the way I was. *You are better than that,* she told me after she hung up. *Better than HER. Smarter. You are MY daughter.*

And somehow I felt I had to choose. Kim or Mom. Pretty or smart. I chose Mom. I chose smart. And I've stuck with it ever since.

"I leave tonight on a seventy-three-hour shift," Dad adds, "and I need to know things are good here at home."

How can things be good when my hair is falling out? But he's waiting for an answer and I've already disappointed him once this morning. "Yes, Dad," I say. "Things will be good. I'll make sure of it."

An hour later I'm not sure I can. I'm sitting at the desk studying Isaac's footage on the camcorder, which I brought home from school Friday, when Ella bursts into my room. After deleting the last visual of my pasty white face from the zoo footage, I turn to her. "There's such a thing as knocking you know."

"Sorry, sorry." But she's grinning like a goofy clown and doesn't look sorry at all. She waves a familiar taupe Nordstrom bag in the air. "Mom bought us some new makeup."

A headache starts at the base of my skull. I have better things to do than play with makeup. Forget makeup. I am obsessed with hair. Even as I played with the footage and tried to focus on content and presentation, I found myself staring at people's heads. Comparing their hair to mine. Wondering what I could do to stop this nightmare. And then mentally beating myself up for being so dumb.

"Come on!" She bounces over to the vanity and digs through the bag, removing a small rectangle that looks like blush. "It's for both of us. Mom said we could try it together."

Of course she did. Kim has involved Ella on purpose. She knows I have a hell of a time saying no to my half-sister. If I complain, Kim will accuse me of overreacting. Imagining things. Being ungrateful. "I don't wear much makeup. You know that."

"That's dumb. Makeup is fun."

If that's all it was, I'd be okay with it. But some women make their appearance their life's work, and I don't want Ella to become one of them. I love her too much for that. "You're too young to wear that stuff." *Even if your mother doesn't think so.*

"No, I'm not." She opens the blush and removes the brush. "I have a cell phone now."

Ella logic. My headache intensifies.

She perches on the small vanity stool. I watch her brush a plum-sized circle of dark pink blush on her right cheek. When she starts on the other side, I jump up to help. "It's too heavy." She looks like a clown. And she's gotten powder on her white sweatshirt too. I brush it away. "You know you don't need this stuff to be pretty, right?" She doesn't. Her cheeks are naturally rosy. Unlike me. I inherited Mom's translucent skin.

"I know."

"You need to be yourself. I've told you that before."

She nods.

"You have lots to offer the world, right?" In my pocket, my phone signals a text message; I ignore it.

"Right." But I've said this to her so many times her "right" sounds automatic.

I feel the heat from her skin, smell the lemony cinnamon scent of her. My own skin prickles with nerves. What if she sees one of my spots? What will I say? Craving distance, I step back and pretend to assess her face. "It's true. It's not what you look like, it's who you are. You're a total brainiac when it comes to math, remember?" She has my dad's math skills.

"Yeah." She leans forward and turns the bag upside down. Pots, wands, and tubes scatter across the vanity. I spot two kinds of eyeliner from a high-end natural makeup line, a Dior mascara, several lipsticks, and three "organic" shadows. How can eye shadow be organic? "It's a total pain because everybody wants to sit beside me in math so they can get my answers." She picks up a pot of plum shadow and shoves it into my hand. "Do my eyes." She lowers her lids.

"It may be a pain right now, but in a few years, it'll mean you could be a scientist or an engineer or a pilot like Dad."

Impatiently she jiggles her shoulders. "My eyes, Sloane!"

Clearly she doesn't care. Suppressing a sigh, I unscrew the top and sweep a little colour onto each lid. "There."

She opens her eyes, leans into the mirror, and frowns. "You can hardly see it."

"Less is more." When she opens her mouth to argue, I add, "Unless you're on TV. That's different." It's something I've heard Kim say. And it seems to satisfy her.

She gets up. "Now you."

"I don't think so."

"Oh, come on. Please?"

My cell rings. "I have to answer this." I dig into my pocket.

Her hands go on her hips; her eyebrows form a straight line across her forehead. I stifle a laugh. She looks just like Dad when she's mad. "Hello?"

"Hey, sunshine."

My breath catches. "Isaac?" His voice is deeper, edgier, on the phone. Like dark chocolate with a hot chili kick.

"Yeah. You didn't answer my text and I wanted to make sure I had the right number."

He saved my number from *last year*? As I'm trying to

process that, he says, "I wanted to make sure you're coming to The Ledge tonight."

Ella is watching me with a curious, sly smile. I turn to the wall, stare at the picture of the olive grove. "I, um, I'm not sure. I've been working on the video. There's lots left to do."

"It won't kill you to take a break. Besides, we need more footage before you can do anything substantial." When I don't respond, he adds, "Please come."

I hesitate. I don't like clubs at the best of times. And this isn't the best of times.

"I'd really like to see you."

He'd really like to see me. I could wear the new hat. Use lots of spray. "Okay," I blurt out. "I'll be there." I'll round up Lexi and Harper and a few of the others. We'll make a night of it.

"Who's Isaac?" Ella asks when I disconnect.

My stomach is tangled with nerves. *Isaac called me about tonight. I'm going to The Ledge.*

"Who is he?" Ella presses.

"Nobody."

"Riiiight." She giggles and rolls her eyes. "I have a nobody too. His name is Dylan."

Ten

The lights outside The Ledge cast a bluish tint over Lexi, Harper, and Chloe as we wait in line later that night. "You look great!" Lexi tells me. Uncomfortable with the compliment, I stare over her shoulder at the building across the street. It's covered with an artsy red, yellow, and blue mural, typical for the Mission neighbourhood of San Francisco, which also happens to be Latino Central and sells some of the best burritos on the planet. "I don't know why you were so against wearing the new clothes." We shuffle a few steps closer to the entrance. "You look hot, Sloane. Hotter than you've looked in ages."

"You do!" Harper chimes in. Chloe nods in agreement. I'm relieved they could come tonight. Chloe is hilarious; anytime she's involved, we're guaranteed a good time. Plus, Harper has her mother's car and Kim agreed to extend my curfew to midnight.

"Because I *am* hot." Between the hat and the brown aviator jacket Lexi lent me (my old jacket apparently wasn't good enough to wear over the pink tulip sweater), I am sweltering. I wiggle my thumb under the waistband of the super skinny jeans. They're so tight I can hardly breathe thanks to the platters of food we shared at a taqueria over on 16th.

And my scalp is prickling. I resist the urge to scratch. My hair is thinning at a stupid fast rate. I'm paranoid that someone will notice. And when I'm not paranoid, I'm panicked. Which panics me more. Because negativity begets stress and stress might be a cause.

"If I didn't know better, I'd swear you were wearing blush."

I am. It was a last-minute impulse before I left the house, mostly because Ella insisted. Or so I tell myself. "It's just the lighting," I say as we reach the door. Now I'm a liar *and* a hypocrite.

How sick is that?

After a cursory search and a stamp on our hands, we're inside. The lights are dim, which is a relief. Flaws are more easily hidden in the dark. I shrug out of Lexi's jacket and sling it over my shoulder. Harper and Chloe disappear into a crush of people.

"Come on!" Lexi tugs me forward. "I see Miles!"

Clearly, they are "on again." As we push through the crowd, I'm careful not to bump into people holding drinks. We're almost at the stage when Lexi stops. "Shit!"

"What's wrong?" I peer around her shoulder.

"I don't *believe* it," she hisses. "Look!"

Glancing over a second time, I see Isaac and Miles surrounded by a cluster of girls, including Breanne, who is flashing an acre of boobage in a white halter dress. Bouncing in and out of view, along with Breanne's breasts, is Matt. He looks awkward and nervous, like he'd rather be in the middle of a busy intersection somewhere.

"What is Breanne *doing* hanging off Miles like a total skank? Isn't Matt enough for her? Come on. We're moving in." Before I can protest, she pulls me into their circle. "Hey, guys!"

Miles whirls around. "Lexi, hi." Even the dim lighting can't hide the flush that hits his cheeks.

Lexi elbows Breanne aside and slides between them. Stifling a smile, I look at Isaac. He's wearing jeans, red high-tops, a fedora like mine except black, and a pale blue Jagged Five T-shirt. Green letters spell out "The Best New Band on the Planet."

"You made it!" He smiles.

"Yeah." Under other circumstances, I'd compliment him on his shirt or ask him where the band is but I'm conscious of the crowd ... of Matt watching me ... so I just smile back.

"It's good to see you," he says.

My stomach muscles clench. This time it's not the super skinny jeans. It's the way Isaac is looking at me. Like I'm the only girl in the room.

"You have quite a crowd here," I say.

"Isn't it great!" Breanne tosses her hair and inches closer to Isaac. Matt's lips twist into a fixed, "I'm pretending to be cool with this" smile. "I can't wait to hear Jagged Five," she adds. "When Isaac texted me, I couldn't say no."

Isaac *texted* Breanne?

Her eyelashes whir like mini chopper blades. "He said he really wanted me here."

I look at him. He did?

"The more people we pull in, the better it is for the guys," he explains as a rail-thin man wearing a headset bounds up onstage to check the DJ equipment. "We have a couple of agents in the crowd tonight so this is a big deal for them." At the far end of the stage, I see drums, guitars, a fiddle: the band equipment that will presumably be pulled out once Isaac warms up the crowd.

Breanne is staring at me. "You're wearing new clothes."

I've mentally rehearsed my spiel. "Lexi and I went shopping. I decided it's time to change things up a bit."

"Huh." Her critical gaze sweeps over me, lingering on the too-tight jeans. My on-again, off-again stomach pain returns.

"Now I get why you bought the fedora," Matt says.

"What are you talking about?"

He inclines his head to Isaac. "You're going for the twin thing."

Breanne giggles. "Oh my God, Matthew, you're right!"

Heat races into my cheeks. If I'd known Isaac was going to wear a fedora, I wouldn't have worn mine.

The guy wearing a headset taps the microphone. "Test, test." I wince at the screech of feedback.

"I'm not sure how I feel about that," Breanne adds.

Matt's lip curls. "I think it sucks."

My self-control snaps. "I'm not sure I care." What I wear, how I look, is not up for discussion.

"I like it." Isaac slides closer to me. "I think Sloane looks great." And then he drops his arm across my shoulder, and I stand there like a statue that's on fire and wonder what is up with him touching me all the time? What is up with me loving it?

"Ladies and gentlemen," booms the guy with the headset.

"Let's get this party started. Put your hands together for Isaac Alexander!"

The crowd starts to clap. "Ohhhhh!" Breanne squeals. "You're up!"

I go to move away but Isaac won't let me. Instead, he leans down and drops a quick kiss on my lips. My innards do a little dance. "For luck," he says.

"For luck," I blurt out, giggling awkwardly. I'm conscious of people staring—Lexi with her open mouth; Matt with his narrowed eyes. But for once I really don't care. "Good luck." I sound like a babbling monkey, one of those primates we filmed at the zoo the other day.

Isaac takes the stairs two at a time, slides behind a mess of black equipment, and leans into the mic. "Welcome to The Ledge," he shouts in his sexy-deep baritone. "And tonight's special appearance by Jagged Five."

I stare up at him. What just happened? Why did he kiss me?

"He's way out of your league," Breanne mutters into my ear. "Besides, that kiss was just for show. He kisses all the girls."

Maybe. Maybe not.

Onstage, Isaac directs a smile my way. "First, we're gonna rock out!" He flicks a switch. I hear music. What kind ... what band ... who knows? I don't even know for sure if Isaac is singling me out with his smile or smiling at the group of us. But I'm fine with that.

Because he didn't kiss any other girl tonight. He kissed me. And right now, that's enough.

The only thing that forces me out of bed Monday morning is the thought of the video. My submission to Clear Eye is due a week Wednesday. If it wasn't for that, I'd pull the covers over my head and get up sometime next year.

Isaac's kiss last night wrecked me. Lexi wouldn't shut up about it. Matt kept staring. Breanne wouldn't stop smirking.

I head for the shower, reliving events at The Ledge. My euphoria after that kiss. My daydreaming as I'd watched him DJ. We had a connection, I'd decided. Chemistry. Maybe, just maybe, me and Isaac weren't so far-fetched after all.

But when the band came on and Isaac came off and he dropped his arm around another girl's shoulders, my imagination screeched to a halt. And when he leaned over and kissed her on the cheek, I crashed to earth in a furious ball of disappointment.

After I got home, I was too keyed up to sleep. Instead I'd spent over an hour googling Isaac Alexander, looking for anything I could find on his personal life. I'd come up empty. How dumb is that?

Breanne was right. I turn on the tap, adjust the water temperature, and step under the spray. His kiss meant nothing. The Voice's default button is set on flirt. Who needs a guy like that? I don't even *like* guys like that. I reach for the extra gentle, non-toxic shampoo and start lathering. The herbal scent of lemongrass and thyme fills the shower stall.

Seconds later, I feel it—a familiar smoothness on the right side of my head.

Another one? My knees start to shake. Not again. I sink to the edge of the tub and sit down. That makes five. When will this end?

After a minute, Mom's words echo through my mind. *You*

can handle this. I know you can. Her confidence steels my resolve. I switch to autopilot. I finish my shower and strategize as I towel off. I'll up my vitamins. Cut out sugar. Do more online research so I'll know what to ask Dr. Paxton when I see her.

Back in the bedroom, I'm in the middle of my morning ritual: standing in front of the mirror going over my head inch by careful inch when my confidence turns to horror. I find a sixth spot on the left side of my head, a virtual twin to the one I just discovered on the right.

My hands start to shake. I twist and rearrange my hair, trying to cover this latest spot.

I can't. This one refuses to be concealed.

Tears well behind my eyelids. Holy shit.

Clutching my towel, I sink onto the edge of the bed and stare at my reflection in the mirror. My skin is still flushed from the shower. My eyes are overly bright. I blink back my tears and stare at my image. I look different. Not like me anymore. I lean closer and study every inch of my face. I'm trying to figure out why bald spots on my head would make my face look so strange.

You're imagining things now. I jump up. *You're being stupid.*

But as I reach for the familiar comfort of my cargo pants and deliberately turn my back on the pot of blush resting on the vanity, again I'm struck by an overwhelming urge to stay home.

Only I can't. We have that interview with the professor at USF later today. The laughter yoga shoot to line up. Plus, I'm reading at the hospital this afternoon. I can't miss that. I need to talk to Jade's parents.

I'm so late getting to school I miss homeroom. I slink into math and take a seat at the back of the room, praying that the teacher doesn't notice me or, more specifically, my hat. For once, luck's on my side. He's too busy explaining today's lesson to care.

My quasi calm lasts until Mandee leans across the aisle and whispers, "Did you get your hair cut?"

My heart starts to thrum. "No."

"Huh." She gazes at my hat, the hair that's visible below. "It looks shorter."

The bottom falls out of my world. "It's not." There's a thousand-pound weight on my chest. I can hardly breathe, never mind talk. "It's probably the hat."

She nods. "Probably."

The rest of the class passes in a blur. *It looks shorter.* Different. My fingers slide up to check that the spray is holding. It is. My hair is as hard as a baseball; the spots are hidden by the hat. So what did Mandee see?

My worry roars back. What will others see?

As if I don't have enough on my mind, Isaac doesn't meet me in the foyer after math as we planned. Doing voice-over work probably. I wait ten minutes and then text him. *Where are U?*

Running late, he replies. *Meet you out front soon.*

The delay ratchets up my unease. I call the university and push back our interview by an hour. Good thing too because it's another twenty minutes before Isaac pulls up. By then my stomach is a mess of butterflies and I am pacing back and forth in front of the entrance. "Good morning, sunshine," he says when I open the door to his beater van. "Sorry I'm late."

"I can deal. I pushed our interview time back." I cannot meet his gaze; I swear I still feel the imprint of his kiss. "No doubt one of your adoring fans kept you busy, Flirt Man." I shove a pile of papers off the passenger seat and sit down. A Styrofoam coffee cup crunches under my foot.

He winks and smiles. "You have no idea."

A funny kind of heat swirls through me. *Who was she and why did you kiss her and for that matter why did you kiss me?* "Oh, I think I do. Clearly you were too busy to shave." I yank on the seat belt, annoyed that he looks even better this morning than he did last night. Between the stubble and the gold hoop winking out from under his dreads, he looks like a pirate. A damn hot one. Better than Johnny Depp in *The Curse of the Black Pearl.* I force those thoughts away and scramble for neutral territory. "Hey, you know that video I was telling you about? The one about the deaf artists? *See What I'm Saying.*"

He throws the van into drive and pulls away from the entrance. "Yeah?"

I look everywhere but his lips. "Well, I happened to be online the other day"—*last night when I was obsessively googling you like a stalkerish fan girl*—"and you can buy it on Amazon, plus there are four copies in the San Francisco Library. Two are available right now. One at Noe Valley and the other at Glen Park. So if you want to see it ..." *With me, maybe.*

"Sounds like a plan. But not for a while. I'm super busy this semester. I'm juggling trig and physics."

Mr. I'll-Coast-on-my-Charm wouldn't last five minutes in Mr. Barrett's physics class. "Get serious."

He laughs. "I *am* serious. You should see the prerequisites for architecture school."

Architecture school? I shoot him a look. "Really?"

His grin deepens. He coasts to a stop at a red light. "Hey, I'm more than a pretty voice."

"Could've fooled me." The directness of his gaze makes me uneasy. I look out the window at a woman walking her grey Weimaraner.

He reaches behind me, grabs something from the back seat, and drops a grease-stained brown paper bag into my lap. "I brought breakfast. Brioche."

The bag is still warm. My traitorous mouth starts to water. I have a weakness for brioche surpassed only by my weakness for film. Simply put, I could live on brioche for the rest of my life and not miss food.

"Consider them my penance for being late. Does that help?" he asks.

It's only coincidence that he has brought them. My logical side knows it. But my emotional side, the side that roared to life after he kissed me last night, wonders if maybe we're soulmates after all.

Not.

In spite of myself, I start to laugh. "My God, I can't believe it. You're buttering me up with bread? Seriously? Do you know how pathetic that is?" I put the bag on the console between us. *And do you know how gorgeous you are? And how crazy that makes me?*

"You know you want them."

"I'd rather have a guy who's reliable and shows up on time." Like Matt. He was never late. He never flirted with anybody when we were together either. Only when I turned my back. Then he got naked in the library stall.

He laughs. "Boring."

Come to think of it, Matt *was* a little boring.

The light changes; he steps on the gas. "Would it help if I told you I stopped to check out that laughter yoga class?"

A cottony warmth balloons in my chest. "You did?" I'm stunned he's taken the initiative.

"Yeah." He shakes his head. "And we just saved ourselves ninety minutes because it's not going to work."

I wait as he slows to let a car merge in front of us. "Why not?"

"They sound like those barking seals we saw the other day."

I giggle. "Really?"

"It's totally fake. Something about opening up the diaphragm. Nothing remotely funny about it."

"Okay. I'll start searching for funny outtakes or bloopers from movies and stuff."

"Sounds like a plan." He taps his fingers impatiently on the steering wheel. Then he slides me a sideways look and asks, "Are you really going to let those brioches get cold?"

"I think I could choke one down." I reach for the bag.

—

The University of San Francisco is spread over fifty-five acres on top of Lone Mountain in the heart of the city. If I wasn't determined to go to film school, I'd want to go here. It's a beautiful green space with some cool old buildings, plus there are always tons of hot guys taking law classes. Lexi and I usually come here once or twice every summer, often with takeout pizza or burgers. We grab a bench and eat our lunch in the shade of a date palm, pretending to enjoy the view of the Golden Gate Bridge and the Marin Headlands. Really, we're way more interested in scanning for our ideal guy. Lexi has a thing for Prince Harry types—guys with reddish hair and freckles—while I lean to the more exotic guys. Yeah, like Isaac.

Professor Ng's office is on the third floor of the psychology wing in the School of Education and luckily we manage to find a parking spot in a nearby lot. Inside, we check in with the white-haired receptionist and then wait in the corner by the window. It's starting to rain; water droplets ping the glass.

"Since we're shooting inside now, you'll need to reset the white balance," I remind Isaac.

"I'll activate it once we're in his office." But he pulls the camera from its case and turns off the auto settings in preparation.

"I have half a dozen questions that'll take five or ten minutes. Depending on his answers, I may have more." I'm *hoping* I'll have more. Professor Ng was forthcoming in his email but I don't know how forthcoming he'll be in person.

The door behind the receptionist opens. A small, dark-haired man moves briskly into the outer office. "Miss Kendrick?"

I extend my hand. "That's me." I gesture to Isaac. "This is Isaac Alexander. He'll run camera so I can concentrate on our conversation."

He smiles. "Of course. Please come in."

"I'm sorry we were delayed. I appreciate you pushing the start time back."

"Not a problem. It actually worked out better for me."

Thank goodness for that. The room is small, stuffy, and smells vaguely of onions. Two extra chairs are wedged in beside the desk and piled with books, papers, and file folders. There's barely room for the two of us.

"It's pretty tight," Isaac murmurs. "Maybe we should do the interview in the hall. The lighting would be better too."

He's probably right.

"I'd prefer to do it here," Professor Ng says. "We'll have fewer distractions." He removes the books from the chairs and slides them under his desk. "Sit. Please." He lifts the second chair. "I'll move this into the hall."

Isaac looks at me and shrugs. Then he hoists the camera and takes his white balance from a piece of paper on the desk. "Can you get rid of that picture?" He points to a family portrait in a gold frame. "And maybe move his computer monitor?"

I put the picture on a nearby shelf, push the monitor as far left as I can, and pull out my notebook. "We appreciate you agreeing to this interview," I say when Professor Ng hurries back into the room.

"No problem." He sits down behind the desk. "I'm happy to do it."

"I thought I'd give you a quick rundown of my questions." I flip my notebook open. "While I do that, Isaac will shoot some wide shots of the two of us." Getting generic wide shots before and after the interview will give us plenty of footage for potential cutaways.

"That's fine." The professor leans back in his chair and steeples his fingers.

Seconds after I start to outline my line of questioning, Isaac interrupts me.

"Sloane? Could you take your hat off?"

I turn cold, then hot. *No way.* "Why?"

"It's in the way."

"I'd prefer to keep it on." I scoot my chair over. "There. Try that."

He checks the viewfinder again. "It's iffy."

"You'll make it work." I give him a breezy smile as I turn back to the professor. "I trust you."

Professor Ng is eloquent and surprisingly funny, offering both hard facts on the differences between how men and women perceive humour as well as a cute personal anecdote about his son and daughter. He has some insightful comments about the social benefits of laughter and says it's an excellent way to create bonds with others. Thinking of the upcoming flash mob, I ask him to expand.

"Shared laughter is one of the best ways to keep relationships fresh and exciting," he says. "As well as that, it helps us overcome challenges both in relationships and personally. And it helps us not take ourselves so seriously."

If only it was that easy, I reflect after Isaac and I say our thanks, put away the equipment, and head to the van. If only I could watch a few *Friends* reruns, laugh, and feel better about my hair loss.

If only.

The rain has stopped but the blowing wind sends autumn leaves dancing across the sidewalk in front of us. "That went well, don't you think?"

"Uh-huh."

His silence since we left the office is making me uncomfortable. "He gave us some really great stuff."

"Yeah."

I shoot him a look. "What's with the monosyllabic answers?"

"What's with you and that hat?"

My heart skips a beat. "What do you mean?"

"Why did you insist on wearing it? It really was in the way."

"I like me in it." The second the words leave my mouth, I want to take them back. *Like me in it.* How lame.

"I didn't think you were like that."

"Like what?"

"Worrying about how you look."

I attempt a giggle but I end up sounding more like a snorting pig than anything human. "All girls do."

He shakes his head. "Maybe, but I figured you had more confidence."

My unease morphs to anger. How dare he poke around in my psyche? "I have plenty of confidence."

"Then why are you so freaked about going on-camera? And why hide behind a hat that's in the way?"

I concentrate on speaking calmly. "I like my hat. That's all. End of story." But I am clenching my purse so hard my nails are jabbing my palms. I force my fingers to relax. "Seriously, Dr. Drew. Find someone else to analyze."

He shrugs. "Right. Whatever."

He doesn't believe me. I'm about to argue my case further when he stops in the middle of the sidewalk and turns to face me. He's standing so close the denim from his jeans brushes my knees. So close I could count the tiny gold flecks in his brown eyes. "You're beautiful, Sloane. I told you that the other day."

You're way hotter than Breanne.

"With or without the hat," he adds. "But you need to own it, that's all."

My breath hitches in my throat. If only he meant it. I manage another snort-giggle. "Yeah, right."

His eyes darken; the gold sparks dissolve. His head dips towards me; my legs turn to licorice. *He's going to kiss me again. He is.*

And I can't let it happen. Not again. I step back and shoot him a shaky smile. "That's me, a regular beauty queen. And you're a famous DJ." I start to walk. "Come on. Your limo's waiting."

Eleven

By the time we get back to the car, it's almost one thirty. Rather than going back to school for an hour, Isaac drops me at the hospital a little early. My cell phone rings seconds after I walk through the entrance. The words *unidentified caller* pop onto the screen. My heart skips a beat. "Hello?"

"Sloanie?" Mom's voice is tinny, like she's calling from the moon.

Tears well at the sound of her voice. I stop so suddenly a man in a suit smashes into my back and gives me a dirty look. "Where are you?"

She starts to answer but cuts out. "You're blocking traffic," a woman says. The purple flowers she's carrying hit me as she brushes past.

I hurry back to the front door. Reception can be spotty in the hospital; I'm not taking any chances.

"Are you there?" Mom asks.

"I'm here." Outside, the clouds are low and threatening; the wind cuts through my hoodie. Needing to generate heat, I speed walk past the drop-off lane to the street. "Where are you?" I ask a second time.

Another delay as my words travel halfway around the world. "At the teaching hospital in Juba ... got here yesterday ... gathering supplies ... going ... village tomorrow ... you okay?"

Okay? My hair is falling out. Isaac is making me crazy. My video is nowhere near done and it's due in a little over a week. And then there's Jade waiting upstairs. There's so much to say, but I don't know where to start, so I say, "Yeah."

Another pause and then, "How are you feeling?"

Terrified. Angry. Confused. I turn at the corner, falling in with a group of people carrying briefcases and designer bags. I see my reflection in a store window. *Beautiful.* Isaac called me beautiful. I glance at my hat. At my hair poking out the bottom. What a joke.

"Scared," I whisper into the phone. I can't believe how much my life has changed in a little over a week. The last time I read to the kids, I didn't know I had alopecia. "And pissed off." I'm so angry it's like I'm PMSing all the time.

A strange emptiness fills the line. She's gone again.

The crowd I'm with makes another turn, steps off the curb, and surges across the street. On autopilot, I follow the woman in front of me, noting her purposeful strides, the royal blue Hermès scarf tied casually to her leather bag. I remember a picture Mom showed me of her last trip to Sudan—the dusty red soil, the thatched huts, the desperation in the eyes of a mother cradling a baby. The poverty.

Tears prickle behind my lids. The two of us are worlds apart.

But then she is back. "... love you, Sloane."

"Love you too, Mom. Miss you."

"Will ... email ... call ... few days."

She is gone. This time, for good. I stare at the unfamiliar

buildings looming on either side of the street. And I am lost. The irony doesn't escape me. *Oh, get over yourself.* I don't have time for a pity party. I pocket my cell, swallow my tears, and begin to retrace my steps.

—

"One of the nurses said you wanted to talk to us," Jade's mom says as we watch the lab tech draw blood from Jade's arm.

"I did but—" I avert my gaze as the tech reaches for vial number four. This feels opportunistic. "I'm not sure now."

Latanna straightens the fuzzy pipe cleaners scattered on Jade's portable hospital table. The pale yellows, pinks, and purples remind me of Easter. "What was it about?"

"I'm doing this school video on laughter."

The lines at the corners of her eyes crinkle when she smiles. "That sounds interesting. I can't wait for Jade to get to high school and do all those wonderful things."

Her sunny optimism makes me want to weep. Jade is back on chemo. She's wearing her favourite green bandana with a sticker: "Chemo. All the cool kids do it."

"But what does that have to do with us?"

I turn my back to the bed and quietly say, "I was going to ask if I could film Jade the next time the clowns perform for the kids."

Latanna gazes at me, her warm brown eyes open and trusting. So like her daughter. A nugget of shame blooms in my chest. "Because she laughs. All the time." Even today when I walked through the door and saw her making a pipe cleaner bracelet, she was giggling. "But it's okay."

Because no matter how much I want my video to shine, reducing Jade to a frame or two of laughter feels wrong. She is so much more than that. I can't do it.

"Done," the lab tech announces. I turn around as she pops a Hello Kitty Band-Aid onto Jade's arm.

"And, anyway, we're doing a laughter flash mob so we'll probably have enough tape."

"I saw a flash mob on YouTube once and it looked waaaay fun," Jade says as she rests back against her pillow. Her voice is so weak the word *way* comes out in a breathless whisper. "When are you doing it, Miss Cookie?"

"At the end of this week." I reach for my stack of books. "Which story today, Miss Jade?"

But she isn't interested in my books. Smudgy shadows circle her ebony eyes as she stares up at me. "Can I come?"

I tweak her nose. "Don't you have better things to do?" *Chemo? Getting better?*

"No." Her head makes a *swish swish* noise against the pillow when she shakes it. "Can I?" She looks at Latanna. "Please, can I go? Please?"

"I don't think the doctors will let you but Miss Cookie asked if she could bring her camera here and film you the next time the clowns come. What do you think of that?"

Her eyes widen. "A real camera like they use for movies?"

I grin. "Yes, a real camera like they use for movies."

"And I could be *on* it?"

I nod. "Yes."

She beams. "That would be so, so fun. *So fun*," she repeats in case I didn't get it the first time.

Latanna brushes the hair off her forehead. "And something for you to look forward to, right?"

"Right!"

I hadn't thought of that. "If you're sure."

"We're sure!" Jade says.

Latanna laughs. And, in spite of my misgivings, I do too.

———

"You're late," Kim snaps when I step through the front door just before five. Her stilettos beat out an angry *tap tap* rhythm against the hardwood as she hurries to the closet. She's perfectly made up—big surprise—but her lips are tight, her movements jerky. "I texted you. Didn't you get my message?"

"No." My knapsack hits the floor with a thump.

She glances down. "That doesn't belong there."

I pick it up.

"Don't you check your phone?" she asks.

"Not at the hospital."

She lifts a brow. "Honestly, Sloane, you should check your phone *regularly* in case the specialist calls and can see you sooner. What's the point of having a phone if you don't use it?"

I refuse to be baited. "You didn't say anything this morning about having to go out tonight and I didn't think dinner was until six."

"I don't have to clear my schedule with you." She thrusts her arms through a butterscotch-coloured leather jacket, smoothes her black skirt. "Something's come up. I needed you here an hour ago."

"Sorry." But I'm not. Not until Kim turns away and I

catch sight of Ella slumped on the living room couch. Her arms are crossed; she is pouting. Crap. Don't tell me Kim's taken out her anger on my little sister?

Kim grabs her purse from the hall table. "There's a vegan bean casserole in the fridge. It'll need about forty minutes in the oven, which is already on." Her keys jangle when she picks them up. "You can grate some cheese for Ella but I'd pass on the cheese if I were you." She studies my face through narrowed eyes. "You look like you're putting on weight and that's the last thing you need at a time like this."

I stiffen. Nice.

She opens the door. Before she steps outside, she looks back and says, "If there's an emergency, call my cell. Unlike some people, I answer mine." She slams the door behind her.

I toss my knapsack in the corner and walk into the living room. "How're you feeling?" I ask Ella as I flop in an easy chair across from her.

She's picking at a random thread on a pale blue pillow. Her eyes are puffy, like she's been crying. "Bad. Sad. Mad."

Right back at you, sister. "What's wrong?"

"Mom won't let me go to Hannah's sleepover." As Ella tells me who else is going and what Hannah has planned, Jade's face floats through my mind. There'll be no sleepovers for her. Not for a while anyway. Maybe never. I shiver. All the little moments of life we take for granted when they're happening. Like this. Right now. Being with Ella.

"Why won't she let you go?"

Ella's lower lip folds down. "She says I'm too young for sleepovers."

Too young, my ass. Kim buys Ella purses meant for twenty-year-olds. Lets her wear makeup. She just doesn't like

Hannah's mother because she's on welfare. I heard her say that to Dad last week.

"She bought me a hat instead."

I stiffen. "A hat?"

"Instead of the sleepover. She said it would make me feel better." A tiny frown creases her forehead. "Don't feel bad, Sloane. She got you one too. Mine's brown, yours is blue."

I clench my teeth so hard my jaw hurts. First makeup and now hats. What's next? Matching outfits? "I'll talk to her."

Ella brightens. "Really?"

"Yeah, really." It probably won't do any good, but if it'll make Ella feel better, there's no harm. Plus I need to tell her what she can do with her hat. "When she comes home tonight." I toss a leg over the side of the chair.

"Mom would kill you if she saw you doing that."

"I know." I toss my other leg over, swing them back and forth.

Ella giggles. And then she turns serious. "Are you sick?"

I stop swinging my legs. "Why are you asking that?"

"Mom said you had to see a specialist. That's for sick people." She stares at me. "You aren't sick, are you Sloane?"

Sick? Not sick like Jade or any of the other kids I saw today, although Kim's buying sprees are making me nauseous. "I'm not sick now but I'll barf if I have to eat beans for dinner. You want to go for a walk? I'll buy you McDonald's."

Ella jumps off the couch. "Yes!"

═══

Later, when I'm getting Ella to bed, Dad calls. He seems surprised when I tell him Kim's not home, especially when I say I'm not sure where she is. I quickly change the subject and talk about the video project instead, telling him about today's shoot at the university and our idea for the flash mob. Before he can ask how I'm feeling, I give the phone to Ella and she pleads her case for the sleepover. It takes me a long time to get her to bed after Dad's call. Finally she settles down, and I get to work on the video. Kim doesn't get home until almost midnight.

"Isn't it a little late for homework?" she asks when she walks into the kitchen and sees me sitting at the table with my laptop and notes. Isaac put the footage on a key and I'm already culling the good from the bad, even though we're still missing a couple of key scenes. "Shouldn't you be in bed by now?"

"Yeah, probably." I power down the laptop. "Dad called. So did some guy named Martin. Just after you left." We were halfway out the door when the phone rang. Ella didn't want me to go back. I shouldn't have.

"Right. I know." She slides out of her heels and pads over to the counter where she reaches into the cupboard for a bag of coffee. "I connected with both of them."

Oh man. *And did you tell Dad about Martin?* I give her a hard stare. "I'll just bet."

She measures beans, pours them into the grinder, and turns to face me. Her eyeliner is smudged; she looks tired. "I don't like the implication behind your tone of voice, Sloane. We have to live together for the next two months. You need to be more civil."

You need to show some loyalty to Dad. "And you need to stop buying makeup and hats and pretending they're for Ella when we both know they're for me."

She flicks on the grinder. After the whirring stops, she says, "I bought the hat for Ella because she was upset. She insisted on getting one for you."

Right. "I'm not allowed to wear hats at school." With the exception of math and study hall, most teachers don't care but Kim doesn't need to know that. "And Ella was upset because you won't let her go to the sleepover. She told me."

She measures grounds into the machine. "That's correct." The rich smell of coffee fills the air.

"Ella is ten. She's old enough for sleepovers."

"When you're a parent, you can make those decisions. Right now, I'm in charge."

The anger I suppressed over her earlier comment about my weight coupled with my fear that she's cheating on Dad—it would kill him if he knew—flares. "So you'll buy Ella makeup and facials and let her do stuff most ten-year-olds don't, but when it comes to something normal like a sleepover, you say no. I don't get you."

"And I don't get *you*. You make no effort at all. None." She gazes at my pyjamas, glances down to my bare feet. "It's no wonder you and Matt didn't last."

My breath hitches. "That's mean!"

"Maybe. And I'm sorry if I hurt your feelings. But honest to God, Sloane, someone has to tell you a few simple truths. People judge you on your appearance. You may not like it but it's true. And now—" She glances at my head and quickly averts her eyes. "With your hair falling out, you have to try harder. You have to do *something*."

Isaac thinks I'm hot. Beautiful. Isaac is also a flirt. "Let me tell you a few simple truths, *Kimberly*."

She flinches at the use of her full name.

"There's a little girl in the hospital dying of cancer." My voice is so thick and low I don't sound like myself. "Her mother would probably cut off her right arm if it meant her daughter could go to a sleepover. You may not believe it, but it's true. Because that's how some mothers are." Moisture clouds my eyes. I grab my laptop and jump up from the table. I won't cry in front of her. "Ask *her* if appearances matter." I bolt for the hall.

Kim's voice floats after me. "You forgot your notes."

Bite me.

=

Kim's comments send me straight to the bedroom mirror. I stare at the contours of my cheeks. I don't think I've gained weight. I tug on the waistband of my pyjamas. If anything, my clothes are looser. Probably because I can barely choke down Kim's crappy health food.

But as I study my face, a lava flow of hot panic bubbles up. I *do* look different. Not quite myself. It's not the spots. I can't see them from this angle. I turn my head. There they are. I straighten my head; they disappear. And yet ... I stare into my face, now flushed with worry. Maybe my thinning hair is changing my appearance. Making me look heavier.

Desperate for I don't know what—support, reassurance, ideas to keep myself looking *like* myself—I crawl into bed with my laptop and visit a different alopecia chat room, one I've never checked before.

Big mistake.

I'm both horrified and fascinated by the incredibly personal details people share. The entries from guys moaning about their receding hairlines make me wish they were here so I could slap them (a receding hairline? Please!). Messages from the serious sufferers talking about treatment side effects make me want to vomit. But the entry that hits me hardest and makes me cry is from a twenty-seven-year-old Irish woman who says her life was ruined when she went from a full head of hair to bald in a month.

Her words slam into my chest like a physical punch. *A month?* I curl into a fetal-like ball and resist the urge to run back to the mirror to see if I've lost more hair in the last ten minutes.

Eventually I pull up YouTube, where I watch our stupid shoe video about a thousand times until the sharp pain in my chest shrinks back to the small knot of panic that's taken up permanent residence behind my breastbone. And then, with images of yellow shoes dancing through my head, I turn out the light and try to sleep.

The next morning, I wake up with a sick, heavy feeling in my stomach. Once again, I consider skipping school, but I can't. I need to go to math and we're getting down to the wire on the video. Isaac and I need to check out a juggler down on Jefferson. With any luck, he'll be good enough to replace the laughter yoga shoot.

Still, I'm uneasy in my own skin. I don't know why. Kim's comments maybe? Or the memory of how Isaac looked at me yesterday? My worry that he'll get close again?

For reasons I choose not to analyze, I put more effort into my appearance. When Ella's in the shower, I sneak into her room and grab one of the lipsticks and liner Kim bought. I pull on my new jeans and a pale blue top with floaty sleeves. I spray down my hair, position the fedora just so, and carefully outline my lips before applying lipstick. I study my reflection in the mirror. Gross. My lips are huge. I can't believe women pay big bucks for this bee-stung look.

Whatever. At least I look different now for a reason.

I feel okay until I get to school and see Mandee Lingworth. When she waves, I remember her words—*You look like you're trying to be pretty.* I tell myself that's got nothing to do with it. But still. My doubts and insecurities roar back. Instead of slowing down to talk to her, I wave and pick up my pace.

For the next few hours, I find myself avoiding eye contact with people. I slip into math at the last possible minute, keeping my head down while I do my work, and getting back out without talking to anyone. I spend first and third block hiding in study hall writing an intro for the video. Or I try to. In truth, I am so obsessed with my hair that I cannot concentrate on my script. And that scares me. I am more than the hair on my head. More than my looks.

I need to remember that.

Isaac has an appointment with his adviser at lunch, which means we can't link up until one. Normally I'd hang in the cafeteria with Lexi, but the less time I'm around people, the fewer potential questions I'll have to endure. So I go for a walk instead, treating myself to a lobster roll from a street vendor; I chase it down with a double cappuccino. It'll give me the energy I need for the afternoon with Isaac. When I get back to school, I duck into an out-of-the-way bathroom to check my hair and reapply lipstick before meeting him in the foyer.

And I run straight into Lexi.

"Where have you been?" She's at the mirror, smoothing her eye shadow. "I've been looking all over for you."

A freshman is washing her hands at the sink beside us. I wait until she finishes and heads for the door. "I have cramps and I needed some painkillers so I walked over to the pharmacy."

"Why didn't you go to the nurse?"

"I needed some air." I straighten my hat; stare at my reflection in the mirror. The lipstick and liner I put on this morning is gone. Either I've chewed it off or my skin absorbs the stuff like a sponge soaking up water.

"I could have gone with you."

"Kim's driving me nuts." I dig around in my knapsack for a comb. "I needed some time alone to process."

Her eyes meet mine in the mirror. "Too much tofu, huh?"

I manage a grin. "Something like that."

Lexi drops the shadow compact into her bag. "She's such a hag, making you stay there for the whole two months."

A sliver of guilt twinges but only a sliver. Given how nasty Kim is, I figure she's fair game as my excuse for not staying with Lexi or Harper, who also offered to call Kim when I told her the whole sad, made-up story. "Yeah, she's the original wicked stepmonster."

She laughs.

I want Lexi to leave so I can fix my lips and hair privately. I keep digging through the knapsack, pretending I can't find my comb. After what seems like a century, the bell rings in the hall. "You go ahead." I'm almost giddy with relief. "I'll see you later."

"I'm in no hurry." She puts her bag down. "I'll wait."

Damn. I can't take my hat off now. Feigning indifference, I comb the ends of my hair before pulling out the lipliner.

"Whoa!" Lexi leans over. "Is that Dior Rouge?"

"Yeah."

"When did you start wearing *that*?"

"When Kim bought it for me and Ella." My hand is shaking as I outline my top lip.

She wrinkles her nose. "For *Ella*?"

"Yeah. You know Kim." I finish my upper lip and go to work on my bottom one. When I'm finished, I toss it in my knapsack and dig around for the lipstick.

When I pull out the black tube, Lexi gives me a sly grin. "At least he's inspired you to ditch that stupid lip gloss."

My heart starts to thrum. "What are you talking about?"

"Oh for God's sake, Sloane." She giggles. "Isaac."

"This isn't about Isaac."

She lifts her eyebrows. "Riiight."

"Seriously. It's not."

She giggles. "Give it up, Sloane. We've known each other since grade two. You can't fool me."

I open my mouth to protest further but Lexi adds, "You could use a little mascara and shadow but otherwise you look pretty good, Sloanie Baloney."

The old nickname makes me grin.

"Even that hat's growing on me." A tiny frown creases her brow as she assesses me in the mirror. "One thing though."

"What's that?"

"You shouldn't pluck your eyebrows so much."

I stare at my reflection. The air leaves me in a giant *whoosh*. My heart starts to race.

"That thin look doesn't suit you," she adds.

Blood roars into my head. I cannot breathe. I'm not plucking my eyebrows. They're falling out.

Twelve

"Oh my God."

"What's wrong?"

I realize I've spoken out loud. I clutch the edge of the counter and stare at my wispy brows. How did I miss something so obvious? No *wonder* I look different.

Lexi touches my arm. "Are you okay?"

My chest feels like it's going to explode. It's not normal for a heart to beat this fast. Maybe I'm having a heart attack.

"You're really pale all of a sudden."

She sounds so far away. Somehow I find enough breath to say, "I have cramps." I bend forward, clutch my middle. "I need to go home. You need to tell Isaac for me."

"Okay." She chews the corner of her mouth. "But you know something? You've been getting cramps a lot. You might have endometriosis. I read about this girl once—"

"Lexi, please! Just go find Isaac." I need to get out of here. I need to talk to Mom. That thought makes me want to cry, except then Lexi will probably insist on calling an ambulance. "Tell him he'll have to shoot the juggler without me." I grab my knapsack and bolt for a stall. "He's waiting in the foyer."

"Don't go anywhere," Lexi orders as I lock myself in and lean against the door. The steel is cold through my flimsy new top. It makes me shiver. I take slow, deep breaths. "Okay?" she calls. "I think the school nurse should see you before you leave."

When I don't answer, she bangs on the stall. I jump. "Okay?" she demands again.

Pressing a hand against my chest, I will my heart to slow. "Yeah, okay." Seconds later, I hear the soft thud of the outside door signalling Lexi's departure.

Silently I count to ten. That should give her enough time to get down the hall and around the corner to the foyer. When I'm sure she's gone, I make my escape, heading in the opposite direction for the nearest outside exit. I'm not seeing the school nurse. I'm going home.

The sky is the colour of a trash can as I head north to get the number 1 bus instead of going south for my usual number 27. It means making a second exchange downtown but it's a small price to pay for privacy. When Lexi realizes I've left, she's liable to come after me and I don't want to talk to her.

What can I say? *Oh, by the way, I'm going bald?*

A bead of moisture hits my cheek. Then another. And another. Great. It's starting to rain. And I don't have an umbrella. I pick up my pace, hurrying past a trio of kids who study me over the tips of their cigarettes as I walk by, and an older couple checking something on an iPhone.

Once they're behind me, I dig out my cell and pull up the number Mom programmed in when my appointment was confirmed.

"Dr. Paxton's office," a nasally voice answers. "How may I help you?"

"I have an appointment with the doctor on the twenty-seventh," I respond. A drop of rain hits my eye; I brush it away. "But I need to get it moved up."

"Who's calling please?"

"Sloane Kendrick. Dr. Thibodeau referred me."

"One moment while I pull your file." She puts me on hold. Canned music fills my ear. The rain is heavier now; it slices into my hoodie like sharp chips of ice. Shivering, I stare down the street past a little Thai restaurant, a laundromat, a mailbox. Where *is* the bus stop?

After a minute, the woman returns. "I'm sorry, Miss Kendrick. The twenty-seventh is the best we can do."

She *has* to fit me in. I struggle to say something, but I'm breathing so hard I'm almost hyperventilating.

"Miss Kendrick? Are you there?"

Panicked, I turn in a circle, trying to get my bearings.

"Miss Kendrick?"

"I'm here." I take cover under the black and gold awning of a small brick apartment building. "What about a cancellation list? Do you have one?"

"We do but it's reserved for emergencies."

"This *is* an emergency."

"And what is the nature of—" She hesitates. "The emergency?"

I wait for a man walking a tartan-coated Westie to pass. "I'm losing my hair," I blurt out. "My eyebrows too."

"I'm sorry but that isn't classed as an emergency."

What the f—? How can she not get it? "Fine. Okay." No amount of arguing will make her understand and I can't afford to piss her off. "Could you please just check again to see if you can fit me in any time before the twenty-seventh? I'll come in at lunch. Early in the morning. Last thing at night. I don't care."

"One moment." She puts me on hold a second time.

I peer down the street. No bus stop. I stand on my toes and look behind me. There, almost a block away, is the familiar red-topped bus shelter. I went too far. I walked right past it.

With a sigh, I pull my hoodie tight, step into the rain, and start retracing my steps.

"I'm sorry, Miss Kendrick, but the twenty-seventh is the best we can do."

I step blindly off the curb, in front of a black Jetta. An angry honk fills the air.

I wave my apology at the driver of the car and go sideways to allow him to pass. And because I am still not looking where I'm going, I manage to step into the middle of an oil-slicked puddle. "Okay. Thanks." For nothing.

By the time the bus pulls up, I've collected a series of texts from both Lexi and Isaac.

Lexi: *What the F***?*
Isaac: *U ok?*
Lexi: *U said U'd wait.*
Isaac: *Talk 2 me.*
Lexi: *I'm @ yr bus stop. WRU???*

I *knew* Lexi would come after me. My runners squish as I drip my way to the back of the bus and take the last seat. I halfway consider pulling out my phone and googling WebMD but what's the point? It's not like I'll learn anything new.

I am losing my hair. All of it. I don't need the specialist to tell me that. I need her to tell me how to get it back.

I stare out the rain-splattered window. My watery, smudged reflection stares back. If I were directing myself in a movie, I would use this shot, I think dispassionately. It's the perfect combination of art and pathos. My round face framed by snaky tendrils of wet, limp hair. Flickering lashes. A droopy mouth.

My lashes. My stomach flips; I taste the lobster roll I ate for lunch. Oh my God. Will I lose those too? Some people do. I read that somewhere.

Lashes can be bought but can eyebrows? Needing a distraction, I stare beyond my face to the outside world. Across the street, a bus pulls up to the stop and disgorges half a dozen people. They flip up umbrellas: black, yellow, blue.

I probably won't need an umbrella if I'm bald. A hat's probably enough.

My cell phone buzzes, signalling a text. *I'm worried.* Lexi again. *Call me.*

I text her instead. *I'm OK. Talk ltr.* I say the same thing to Isaac but add, *Sorry.* And then I text Mom: *I need to talk to you. ASAP.*

When my phone rings less than a minute later, my heart flutters into my throat. "Mom!"

"Sorry, sunshine," Isaac drawls. "It's me."

Damn, I should have checked call display. "Sorry," I blurt out again.

"Are you okay? Lexi says you're really sick."

"I just need to go home. I'll be okay." Empty words. I may never be okay again. The bus slows to a stop; the front doors slap open.

"You don't sound okay." And then I hear Lexi in the background shouting, "If Midol doesn't work, try ibuprofen."

Oh my *God*. They're *together*? Isaac knows I have cramps?

"My sister swears by warm tea and a heating pad," Isaac adds.

My humiliation is complete. I shut my eyes, press my head against the cold window, and tell myself not to be a fool. What does it matter what Isaac thinks? It's a lie anyway. "Thanks," I manage. "I, um, I'm sorry I can't be there for the juggler this afternoon. Just get some footage, okay? I'll figure out what to do later."

"With this rain, I doubt he'll be outside anyway, so no biggie."

"Oh, right. I guess, we'll, uh, do him later then." Later, when? We only have a week until the scholarship deadline. But suddenly I don't care. The video, Clear Eye, what does it matter anyway? Maybe I should just give it up.

It's a crazy thought, a defeatist thought. The kind of thought I'd never considered myself capable of. Giving up the biggest dream of my life because I'm embarrassed by my looks? That's insane. And yet ...

"... fit him in somewhere," Isaac is saying when I snap back to myself. "If not, we'll get someone else." I hear Lexi mumble something. "Lexi wants to talk to you," he adds.

I don't want to talk to Lexi. "You're fading out," I tell him. "Tell her to text me." And I disconnect.

I shove my phone into my pocket and turn back to the

window. Cars stream past the bus, their windshield wipers tick-tock back and forth like my thoughts.

Give up. Keep going. Give up. I can't believe I'd walk away from a possible scholarship because I'm losing my hair. Because I'm afraid of what people will think. I pull my gaze from car wipers. My blurry, smudged reflection stares back.

I give my head a little shake. Wet tendrils of hair slap my cheeks. I don't recognize myself anymore. Not physically. And not mentally either.

I've never been this obsessive. And I've never been a quitter. Not ever.

Giving up my shot at Clear Eye would be like giving up a part of me. Another part. How can I do that? I can't. I won't. I may not be able to stop my hair from falling out, and I may not be able to stop thinking about it all the time, but I can work a lot harder to stop people from noticing.

And I know exactly where to start.

Kim's studio.

—

The driveway is empty when I reach Dad's house, but he and Kim park in the garage so that's no guarantee they're not home.

I open the door and step into the foyer, prepared with my excuse (cramps) if one of them is there. The door shuts with a soft click. I cock my head and listen. A yawning silence greets me. The telltale silence of an empty house.

I slide out of my wet runners and socks and do a quick walk-through anyway, checking the kitchen and den, poking my head through the door that connects the garage with the living room. Satisfied that the house is empty, I ditch my knapsack and wet clothes in the bedroom before heading down the hall to Kim and Dad's room.

But when my fingers fasten around the doorknob, I hesitate.

What I'm about to do is a breach of privacy. And privacy is something I've been taught to respect. On the other hand, it's not like I've never been in Kim's room before. Hell, half the models in San Francisco have been in Kim's room. Or, more specifically, the studio attached to the bedroom. Only they've been invited in. And I haven't. Not today.

But still. The end—getting what I need without involving Kim—justifies the means.

I turn the knob and step inside.

Decorated in a quasi–French provincial theme with pale blue walls, cream furniture, and reams of curtains, the bedroom smells faintly of Kim's floral perfume. The thick cream carpet muffles my footsteps as I hurry past the bed and around the corner to the door that leads to her makeup studio.

I need new brows. If Lexi noticed they're thinner, it won't be long before other people notice too. Mandee for sure. Isaac probably.

You're beautiful.

Yeah, right. Beautiful without brows. It sounds like the lyrics to a bad song. I need to hide the evidence. Hide in plain sight, that's what I'm going to do. I plan to get my Ph.D. in it.

I flick the switch, flooding the room with intense, bright light. Unlike the bedroom, this room is black, white, and businesslike.

Two black director's chairs sit in front of the makeup stations. A four-tier, stainless-steel shelf unit rests between them, holding trays of shadows and brushes and pots. Framed images from Kim's portfolio line the wall. The eyes of a dozen models follow me as I move quickly past the airbrush station and the outside door that allows clients independent access, to the built-in shelves where Kim keeps her supplies.

I scan the jumble of boxes and baskets, plastic totes, suitcases. Some are labelled. Others aren't. And I don't know where to start. But I do know what I want. False eyelashes for sure. A dark brow pencil. Some foundation and blush. Maybe a shadow or two.

If you buy a hat and the rest of you looks shitty, people will stare for all the wrong reasons, Lexi had said.

And if I only get brows, people will stare at the rest of my face and see all the flaws.

The lights are freakishly hot. A bead of sweat trickles down my spine as I pull down a tote labelled "FX." Peering inside, I see liquid latex, fake blood, hairpieces, and wigs. It takes me a minute to make the connection. FX for special *effects*. As my mind spins with possibilities, I pick out a hairpiece close to my own hair colour. Who knows? Maybe I can do something with it.

I go through two more totes, selecting a couple of lipsticks, a foundation, and some powder before I open a small, white cardboard box and find them.

False eyelashes.

I stare at the jumble of black and brown and fuchsia and turquoise. The range of colours and shapes amazes me. Thick strips. Individual wisps. Half lashes. Every possible combination and some I've never even thought of. Lashes that look like feathers and some that are decorated with glitter. They feel like silk sliding through my fingers.

They're frivolous. Verging on ridiculous. But they make me smile. For some reason, I think of Jade. She would love them.

I dig for something that matches my colouring, eventually selecting a couple of strip lashes, a sleeve of half lashes, and a handful of uber-curly individual lashes I figure I can cut down. Impulsively I pick out a set of feathery turquoise and gold lashes for Jade too. After retrieving a white tube of eyelash adhesive, I fasten the lid on the box and reach up to put it away. All I need now is some shadow and a brow pencil and I'm good to go.

"What are you doing?"

I gasp. Kim! The box slips from my fingers. The lid pops off. Lashes, adhesive, and tweezers scatter across the black and white tiled floor.

Heat floods my cheeks; I turn.

Kim stands, hands on hips, wearing her faux fur vest and leggings with her favourite thigh-high boots. She scowls at the stash I've accumulated at my feet: the hairpiece, the lipsticks, the various pots and tubes. "Why are you taking my stuff?"

"I—Um." I'm tempted to lie—lately I'm quite skilled at it—but of all my family, Kim is the most suspicious and the most perceptive. I'm rarely able to fool her.

As I'm about to blurt out the truth, she drops her hands from her hips and says, "We have boundaries in this house, young lady. You, of all people, should know that."

I glance away, shutting her out. I don't have the energy for this. "Whatever."

She begins gathering up the things on the floor. "If you want something, all you have to do is ask." Her voice is soft, kind almost. Tears jam the back of my throat. It'd be easier if she screamed at me. Called me more names. I could hate her then. And right now, I want to hate her.

"You've never been a coward, Sloane. Don't start now." She shoves the random collection of lashes and tubes and wigs into my hand. "Sometimes the most courageous thing we can do is ask for help."

Kim is wrong, I think, as I bolt for the privacy of my bedroom. Sometimes the most courageous thing we can do is pretend to be something we're not.

Thirteen

"Sloane, Sloane!"

I'm in water. Swimming and diving with Isaac. My hair flows out long and thick behind me. But Isaac doesn't care about my hair. He's looking at the rest of me, pulling me close. Then the pool is shaking. The entire world is shaking.

"Sloane!"

I surface from the edge of dreaming. The *bed* is shaking. Earthquake?

"*Come on,* Sloane. Wake up!"

It's not an earthquake. It's Ella, pounding on my shoulder. I peer at her through sleep-crusted eyes. "What?"

She laughs, and her pink braces gleam. "Mom says I can go to Hannah's sleepover now!" She throws her arms around my neck. The scent of her citrus soap nudges me closer to consciousness. "Thank you, thank you, *thank you.*"

I suspect Dad had more to do with that than me. "You're welcome." She's hugging me so hard I'm sure she'll do ligament damage. Pulling away, I search the bedside table for my cell. It's still dark outside but I smell coffee. And Ella is already dressed. "What time is it?"

"Six fifteen," she chirps in a wide-awake voice. "We have a field trip today. I have to be at school early."

I groan. It's practically the middle of the night. "Go away." I burrow down and yank the covers back up. "I still have fifteen minutes."

She nudges my hip. "Don't be lazy. Mom's making waffles. The real kind. Not the toaster shit kind."

"Ella!" I pop my head out of my cozy hole and glare at her. "Watch your language!"

She giggles. "Why? That's what Mom said."

Knowing my chances for sleep are nil, I wiggle up and prop a pillow behind my shoulders. At least there's cream for my coffee. Sometime in the last couple of days, a small carton magically appeared in the fridge. "Well, it's not very nice." But I give her a tiny smile.

Hands resting on her jean-clad legs, she studies me for a minute. "Why do you have no eyebrows?"

Oh God. Don't tell me—

Her gaze shifts higher. Her blue eyes widen. "And bald spots on your head?" Panic skitters across her face. "You *are* sick, aren't you?"

I swallow and lick my lips. "No." I don't want Ella to know. I don't want anyone to know. That's the only way I can cope. "I'm not sick."

Slowly she eases herself backwards off the bed, never taking her eyes from mine. "Then what's wrong?"

I want to reach up and touch my brows. Are they *all* gone or the same as yesterday? But the look of fear on Ella's face stops me. "They aren't exactly sure, but it could be a disease call—"

"I *knew* it!" Before I can finish, she bolts from the room yelling, "Mom! Why didn't you *tell* me?"

I need to go after her. I can't let her be afraid.

But first, I toss the covers aside and swing my legs to the floor. I walk slowly to the mirror.

Oh my God. A nasty, metallic taste floods my mouth. It's the taste of panic.

My eyebrows are completely gone.

—

"They don't know *for sure* what's making me lose my hair," I tell Ella as we sit across from each other at the kitchen table. It's set with Kim's cheerful yellow breakfast plates, a bowl of strawberries and honeydew melon, and a small bottle of agave syrup, clearly Kim's idea of an Aunt Jemima substitute. "They think it could be something called alopecia. But they're sending me to a specialist and I won't know for sure until then."

Ella's blue eyes are huge in her milk-pale face. "Could I get it?"

"No. It's not something you catch like—" *Like lice* I was going to say. "Like a cold or anything. It's just me." Just. Me.

Her relief is palpable. "Good. 'Cause I don't want to lose my hair or anything."

Yeah, no shit. The sound of morning birdsong floats through the window. Yesterday's rain is history. It's going to be a nice day.

"It's nothing to be afraid of," Kim interjects from the counter where she's cooking the waffles. It's the first thing she's said since I walked into the kitchen. To give her credit, she's let me handle every single one of Ella's questions.

"I'm not afraid." Ella wrinkles her nose. "It's just ugly, that's all." She is staring at my head.

Ella sounds so much like Kim I want to slap her. I hate the way she's staring. I should have worn my hat to the table.

"You won't lose all your hair, will you?"

The $64,000 question. "I don't know. I could."

She leans over and looks at the side of my head. "You've lost a lot already." She looks totally grossed out.

"Yeah, I have. Sucks to be me." I try to smile but it's a pathetic attempt. It's taking all I've got to be strong for her, not to fall apart. "But you know what I've always told you, Ella, appearances aren't everything, right?"

"Right." The flat tone of her voice tells me she doesn't buy it. "Except people will stare."

"I'm not telling people. At least not until I see the specialist." And maybe not ever. "So I need you to keep quiet about this, okay?"

She nods. "Sure. When do you see the specialist?"

"In a little over two weeks."

She makes a face. "It sucks that you have to wait."

"Yeah. Well." I shrug. "I'll wear my hat and no one will know." Except for the problem of my eyebrows falling off ...

Ella brightens. "And Mom bought you the other hat, remember? That blue beret. We can be twins."

"Right." I'm not going within a hundred yards of that dumb thing. But I do have an imminent date with some false eyelashes.

Kim places a cup of coffee in front of me. With cream. A lump swells in my throat. It's a small kindness, the sort of thing Mom would do. And that reminds me. Mom still hasn't called. "Thanks." I glance up just in time to glimpse the back of her sweats as she turns away.

"You're welcome." She flicks open the waffle iron, presses a peach-tipped nail into the dough. "They're almost done. Just another minute. You can eat before you shower."

"I'm not hungry." I pick up my mug and stand.

"You have to eat, Sloane." A note of irritation creeps into her voice as she shoots me a quick look. "You can't go to school without breakfast."

"Oh yes I can."

Back in the bedroom, I punch out another text to Mom: *Call me ASAP. It's really important.*

Out in the hall, Kim laughs at something Ella says. The sound stabs me like a physical blow. My life is falling apart but everybody else's life is exactly the same. I need Mom. She's the only one who will understand.

I take my cell into the bathroom when I shower. After Kim leaves to drive Ella to school, I carry it with me into the kitchen to get a second cup of coffee and a cold waffle. In spite of what I said to Kim, I am hungry, almost jittery in my need for food. Catching sight of my reflection in the stainless steel of the microwave, I quickly avert my gaze. I know how bad I look.

I don't need to look again.

When I get dressed, I automatically reach for comfort clothes (old jeans, a soft hoodie) because—let's be honest—new clothes just don't go with the bald forehead look. My jeans are half on when my cell buzzes.

I hop-run to the bed, stubbing my toe as I lunge for the phone. "Shit!" The screen says it's an unidentified caller. Thinking of Isaac and how he surprised me yesterday, I say a tentative, "Hello?"

The line hums. My heart leaps into my throat. Please, God, let it be her. "Sloane?" a faraway voice finally says.

Legs trembling, I sink onto the bed. "Mom! I miss you." My tears are back, clogging my throat, clouding my vision.

"Got your messages ... been travelling ... just back at base tonight."

"You're cutting out." Suddenly I am furious. At the phone lines, at Mom, at my throbbing toe. "I need to *talk* to you." *My eyebrows are gone. How am I supposed to live? Go to school? Do the video?*

"Hold on," she says. There's a click before the line once again offers up its empty hum.

Clutching the phone in one hand, I pull up my jeans with the other. I'm doing up the snap when Mom comes back.

"I'm in the office on the other line now. That should be better."

It is. The hum is still there but it's not overwhelming. And her voice is clear and strong. "I've been trying to get you since yesterday."

"I'm sorry, babe, I only saw your message a few minutes ago. There's been a flu outbreak or something in one of the villages. We've sent blood samples to London for analysis. Anyway, we've been swamped. Four people have died and we brought three people back with us. They're critical."

Death. Flu. African poverty. And I think my world is ending because I have no eyebrows. I am such a tool. "You sound tired."

"Yeah, well." A soft chuckle floats down the line. "I didn't come here for a rest."

My eyebrows are gone. Tell me what to do.

"You must be on your way to school. Isn't it after eight there?"

"Just after seven. I'll leave in forty minutes or so." It's easier to talk about the mundane. "Isaac and I are doing a shoot at the hospital today for the video. Then we'll work on the footage and plan more for the laughter flash mob this coming Sunday."

Isaac. In my dream, we were going to make out. I wanted it. He did too. An ache unfurls low in my belly. Once upon a time, even with all his crazy-assed flirting, I'd thought me and Isaac ... But not now.

For sure not now.

"Laughter flash mob. That sounds interesting."

"Yeah, except I have to be on-camera for it."

"That's not so bad," she says.

"My eyebrows are gone."

"So it's getting worse."

"Yeah. I've got eight spots now." My voice comes out all wobbly. "Ella found out this morning."

She sighs. "I know you wanted to keep this private, but maybe it's best this way. It may get to the point where you can't hide it." She hesitates. "Or are you at that point already?"

"Not quite. Two of the spots are almost too big to cover with hair, but if I wear a hat, I'm okay." I eye the makeup, lashes, and hairpiece waiting on the dresser. "I'm trying a few other things too." I know better than to say more. "And I've been checking out my treatment options online."

"You can't believe everything you read on the Internet,"

Mom cautions. "And whether you're able to stop it or not, the hair you've already lost may not come back for a long time. If at all."

Heat surges into my face. "Don't be so negative. I read about this guy whose hair started to grow back *two weeks* after he had some kind of shots. You never know what's going to happen."

"True, but I don't want you to get your hopes up and be more disappointed. You need to face facts, Sloane. You need to be realistic."

Realism sucks.

The hum on the line swells, and for a minute, her voice is lost. Then she says, "Like I told you last week, you have good friends who will support you. They love you and they'll continue to love you. Hair is nothing. Not in the big scheme of things."

Maybe not in the African scheme of things. But in North America, seventy-five percent of women polled would rather lose their left arm than their head of hair. I read that in the chat room.

"I'm not telling my friends. They'd be grossed out, like Ella."

Mom sighs again. "Not true friends. Besides, you've never worried about what people thought of you before."

I was never bald before.

"You can't start now."

I already have. I have turned into someone I hardly know.

"You need to give people a chance," she says. "Not everyone is as judgmental as you might expect."

Yeah, some of us know better than to judge on looks, but it's the ones who don't I'm worried about.

And then Mom says, "I'll be right there."

For a heartbeat I think she's talking to me. But when she adds, "I'll phone London right after I check on him," my tiny kernel of hope dies. Someone else is in the room with her.

"I have to go," she says.

"I know." Disappointment rises up. I need more. More time. More her. More support. "I love you, Mom."

"I love you too, Sloanie. Hang in there. Remember you've got your specialist's appointment in a few weeks. I'll call before then. Promise. Sending you hugs." She makes a smacking sound. "Kisses too." And then she is gone.

I don't have much time to fix myself before I need to leave for school and yet I procrastinate, wasting five minutes putting everything into my knapsack and then sending an email to Leslie reminding her I'll be at the hospital with Isaac that afternoon.

But I am only postponing the inevitable. Telling myself to approach this like a film subject, I go to the mirror and pretend I'm seeing a stranger for the first time.

My insides drain away.

No wonder Ella was afraid. Without my eyebrows, I look washed out and sick. Truth lodges, cold and bleak, in the pit of my stomach. I do look gross.

Pity slams me, followed by disgust, fear, panic, your basic smorgasbord of nasty. Taking a deep breath, I lean into the mirror and inspect my lashes. Are they thinning? Or is it my imagination?

I can't tell. I've lost all perspective where my looks are concerned.

As I pull out the false lashes, I hear Kim's car pulling into the garage. Damn. I wanted to be out of the house before she came back from driving Ella to school. Frowning, I stare at a marbled grey compact. I don't remember taking it. Popping the lid, I see a trio of shadows: soft green, glittery gold, shimmering brown. So pretty. I touch my finger to the gold shimmer and smear it on my wrist, releasing a faint, sweet scent. It's a touch of pretty in a morning of ugly. No wonder women like this stuff. I snap the case shut.

Putting the compact aside, I pick up the strip of uber-curly lashes and go to work. Yesterday I planned to cut them down and glue them into the brows I had left.

But today, without any other brow hairs there to act as a frame, they look stupid. And the glue is way too thick. Dismayed, I stare at the freaky mad-scientist look on my forehead. Maybe I need to cut them down more.

There's a knock on my door. "Sloane?"

It's Kim. I don't answer. Instead, I tiptoe over and quietly lock the door. For someone who's big on boundaries, she doesn't seem to have a problem walking in on me whenever she wants. Deciding the lashes I tried are too curly, I pick out a straighter pair of half lashes. Maybe they'll look better.

A few minutes later, Kim knocks again. "Sloane? I need to talk to you."

"Later." Now I look like I have earthworms marching across my forehead. "I'm busy." This isn't going to work. Plus, I'm going to be late for school. Disgusted, I rub everything off and pick up the brow pencil.

Honest to God, who knew? It's like trying to draw a fine line with a baseball bat. My lack of attention to the finer art of makeup is clearly biting me in the ass.

I'm in the middle of trying to wipe it off when my cell phone signals a text. I glance down. It's Kim. *I need to talk to you.*

I wipe my fingers and punch out a reply. *Later.*

Half a minute later my phone buzzes again. *I got your dermatologist's appointment moved up.*

My heart flips. I drop the wad of tissue clutched in my fingers. How did she manage that when I couldn't?

I text her back. *How? When?*

Come out, she responds. *And I'll tell you.*

Piss. Trust Kim. But my need to know overrides my annoyance, so I go to the door and open it.

Fourteen

Kim leans against the wall, arms crossed, still in black sweats and fuchsia flip-flops. "You have brow pencil smeared all over your forehead."

"Really? Thanks for telling me."

She frowns. But it doesn't carry the usual "you disappoint me" vibe. Maybe because she's not wearing makeup, she looks almost human. "When do I see the specialist?"

"Tomorrow."

I blink. What the—?

"She'll fit you in before her first appointment."

Tomorrow. My knees start to tremble. *One more day.*

"I told them it was an emergency."

My euphoria is tempered by a squirm of unease. Kim managed to get me into that office when I couldn't. I owe her. "Thanks."

"You're welcome." She turns and heads for her bedroom. "I'll write you a note. You'll miss first block and possibly part of second."

I follow her down the hall. "That's not an issue. I have film first thing tomorrow. And there's a transit stop half a block from her office, so I should make it back in time for math."

"I'll drive you both ways. It'll be faster." She walks past her bed with its jumble of pale green sheets. "I'll go in with you too. Your dad would want me there." She disappears around the corner into her studio.

I am *not* seeing the specialist with Kim. No matter how grateful I am. Biting back my frustration, I stop in the doorway. "The ride in would be nice but you can just drop me."

"Dropping you isn't an option. Like I said, your dad would want me there. So would your mother." She pulls out a black director's chair and inclines her head. "Sit."

I don't want to sit. I need to get to school. "Why?"

Kim raises her brows, reminding me all over again of my own lack thereof. "Unless you want to go out in public with brow pencil on your forehead?" She turns to her supply shelf and starts opening boxes.

Feeling a strange mix of relief and discomfort, I sit.

"If you'd told me what you were looking for yesterday, I could have helped you." She turns around, a clutch of makeup pencils in hand.

I didn't want her help. Not when it comes to makeup and stuff like that. I still don't. Only now, I'm truly broken and smart enough to realize I need it.

She turns on the lights framing the mirror. The temperature in the room shoots up by about a thousand degrees. "Whoa."

"Sorry. I need good light to see what I'm doing." She squirts some clear liquid onto a white makeup pad and quickly cleans my forehead. Then she says, "Hold out your wrist."

She draws three lines, appraising them through narrowed eyes, glancing back and forth from my face to my wrist. "Given your dark hair and pale colouring, none of them are ideal. But if I even out your skin tone with foundation, they'll look better."

I'm already halfway to Freakville. If I let Kim near me with makeup, I'll end up looking like the mayor of Freakville. "Just the brows."

She picks a pencil, leans close, and goes to work.

I stare at her skin, surprised to see tiny round scars on her cheeks. There are a couple of small scars on her chin too. Odd. Kim's skin always appears so flawless. But then, I don't think I've ever seen her without makeup on.

"Some women prefer brow tattoos to brow pencils." She's making small, feathery strokes across my brow line. "You might want to consider it."

I didn't know they existed until I read about them in the chat room. They sound disgusting. "I don't think so."

"They can be really beautiful. And done right, you can't tell the difference. I know somebody—"

"I'm good. But thanks."

Wisely she says nothing more until she finishes. "It's not my best job." She stands back to assess me. "Brow pencils are more for fill in and definition. I could try for thinner but the thin look doesn't suit you."

I stare into the mirror. A waterfall of relief rushes through me. Kim has attempted to give me back my original, slightly thick, brows. I look almost normal again. Involuntarily my gaze is drawn to one of my spots. As long as I don't look at my hair.

"They look fine." Slightly fake but way better than the Brazilian I had on my forehead a few minutes ago. "Thanks."

"Take it with you." Kim presses the brow pencil into my hand. "You'll probably need to touch up during the day."

"Okay." I slide from the chair.

"If you feel too washed out with the dark brows, try wearing blush or that new hat I bought you," she adds. "The colour would be great with your skin."

"I can't wear hats in most of my classes," I tell her. Math + study hall = most. "And I've got the fedora anyway. But thanks for the suggestion."

I have accepted enough help from Kim. I don't need more. I am still my mother's daughter. Smart still matters more than pretty.

At least I used to think so. Now, I'm not so sure.

—

"Isaac is good with them," Leslie says later that afternoon when we finish shooting. We're in the long wing waiting room and Isaac is surrounded by a group of laughing kids. They're watching *Crash*. The clown is repeating his walking-the-dog mime routine where he trips, falls, and crashes as he tries to get an invisible, oversized poodle named Crayon to behave. And, like they did when we filmed them, the kids are eating it up. "Most guys his age would be uncomfortable in this kind of environment but he's taking it all in stride."

That's an understatement. Isaac is on the floor, jean-clad legs sprawled out in front of him, framed by half a dozen little girls. My heart tumbles at the sight of all those shiny, bald heads. One girl, wearing a yellow robe, grabs at his dreads. He pulls back and gives her a look of mock horror.

She laughs. "He's a flirt," I say. But I can't help smiling. If any kids could do with some good-natured flirting, it's these ones. Out of the corner of my eye, I see Leslie studying me.

"You okay, Sloane?"

Isaac asked me the same thing when we met this afternoon. When I said I was fine, he added that I looked pale. Being pale was the least of my worries. Hiding in plain sight at school for most of the day proved harder than I thought it would be. "I'm fine," I tell her. And I quickly change the subject like I did with him. "I'm pretty sure we got some great tape." I tell her about the laughter flash mob this coming Sunday, how it's the last shoot we need before doing the final edit. She asks if I've heard from Mom and we spend a few minutes talking about Africa. Then she looks at her watch and says, "Jade has a scan in fifteen minutes. I need to get her ready."

I glance to the corner where Jade sits with a couple of kids in wheelchairs. Isaac has joined them. He's crouched beside Stacey, a six-year-old burn victim who's in for more skin grafts. And he's signing. "I didn't know Stacey could sign."

"She can't." Leslie retrieves an empty wheelchair from the alcove near the door. "But since her hearing was damaged in the explosion, her mom is trying to teach her. Somebody must have told Isaac."

When we reach them, Jade looks at me and giggles. "You look so silly without your hat, Miss Cookie!"

Isaac gives me a tiny half smile. *Miss Cookie,* he mouths.

I give him the death stare before turning to Jade. "Remember what I told you when I came in today and you didn't recognize me at first? I only wear it when I'm reading to you." Today I'm back to the sage-green ball cap. I don't care if it makes me look jaundiced. It hides more than the fedora.

"You have an appointment downstairs, Jade. The tech will be here any minute to pick you up." Leslie pats the wheel-chair. "Your limousine awaits."

"I want him to push me." Jade points at Isaac.

Leslie gives her weary smile. "The word *please* might be useful."

"Pleeeease!" Jade squeals.

Isaac looks at me. "We're done here, right?" I nod. He takes the wheelchair and waits while Jade gets settled before steering her to the door. Jade waves at her friends. "See ya later, alligators."

Two of them answer. "In a while, crocodile."

Stacey says nothing. But as she lifts a hand in farewell, a faint smile floats across her taut, scarred face. The image haunts me as Leslie and I follow Isaac and Jade into the hall.

"Poor Stacey," I mutter softly.

Jade hears me. "Stacey's not poor. She lives in a big house with a heated pool, and last summer her parents took her to Disney World."

Isaac looks back at me. "And there are worse things than being deaf."

Deaf is only part of it. Stacey's whole face is burned.

"Yeah, like being blind," Jade says. "Then you couldn't see *anything* at Disney World. That would be awful."

As the two of them debate the merits of Disney World over Disneyland, Leslie and I fall behind. "Sometimes it takes a five-year-old to give me a slap upside the face," she says.

"What do you mean?"

"It's easy to pity these kids. I fall into the same trap at times."

"It's not a trap." I can hide my hair loss. Stacey's problem is front and centre. "Most people would feel sorry for her."

Leslie sighs. "I get what you're saying, Sloane. I do. But pity implies they're somehow less than their whole selves. And Jade understands that."

Up ahead, Isaac leans down and whispers something in Jade's ear. She laughs. "Oh come on, Jade's five years old."

"So?" She snorts. "Trust me, some five-year-olds are wiser than a few adults I know." She turns serious again. "It may not be conscious, but at some level, Jade understands she's not her cancer and Stacey isn't her burn. And Stacey's hearing loss may or may not be permanent; the doctors aren't sure yet."

That's good news. It suddenly occurs to me that I've been more upset by Stacey's scarring than her hearing loss. What does that say about me? Nothing good. I push back a niggle of shame.

"Either way," Leslie adds, "Jade doesn't feel sorry for Stacey because she doesn't see her as a victim. She sees Stacey as Stacey."

I didn't. My shame deepens. "You know what people are like. That poor kid is in for years of stares and comments and general nastiness. People will see her as 'less than,'" I put invisible quotes around the last two words, "because of her burn." Just like some people will see me as less than because I'm losing my hair.

"I know." Leslie and I watch Isaac wheel Jade up to the nurses' station. "Both girls have a hard road ahead. Jade has to heal and Stacey has to learn to endure."

Learn to endure. What a nasty phrase. "It doesn't seem fair."

"No, it doesn't."

When we reach the nurses' station, a tech wearing neon green nursing clogs is checking the white patient ID bracelet on Jade's bird-thin wrist. "You're just the person I need to see." He quickly confirms her name on his clipboard and releases the brake on her chair.

"Bye, Miss Cookie," Jade says. "Bye, Isaac. Bye, Leslie."

"See you soon, Jade." After thanking Leslie and saying goodbye, Isaac and I head for the elevator.

"You guys seemed to be having a pretty heavy-duty conversation." Isaac shifts the duffle to his other hand and pushes the button. "*Miss Cookie*."

His tone is light and teasing but I still blush. "When I read to them, I bring the kids cookies and wear this wig ... so they started calling me that and ... it just kinda stuck." My voice trails away.

He grins. "It's cute."

"Whatever." My blush deepens. To hide my embarrassment, I watch the floor countdown of the elevator car.

"So what were you and Leslie talking about?"

"Mostly about Stacey. Leslie was saying I shouldn't pity her."

"You shouldn't."

"Oh God. Not you too."

He holds up his hand. "Relax. Don't lose your shit."

The elevator pings. "I'm not losing my shit but I don't get you and Leslie." The doors whoosh open; I step aside to let a woman and a man get off before following Isaac into the elevator. "That poor kid is in for a lifetime of hell."

"The skin grafts won't go on forever."

I punch the button for the lobby. "I'm not talking about the operations. I'm talking about how people will treat her."

The car starts moving. "That's their loss, not hers."

Part of me admires his laid-back attitude, but the other part is annoyed that he can't see where I'm coming from. "I feel sorry for her. Any compassionate person would."

"Pity is just another form of judgment." He shrugs. "It's disempowering. It doesn't help Jonas when people feel sorry for him. It won't help Stacey either."

And if life unfolded according to the logic of Voice Man, my hair loss would be no big deal either.

The car stops to let a crowd of people on. Isaac steps closer and accidentally knocks my hat. Panic turns me cold. I straighten it and inch closer to the wall, but there's really nowhere to go. "So we'll go view the footage now, right?" His breath is hot on my ear; he smells faintly of coffee and musk.

"Sure."

He is way too close. He gazes at me—at my eyes, my mouth, my eyes again—and my stomach bottoms out. Is it my brows? My hair? What can he see? "I figured we'd go back to my place instead of doing it at school. We have a computer room in the basement and I can kick the other kids out."

His place. The basement. *Alone?* Not a chance. "Actually it might be better if you give me the tape so I can look on my own."

His eyes narrow slightly. "But you just said yes. And we haven't sat down together to view the footage yet."

The elevator bumps to a stop. I follow him into the lobby, mentally scrambling for an out. But Isaac doesn't give me a chance to speak. "Look, I get it okay? I know what's going on."

Fear twists my gut. He can't know.

He tosses the duffle over his shoulder and stares at me. "I'm not totally useless."

Oh geez. "I didn't say you were."

"I know you think you have to control every little thing, and if you don't do it, it won't be done right, but that's not true." He's saying I'm a control freak. Without judgment and in the nicest way possible. And, damn him, he's right. "I know I messed up on that project we did last year and you ended up doing most of the work, and that wasn't fair."

He's *admitting* it?

"This time I want to do my share," he adds.

"For sure. It's just—" *I can't be alone with you. Not today.* "I have an appointment that I forgot about." I gesture to the lab wing. "My doctor referred me and I completely forgot until I saw the tech with all the vials on the elevator."

"I can wait. I don't mind."

Oh shit. Of course he doesn't. Mr. Laid-Back. "I, um, I don't know how I'll feel afterwards so it's probably better if you don't hang around."

A shadow passes across his face. "Oh." Thank God. Like most guys, he's obviously a baby when it comes to illness. "Okay, sure." He pops the tape out of the camera and drops it into my palm.

"Thanks."

"So, I'll see you at school tomorrow then?" His face is shuttered, the warmth of seconds ago gone.

"Yeah. I guess. Probably." I'm not sure why things are suddenly so awkward but they are.

"Because Fisher wants to see what we have before we do the laughter flash mob," he reminds me.

"I know. He wants to talk about the final cut."

"Right." Isaac makes no move to leave. He's too still, too close, too sharply focused on me.

A nervous tic starts at the corner of my mouth. I can't walk out the entrance now that I've lied. I turn towards the lab wing. "See ya," I say.

"See ya. And good luck," he adds.

Good luck? Oh right. The test. I smile and keep on walking.

<hr />

When I preview the footage in my room before dinner, I realize Isaac got some wicked hot stuff. Part of it was his creativity with angles; he even took a few shots lying on the floor. And in spite of the strict hospital rules, he captured some great footage of the kids laughing at *Crash* without focusing on any one patient. I can probably use it without worry. But he also captured a hilarious exchange between three boys who found the word *poopage* and its variations hysterically funny. When the camera pans to Jade, Stacey, and a third girl I don't know, they're studying the boys with complete distain. Their reaction—a perfect example of gender differences—makes me laugh. I definitely need to use it. But do I ask for permission or use it without asking the parent guardians? I'm mulling my options when there's a knock at the door.

"Come in."

When Ella pokes her head around the corner, I hit pause. "Hi, Boo, what's up?"

"Not much." She won't meet my gaze; she looks at the computer instead. "What are you doing?"

"Working on my video." I need to do some editing before meeting with Fisher tomorrow.

She shifts awkwardly from one foot to another. "Mom said to tell you dinner's almost ready. She's making pasta."

"Okay. Thanks." I glance at the computer but Ella doesn't take the hint and leave.

"I went to Beth's after school today," she says.

"Cool." I tap my fingers impatiently on the keyboard. I want this done before dinner.

"And we were talking about your hair thingy and—"

My blood stops. "You told Beth?"

Her cheeks fill with colour. "Yes, but—"

"I told you—"

"Not to tell anyone," Ella interrupts, a flash of impatience in her blue eyes. "I *know* that. But Beth isn't *anyone*. She's my best friend."

"And best friends keep secrets!" chimes a second voice. Beth pops into view like a live jack-in-the-box. She smiles. "And I won't tell anyone. Honest!"

Shocked by Beth's unexpected appearance and Ella's traitorous behaviour, I can only stare. Beth is the yang to Ella's yin. On top of similar dark hair and eyes, they're the same height, same build; they favour the same blue eye-shadowed, lip-glossed look. And now, as they stand in the doorway, they share the same smug, "we have a secret and we're cool with it" smirk. I take a deep, centreing breath.

They're only ten years old. Even if they act like they're fourteen. They don't know anyone I know. They go to different schools.

Except, Ella is incredibly chatty. If she's told Beth, she's probably told someone else. Or she soon will.

Ella pulls out a white book from behind her back. I glimpse blocky pink writing on the cover. "This is Beth's mom's—"

My voice comes out in a squeak. "You told Beth's mom too?"

The two girls roll their eyes in tandem. "No," Beth clarifies. "Ella told *me* and I remembered Mom's book and we think it can help." She plucks the book from Ella's hand and marches into the room.

"*You* think it can help," Ella says.

"Whatever," Beth counters.

I'm suddenly conscious of the fact that I'm not wearing my hat, that I haven't combed my hair. "Here." Beth shoves the book at me. I glance down as my hands fold around it. *Think Yourself Well! The Amazing Power of Your Mind!*

Oh my God. She has to be kidding.

"So Ella wasn't lying." When I look up, Beth is staring at my head. "You really are going bald."

My shoulders tighten. I don't need to answer to her.

"I told you!" Ella walks into the room. "And that's the hat she usually wears." She points to the fedora on my dresser. "Only not at home. But Mom says soon she'll get a wig—"

What? "I'm not getting a wig."

"... and that means she can have a pile of different styles so she'll look different every day of the week. That part's cool, right?"

Beth averts her gaze and takes a step back. "Right." Her voice is thick with uncertainty.

"So it's good?" Ella gestures to the offending book resting on my lap. "You'll read it?"

My head is ready to explode. I'm not sure who deserves my rage more—Ella or Kim. "I'll see," I mutter.

"Mom was right," Ella tells Beth. "We shouldn't have given it to her."

My body turns to stone. "Kim knows about the book. She knows you told Beth?"

"Yeah." Ella glares at me. "And I already got into trouble so you don't need to rag on me too."

"And I promised your mom I wouldn't tell anybody," Beth stresses again.

She's not my mother, I almost say. But my jaw is clenched so tight I doubt I could open my mouth.

"Mom said we shouldn't give you the book because you aren't really sick and we shouldn't treat you like a patient and make you more upset and stuff."

"But my mom is hugely into visualization and positive thinking and aura cleansing, and when we told her we knew someone who wasn't really sick but they were kinda sick and losing their hair, she said this is the best book for the job." Beth smiles. "So I wanted to bring it over."

The words spill out of Beth like water bursting from a dam, and that's how I feel. Like I've been smacked down by a five-ton wall of water. Or, more specifically, by two well-intentioned ten-year-olds. So they haven't told anybody else. Technically. Except, they have. And Beth's mom isn't stupid. She'll figure it out soon enough.

"And even though Mom had a cow, Beth can still stay for dinner as long as we don't talk about your hair when you're around," Ella adds.

When you're around. So I can be the subject of conversation as long as they do it behind my back. I bite down harder on my back teeth. Nice. I turn back to the computer, start the footage again.

"Poopalicious!" shouts a boy in a blue bathrobe as he gestures to the back of his wheelchair. The two boys beside him howl with laughter.

"Ew, *gross*," Ella squeals.

Beth grimaces. "What is *wrong* with him?"

"Patrick has leukemia," I tell them.

"But why does he have to be so *disgusting?*"

Disgusting, like what people find funny clearly depends on their point of view. I pause the video a second time. "You guys need to leave. I have work to do."

"I hope he's not at the laughter flash mob," Ella mutters as they head for the door.

"If he is, I'm not standing beside him," Beth says.

I call after them, "Who said you guys were going?"

"Mom did," Ella says. "It's Columbus Day weekend, plus it's a Sunday so Mom's taking me and Beth and Felicity. If Felicity's mom says it's okay."

I'm not sure how I feel about that. The last thing I need is Kim watching me. On the other hand, I'm seriously afraid only a few people will show up and that'll make for lousy footage.

"Your mom is taking us for pizza first," Beth says as they wander into the hall. "But I have a sensitive stomach, and if I see or hear anything gross, I sometimes puke and it would *not* be funny if I puked up my pizza."

"Especially not on-camera," Ella adds.

That's also a matter of opinion. I toss the stupid book to

the floor and push play. Bursts of laughter fill the bedroom. I stare at the sight of three boys almost hyperventilating with glee. On the floor, the corner of *Think Yourself Well! The Amazing Power of Your Mind!* presses against my foot. I stomp down hard and get back to work.

Fifteen

The waiting room in Dr. Arianna Paxton's office is empty when we arrive the next morning. As we follow the nurse down the hall past the examining rooms, my heart flips at the poster of a woman with an obvious skin disease. I avert my gaze and remind myself of why I'm here. I need a treatment plan. I need to get better. I need my hair back.

The nurse ushers us into the last room on the right. There's an examining bed, a chrome desk and chairs, and a kids' play area in the corner. "I'll let her know you're here."

Kim and I spend an awkward few minutes making polite small talk until a white-coated woman appears beside the door and plucks my file from the wall. She's tall; her face is freckled; and she has frizzy brown hair and thick, gold hoops in her ears.

"I'm Dr. Paxton." She strides into the room. "You must be Sloane Kendrick."

"Yes."

She turns to Kim. "And you must be Sloane's mother."

"Stepmother." Kim holds up her pen and notepad. "Taking notes in case we need to refer back."

"Excellent idea." Her gaze is direct, her words to the point. "I understand your hair loss has accelerated over the last couple of days."

"Yes."

"When did it start? Do you remember?"

How could I forget? "Exactly two weeks ago. At least that's when I first noticed it."

"I see from your file that Dr. Thibodeau ordered some blood work when he referred you?"

I nod.

"Well, your blood work looks good." She smiles, puts the file on her desk. "No worries there."

My heart skips a beat. "Then I don't have alopecia?"

Instead of answering, she says, "Would you mind removing your hat and coming over to the examining table?"

I'm nowhere near bald but I feel so exposed when I take off my hat. As I slide onto the table, she pulls a portable tray close. I see disinfectant wipes, specimen jars, a tiny knife no bigger than tweezers, and latex gloves. "I'll examine your scalp, take a skin specimen for a biopsy, and then pull a few hairs."

Lose more hair? I don't think so. "But—"

"Only two, don't worry." She flicks on a portable light, snaps on the gloves. "I'll pull them from an area that hasn't been affected."

Affected by what? If this isn't alopecia, then what is it?

"Bend your head for me, please."

Her rubbery fingers comb gently through my scalp. She examines the bald patches several times, once asking me to tilt my head farther to allow her a better look.

"Here comes the little scrape." I feel a stinging tug, like

I've pulled off a hangnail. From under my lids, I see her drop a piece of my pale, pink skin into one of the jars. "And now the hair." She pulls. I don't even feel it. But the lump in my throat threatens to choke me when she drops the two hairs into the second jar.

"Look up, please." When I do, she asks, "Did you bring your brow pencil with you?"

"Yes."

"Then I'm going to rub the pencil off to take a look, okay?"

Nothing about this is okay. "Sure." I shut my eyes.

The disinfectant is cold against my forehead. Seconds later, she says, "You can open your eyes now."

She is so close her nose is practically touching mine. "Blink your lashes, please."

I blink, once, twice.

She skims my right eyelashes with the tip of her finger. My eyes start to water. I blink again. She brushes something from my cheek—an eyelash?—and then tells me to look up at the ceiling. When I do, she takes a tiny flashlight from her pocket and shines it up my nose. Then she checks my ears. What the hell?

After a minute she steps back. "That's all. You can put your hat back on."

I return to my chair while she labels the specimen jars. "Have you noticed any hair loss on the rest of your body?" she asks.

"I don't think so."

She walks to her desk and sits down. "Your arms or your legs? Maybe when you shave them?"

I haven't shaved my legs in weeks. Because I haven't

needed to. My stomach knots. Oh my God. "Maybe a little on my legs." My voice sounds as if it's coming from far away.

She jots something down in my file. "What about in your pubic region?"

My stomach cramp intensifies. She *has* to be kidding. "My pubic region?"

"Yes."

"I don't know." It's not like I'm in the habit of examining myself. "You said my blood work is good. That there's nothing to worry about. So if I don't have alopecia, what do I have?"

"The fact that your blood work is good doesn't rule out alopecia." She drops her pen and leans back in her chair. "If anything, it helps us confirm it."

I stiffen.

Kim looks up from her notebook. "How can that be?"

"We do the blood work to rule out an underlying disease or a thyroid condition. Something other than alopecia that could cause hair loss," the doctor tells her. "In this case, nothing showed. Dr. Thibodeau's preliminary diagnosis was alopecia but it's always good to get a second opinion."

Her smile is kind. Respectful. But I cannot smile back. Hate for this woman—her freckles, her frizzy hair, her calm, cool demeanour—swamps me.

"As a matter of routine, I'll send your hair and scalp sample for analysis but there's really no question in my mind that you have alopecia. I've seen hundreds of cases and yours is presenting quite typically."

Deep down, I knew it. Even though a part of me prayed it wouldn't be true. I hug my waist. I'm suddenly freezing.

To-the-bone cold. But I am prepared. I know exactly what I want. "Let's discuss treatments."

"Of course." She pulls two pamphlets from her desk drawer and hands us each one.

"About Alopecia" the blue banner screams. The same brochure Thibodeau gave me. I stick it under my thigh. "I read about some treatments online and I know you have to be careful about online stuff—my mother is a doctor—but I'm talking about conventional medical treatments. Things like prednisone or anthralin or cortisone shots. I've considered them all. And I want to try the cortisone shots."

"I don't recommend it. Not yet."

"Why not?" Kim asks sharply, pen poised over her notebook.

"My recommendation is that Sloane wait until she's through the acute phase."

"Until I lose all my hair you mean?"

The doctor opens her mouth but Kim cuts her off. "How long will that be? Why can't Sloane start the shots now?"

Dr. Paxton twists her silver watchband. "Alopecia is extremely unpredictable in its progress. The pattern of hair loss can take many different paths. Treatment depends on the type of alopecia we're dealing with."

"But you said my case was typical. I've got the smooth, round spots of alopecia areata, right?"

Dr. Paxton's eyes meet mine and skate away. Nerves flutter in my stomach. "Alopecia areata is the most common form but given the swiftness of your hair loss to date, my educated guess is that we're dealing with either alopecia totalis or alopecia universalis."

Oh no. No, no. Totalis wipes out all the hair on your scalp, usually fast. Universalis takes all your head *and* body hair. Both are totally gross. I clutch my stomach. I might be sick. "Are you sure?"

"I can't be one hundred percent sure yet, Sloane. I'm sorry. But given the amount of hair you've lost in such a short period of time, and considering the loss of your eyebrows and the thinning I see on your lashes and in your nasal cavity, I suspect we're dealing with universalis." Compassion shines from her brown eyes. "Unfortunately treatment options for totalis and universalis are minimal and the outcomes are generally poor," she adds softly.

I'm going to lose all the hair on my head and probably all the hair on my body too. My stomach rolls and dips. I'm a fucking freak.

"Keep in mind that alopecia universalis may be acute and short-lived," she adds.

"But it can be permanent too." My voice is croaky. I did my research.

"True," she admits. "But regrowth is always possible even in cases where there's one hundred percent hair loss over a period of years."

Years. Good God in Heaven.

"One of the things you have to be aware of with AU—"

Kim frowns and stops writing. "AU?"

"Alopecia universalis," the doctor clarifies. "And one of the things you need to be aware of is that when people lose their lashes and brows along with the hair in their nose and ears, they're more vulnerable to dust, germs, and the invasion of foreign particles."

I want to throw up. First I lose my hair. Next I'll be invaded by foreign particles. Great.

"Are you saying there are no treatments at all?" Kim asks.

"Certainly there are things we can try. I'll see Sloane every week for the next month. By then we'll have a better idea of where she's at. We're seeing some success with topical immunotherapy, whereby we produce an allergic reaction with irritants placed on the skin. The idea being that hair can sometimes be stimulated into regrowth by irritating the follicles."

I tune her out. I cannot believe this is happening to me. I haven't done anything to get this. I haven't abused my body. Indulged in risky behaviour. Nothing. It's so fucking unfair. There's no treatment. No cure. No way to control this.

Honestly, cancer would be better. At least I could get chemo. And people would understand. Who understands baldness?

"My nurse will give you some information on the National Alopecia Areata Foundation," the doctor continues. "Even though you likely have a different form of the disease, the organization is an excellent resource and will be able to help you."

"I don't need it." I've read enough online. Too much.

"I understand this is hard for you, Sloane. Believe me, I do. Over four million Americans are affected by alopecia. And the effects are primarily emotional and social." She pauses. "Have you shared this with any of your friends?"

"No."

"I would encourage you to confide in someone. Those who cope best surround themselves with a support group. Sharing is so important. The NAAF holds a yearly conference—"

Go to a freak show? No way. I look at Kim. "Can we go now? I need to get to school."

"Not so fast," Kim says. "There's someone else I want you to see. I thought we'd talk to her about your options."

Options? Like I have any? "My video's due in less than a week. I need to finish it." Before I become a card-carrying member of Freaktown and have to stay home forever. "Besides, my options are pretty clear." I stand. "Bald or bald."

⸻

"I don't want a wig."

Half an hour after our appointment with Dr. Paxton, I am surrounded by hair and mirrors. My current definition of hell.

I'd been so stunned by the news from the doctor that when Kim said we had an appointment with another specialist and hustled me into a nondescript office complex off Polk, I assumed she meant another medical specialist.

Instead, I am in a windowless room lined with shelf after shelf of faceless heads topped with every kind of hair you can imagine: short, long, sleek, curly. Red, blonde, brown, black. I glance at a spiky white wig with green and pink tips. Even multicoloured.

"But—"

"No buts." I give Kim a frosty smile before turning to Francine. She's a short, bowling-ball-shaped woman wearing a flowing red caftan. "Thanks anyway."

Before I can stop her, Francine whips off my fedora and slaps a long, dark wig onto my head. "Sit!" She is bowling ball with attitude.

Swallowing my anger, I sit.

The two of them hover in front of me, flipping bits of hair around. I glimpse at myself in the mirror. Small white face, huge dark wig. I look like a vampire playing dress-up. A trickle of sweat runs down my back. Only vampires are never hot and I'm pretty sure they never take this kind of abuse either.

"We'll need to have it thinned," Francine says to Kim.

"And shortened." Kim touches my shoulder. "To about here."

"I'll have to send it out."

I shut my eyes, shut them out. I do not want to be here. I do not want a wig. But I don't have the energy to argue. Besides, Kim can buy me as many wigs as she wants; I don't have to wear them.

After a minute, Francine stands aside. "What do you think?"

The hair is a good colour match for my own, I mentally concede as I stare into the mirror. Even if it feels like I'm wearing a garden shrub on my head. "It's heavy. I'd rather wear a hat."

"So I heard." Before I realize what she's doing, Francine pops the wig off and replaces it with a denim ball cap. A cap with dark hair attached. "This is a lighter, cooler option." She stands back and gives me an appraising look. "It suits you."

Unlike my sage green cap, this one fits snugly. And the attached hair is so close to my natural colour, it totally blends in.

"Can you shorten the hair and maybe thin it a little?" Kim asks.

"That I can do immediately."

"Thanks," Kim says. "We'll take both. I'll pick up the full wig next week."

Francine takes the cap to a table in the corner. Kim pulls her wallet from her purse. "You can wear the new hat to school right now if you want," she tells me.

"No, I can't." I shove the fedora back on my head.

"Why not?"

"Because I have to take my hat off in some of my classes and I'm not taking my hair off too."

<hr>

Forty minutes later, I'm signing the late sheet in the office when the secretary looks over the top of her neon green reading glasses and says, "Miss Kendrick? Mrs. Peterson would like to see you in her office."

Her words chill me. There's no reason for the school counsellor to see me. Unless something has happened. Stomach churning, I hurry to Peterson's office, mentally flipping through the ugly possibilities: *Dad's plane has crashed; there's been a shooting in Mom's Sudanese village; Ella's been in an accident.*

Mrs. Peterson's door is open. Her curly grey hair is bent over a stack of papers. When I knock, she looks up and smiles. "Sloane, hi. Come on in." She gets up to shut the door. "Your mother called."

My unease mushrooms. Mom wouldn't call the counsellor from Sudan unless something *was* seriously wrong. "My mother?"

"Yes." She sits back down. "She told me about your issue with hats."

It's a second before I realize she means Kim, not Mom.

"She explained about your illness and why you need to wear them in class."

My heart slams to a halt. Kim has told *the counsellor* about my alopecia? The gratitude I feel towards her dissolves. What part of "it's a secret" doesn't she get?

"This must be difficult for you," Mrs. Peterson says.

I clench my hands; my nails bite into my palms. Does Kim think going to the doctor's office and stopping at a wig store gives her the right to meddle in my life?

"If you'd like to talk or need a safe place to vent, I'm here," she adds.

Kind and non-judgmental, Mrs. Peterson has been known to let kids sleep on her couch when they've had problems at home. She's as non-threatening as a kitten, and yet right now, she feels like the enemy.

"It's fine," I lie.

"I've already informed your math teacher of the situation."

Oh God! What if he says something to me in front of people?

"But since your mother just called a few minutes ago, I haven't gotten to the others yet. I'll do it at lunch and explain—"

"No!"

"But—"

"Math is the only class where I'm not allowed to wear a hat. The others are fine with it."

"All right."

And then I remember. "And maybe study hall."

She frowns. "I don't see study hall on your rotation this term."

"It's not. But I'm working on a video project for film studies and I've been doing some of the work in study hall." Because the library is now a toxic waste dump of memories.

She scribbles something on a sheet of paper. "I'll talk to her then."

"But I, um. I want to keep the reason for the hat thing quiet." I stare at her. "I *really* don't want anyone to know about the—" I hesitate. "Illness." It's the first time I've actually said that word aloud.

Her gaze is sympathetic. "I understand."

She doesn't. She can't. No one can. "If you could stress that this is a *private* medical issue to those two teachers and that I don't want *anyone else* knowing, I'd appreciate it."

"Of course." She nods. "I'm sorry you're going through this, Sloane. I really am."

Right back at ya, Mrs. P.

"If there's anything I can do to help, please just ask."

"Thanks." Other than putting a muzzle on Kim, there's nothing she can do.

—

The instant I leave Peterson's office, I text Kim. *DO NOT TELL ANYBODY ELSE.*

She answers immediately. *U should be allowed 2 wear hats. Counsellor is discreet.*

I respond: *This is a SECRET. NO ONE else.*

My hands are shaking so much it takes me three tries to

open my locker. Please God, don't let anyone else find out. Tears burn behind my eyelids. I couldn't stand the stares. The whispers.

My wavy distorted self stares back from the tiny mirror on the back of my locker. I lean in to inspect my brows. Kim reapplied them at the wig store, muttering the whole time that her angles were off. And sure enough, the right one looks weird.

I slam my locker shut and head for the nearest bathroom. It's becoming a compulsion, this need to look at my reflection everywhere: subway cars, restaurant doors, puddles even.

But I can't help myself.

Inside the bathroom, I'm assaulted by the smell of pot and raucous laughter.

Oh God. Breanne and two members of the Bathroom Brigade. I turn around. I need to find some privacy.

"What?" Breanne drawls. "Scared of us?"

I turn back. They're leaning against the sinks, lined up like three badly dressed skanks in a chorus line. Breanne takes a toke from a joint before passing it to the girl on her left.

"She's not scared of anything," says the girl with the kohl-rimmed eyes. "She's a Michael Moore wannabe, dontcha know?"

"Only, Moore dresses better." The other girl sucks in some smoke. She's wearing a purple halter top the size of a rice cake. "And those boots with that hat?" Her eyes roll so far back in her head I actually see white. "That's, like, a serious whiff of badass ugly."

More peals of laughter. If I leave, they'll never let me forget it, but I don't want to linger either. "I need to wash my hands." A quick rinse and I'm out of here.

The three of them exchange glances. As if on cue, they double over in convulsions again. "I'm glad you find me entertaining." I shove my way between Breanne and Rice Cake Girl. "Now excuse me."

I turn on the water. While it heats up, I glance into the mirror. My heart picks up speed. The brows are too thick. And the one on the right has a strange arch thing going on. I look like a deranged serial killer.

Breanne straightens, takes another toke from the joint, passes it on. "The boots and the hat are bad enough, but check out those disgusting eyebrows." She glances at me and smirks. "Can you spell tranny?"

Heat races into my cheeks. *Leave. Go.* But I am rooted to the spot. Humiliation has burned me into place.

"Trannies are male."

"No, they're not," says Kohl Girl. "How 'bout Chaz Bono?"

"Bono isn't a tranny," Breanne clarifies, "he's transgendered." In her stoned drawl, it comes out as *traaaaaansgenderrred.*

"Whateeeever," Kohl Girl says. "It wouldn't surprise me if *she* graduated and *he* came back to our first reunion."

Their words slam me like a body blow.

More peals of laughter. Rice Cake Girl chokes on her smoke. Breanne slaps her on the back.

That's it. I switch off the water. I'm outta here.

The door swings open. "I smell pot." Mandee Lingworth clomps into the bathroom. "That's illegal."

"That's *illegal*," Breanne repeats in a singsong voice.

Kohl Girl giggles. "*You're* illegal."

"So is your sweater," Rice Cake Girl adds.

Mandee flushes. Her turquoise sweater has a brown

coffee dribble. "I'm not illegal. I'm allowed to be here. My period started."

Snorts of laughter. "Ewww," Breanne says. "TMI."

Mandee digs in her pocket for change. "It's true. And that's what I told Mrs. Perez when she stopped me in the hall." She plugs a quarter into the dispenser on the wall.

Kohl Girl blanches. "Perez is down the hall?"

"Shit, shit, shit." Breanne bolts for the stall and throws the joint away. "I'm on my third warning. I can't afford another one." She flushes the toilet. "Let's go."

Tranny. I stare at my reflection. Really? *They're stoned,* I tell myself as they giggle their way out the door. Higher than kites.

Except. What if somebody else thinks the same thing? What if Isaac does?

Mandee's gaze meets mine in the mirror. "Did your period start too, Sloane?"

"That's personal, Mandee. But no, it didn't."

"Cause you look sick."

Something inside me shrivels and dies. "What do you mean I look sick?"

"Sick like you're on your period." She removes a small blue packet from the dispenser and sticks it in her pocket before turning around. "Like me." She gestures to our side-by-side reflections. "See."

I've got two inches on Mandee; she's got thirty pounds on me. Her hair sticks up on one side; most of mine is hidden under my fedora.

"You're the colour of mashed potatoes," she says matter-of-factly. "So am I."

At least she doesn't think I look like a tranny. But still.

"I never have any colour when I have my period either, probably 'cause I'm bleeding it all away."

Before I can react with the kind of revulsion that comment deserves, Mandee pulls a lipstick from her pocket and offers it to me. "Here," she says. "You can use this just like blush."

I don't need blush. I need a new set of eyebrows. A full head of hair. A friend. I need Lexi. But I'd be crazy to tell her. Certifiable. "I'm good, Mandee. Thanks."

"You're not good." She unrolls the tube and smears a blob of pinky purple across her cheek. "You look like you're going to throw up."

I feel like it too. One thing about Lexi, she never lies. She'd tell me if I looked like a tranny.

Except I'm not sure I want to know.

Brow tattoos can be beautiful. Kim is in my head. *You can't tell the difference.* Getting my eyebrows back would be a step in the right direction. A move away from Freaktown.

But I can't get tattooed by myself.

You need support. I hear Dr. Paxton's words now. And then Mom: *Your friends will love you no matter what.*

No way. Lexi would be totally grossed out. *I'm* totally grossed out.

Maybe I should go home. I stare at my reflection in the mirror. Kim would understand. Except I have another math quiz this afternoon, and since I failed the last one, I can't afford to miss this one.

Tranny.

I have to make myself look better. I rub at the arch in my brow. Better, but not perfect. As I dig through my bag for Kim's brow pencil, my gaze lands on my cell.

Tranny.

I need help. I need my best friend. Before I can overthink it, I punch out a message. *Can you meet me outside the band wing? Asap?*

"Here." Mandee presses the lipstick into my palm. "I look better now and you can too."

I dab a few spots of colour on my cheeks but only to make Mandee happy. Being pale is the least of my worries.

Tranny.

I'm way more worried about Breanne's comment. That and how I'll tell my best friend I'm going bald.

Sixteen

"What happened to your cheeks?" Lexi demands when we meet outside ten minutes later. Her hair is up in a sloppy topknot; turquoise chandelier earrings dangle from her earlobes. "You look like you got attacked by a purple pencil crayon."

I didn't think it looked that bad. Maybe when you start going bald, your standards slip. More likely I never had any standards in the first place. "It's a long story." I rub at the offending lipstick.

By unspoken agreement, we cross the student parking lot, walk across the street to the bank, and turn the corner to the coffee shop. The smell of dark roast hits me like a welcome slap.

"So what's going on?" Lexi pulls her slouchy grey sweater tight and wraps her arms around her waist.

I don't know where to start. I can't stop thinking about what Breanne said about my eyebrows. How I'll look on tape at the laughter flash mob. What Isaac will say.

"So?" she prompts.

"Do I look like a tranny?"

She gapes at me. "A *what*?"

"Sssh. Don't *yell*!" I tug her past the florist. "A transvestite?" I murmur when the guy arranging the buckets of flowers is behind us. "Do I look like one?"

"What kind of dumb-ass question is that?"

"Breanne thinks so."

"Like I said. Dumb. Ass."

"You haven't answered the question." Losing my hair has turned me paranoid.

"You don't look like a transvestite." But she won't look at me.

My heart does a nasty lurch. "What *do* I look like?"

She's silent.

"Come on."

"Like you're at the awkward first-date stage," she blurts out.

Now *I'm* confused. "What are you talking about?"

We slow down. The coffee shop is only two doors away. "Like that first date when you like the guy a lot but you're not quite sure it's going to work out only you want it to so you try a little too hard."

Huh? Sometimes letting Lexi talk is the only way to figure out the puzzle of what she's saying. But this morning it's not working. "I don't get it."

"It's like you've finally given up pretending you don't care what you look like." We stop in front of the door. "But you're in that awkward 'trying too hard and going overboard and messing up' stage."

If she thinks I'm awkward now, how about when all

my hair falls out? I grab the door handle. "I'm getting tattooed."

She follows me inside. "Are you *nuts*? Have you *seriously* lost your mind?"

Behind the counter, the barista shouts, "One large pumpkin latte, half sweet, double shot."

I glance around the room. More than half the tables are taken. It's way too crowded. And too public. I can't tell her here.

"My God, Sloane, those needles can give you AIDS, hepatitis, even tuberculosis. The Mayo Clinic did this study—"

"Sssh!" I interrupt. Like I need the guy in front of us to hear. "You don't understand—"

"No, *you* don't understand!" Lexi raises her voice to talk over me. "This Mayo Clinic study found people got syphilis, tetanus, one guy even got flesh-eating disease from a tattoo parlour." She stares at me like I've sprouted a third arm. "What is *wrong* with you? First you get a hat, which—" Her turquoise earrings bob when she jerks her head at my fedora. "I hate to say it but it's not your best look." I open my mouth but she cuts me off again. "And don't say Tannis could have found you a better one because she couldn't. Then you pluck your eyebrows until they look like threads. Now you want a *tattoo*?"

The guy in front of us moves on. We step up to the counter.

"What's wrong with tattoos?" the server asks with a smile. Given that she has about a dozen piercings in her face, lime-green shadow framing her eyes, and some kind of twisty creature inked along the right side of her neck, she is not the best person to argue my case.

"I am trying to save my friend from making a ridiculous mistake," Lexi tells her.

"It's not ridiculous if you go to the right place," the server responds. "I know someone—"

Oh *man. Everybody* knows someone. I cut her off. "I'll have a tall strong to go, please." We'll walk over to the playground; I'll tell her there. "And no cream, so top the cup up." I probably should have started with the diagnosis and led up to the eyebrows but my run-in with the Queen of Skanks has left me somewhat—okay majorly—obsessed.

"I'll have a cinnamon dolce latte with a double shot of espresso and extra whipping cream."

"To go," I remind the barista.

Lexi pouts. "Can't we stay? It's cold out."

"No. And FYI, a plain coffee would have been faster."

"FYI back. When my best friend tells me she's about to indulge in potentially deadly behaviour, I need sugar." She pulls out her cell, does a quick surf. "Listen to this. It's from the Mayo site. 'Few states have hygiene regulations to ensure safe tattooing practices and—'"

I pluck the phone from her hand.

"Hey!" She lunges for it.

I put it behind my back. "I'm not talking about a body tattoo. I'm talking about my forehead."

"Last time I checked, your forehead *was* part of your body. And who gets a permanent tattoo on their forehead anyway? That's just stupid."

A middle-aged blonde in black sweatpants taps me on the shoulder. "You have to be eighteen to get a tattoo in the state of California," she says. "At least from a place that's legitimate."

Oh my *God*. Is nothing private? I shove Lexi's phone in my pocket.

Her jogging partner pipes up. "But your mother can write you a note, dear. I did for my daughter. She got a green and blue dragonfly." She smiles. "It's pretty but I think she should have picked the ladybug."

Lexi and I exchange glances. The server returns, rings in our order.

"I'm seriously worried about you," Lexi whispers after we pay and walk over to the barista bar. At least she's whispering. "Do you have a vitamin deficiency or something? You're acting totally weird."

"Skinny peppermint mocha," the barista yells. I wait for a woman in a beige trench to take her drink and leave. "There's a reason," I murmur.

"Yeah, yeah, I know. You're the smart one and you'll never be pretty but you don't care what you look like because you're better than that and it's substance over style." She waves her hands in the air. "Blah, blah, yada, yada."

Her words jolt me. It's like listening to a tape of myself. A self I hardly recognize anymore. I wish I could turn back time. Be who I used to be.

"But I can't believe you'd get a tattoo just to make a dumb point about beauty." Lexi's face is flushed with colour; her nostrils are flared. A total giveaway that she's slipping into what my mom calls her overwrought, histrionic state.

"Double espresso." A guy in a yellow construction hat steps up to the counter. We take a few steps forward; our drinks are up next.

"Tattoos can lead to scarring."

My God, if she's having a meltdown over a tattoo how

will she handle my hair loss? More to the point, how will I handle her? Maybe I shouldn't tell her.

"They can lead to dermatitis. Psoriasis even." Her voice is starting to climb. The two women in jogging suits are behind us again. I motion for Lexi to tone it down. "They'll be a problem if you ever need an MRI," she adds in a slightly lower tone. "One girl I know said hers set off the airport security alarm. And who wants *that*?"

I need to tell someone. I can't go through this alone. Especially not with people like Breanne staring at me and making my life miserable. And who better to hold my hand when I get inked than my best friend? The fact that she's a histrionic hypochondriac is a plus. She'll insist the needles are clean and she'll be the first to tell me if they're screwing up.

But now that I've thought through some of my anxiety, I realize the tattoo isn't my only worry. My more immediate worry is getting through the rest of today. Sitting through math. Seeing people. Breanne again. Isaac maybe.

"You need to rethink this, Sloane." She holds out her hand. "Give me my phone back."

I hand it over, and reach for my own. I can't say this out loud. I just can't. So I text her.

I have something to tell U.

She shoots me an "are you for real?" look. "Seriously?" she screeches. "You're standing right beside me and you have to *text* me?"

The blonde behind me says, "Oh, my daughter and her boyfriend do that all the time." Her friend laughs.

I text: *That's why.*

Lexi answers: *R we 5 yrs old now?*

My fingers fly over the keys. *I'm losing my hair.*

She starts to laugh. "Right. Like I believe th—"

I pinch her arm.

"Oww!" she yelps.

The barista slaps our drinks onto the counter. "Tall dark, filled to the top. Cinnamon dolce latte, double shot, extra whip."

"Get a lid," I tell Lexi. "We're going for a walk."

═

"So tell me. What kind of weird-ass disease makes your hair fall out?" Lexi demands when we're sitting in the park.

The picnic table is hard beneath my butt. I stare across the playground to the swings where a little girl in a bright red jacket is being pushed by her mom. Nearby, a boy in yellow rain boots claps his hands and runs after a black crow. I refused to tell Lexi until we got here, but now I can't bring myself to say the word.

She scoops impatiently at the whipping cream in her coffee. "Come on. What is it?"

Here goes. I sip my coffee for courage and then say, "It's called alopecia and I've been to two doctors and it's been confirmed so don't even think about suggesting I have something else."

"And it makes you bald?"

My heart skips a beat. "Yes."

Her stir stick stops moving. "Let me see."

My stomach clenches. I glance at the mom and her two kids. They aren't looking. And even if they were, they're far enough away. I look back at Lexi. She's waiting.

I've come this far. There's no going back. I take off my

hat, run a finger through my hairspray-crusted strands, and slowly turn my head from side to side.

Lexi stares. Her eyes go wide and her mouth opens. Then it closes. And opens a second time. She looks like a guppy. "Oh. My. God." When she leans forward to take a closer look, her breath is hot on my neck. "I think I read about that once. Don't you lose your fingernails and toenails too?"

What? "No. Just my hair." *Just.*

"All of it?"

My throat constricts. I take a deep, steadying breath. "Yeah, apparently so. The question isn't *if*. The doctor's ninety-nine percent sure it'll all fall out. The only question is *when*."

She blinks up at me, her face inscrutable.

"You can't tell anybody," I say.

"Okay."

"Seriously. *Not anybody*," I repeat fiercely. "Kim called Peterson and told her and she's telling some of the teachers so they'll let me wear a hat in class."

She groans.

"I know, right? And you know how teachers talk. This is *private*. Nobody finds out."

She bites her lip. "Hiding it's going to be hard."

"Yeah, well. I'm used to hard." I look away, watch the mom lift the little boy onto the teeter-totter.

"No wonder you wanted a hat."

"Yeah."

Lexi continues to study me; my scalp burns under her scrutiny. Just when I'm about to tell her to quit looking, she says, "A bald model opened a fashion show in India last year. And one of my boss's favourite supermodels of the nineties—I think she was Canadian—was bald with ink on her head."

Lexi's trying to make me feel better. I bite my lower lip, fight the urge to cry.

"Being bald isn't the end of the world," she adds matter-of-factly.

"Maybe if you're a famous supermodel." But the knot in my throat starts to dissolve. She's not as grossed out as I expected. "Or a fat, middle-aged man."

She giggles softly. Then her eyes widen. "You didn't *pluck* your eyebrows. You *lost* them."

"Bingo. Give the girl a prize."

"That means—"

"Yeah," I interrupt. "My lashes are probably next. And that's more of an issue because, according to the doctor, that can lead to complications."

"Like what?"

I shiver. Damn, it's cold. I put my hat back on. "Colds, foreign particles in your eyes, that kind of thing."

"What about your body hair?" she blurts out. "Will you lose that too?"

I hesitate. Here comes another gross-out factor. But if I can't tell my best friend ... "They don't know for sure." I clutch my coffee so hard the paper cup dimples. "But probably."

Another nervous giggle. "Think of the pain you'll avoid from waxing." She won't meet my eyes. Instead, she stares into the milky brew of her coffee. "So, like, will you ... are you ...?"

"I'm not contagious, Lexi."

She flushes. "That's not what I meant."

"But you were thinking it."

The flush spreads down her neck. "No, I wasn't. I was wondering"—her voice starts to tremble—"if it's the sign of something more serious and you'll get worse and die."

I'm touched. And surprised. I hadn't expected Lexi to make that connection. I've underestimated her. "I'm not going to die. It's not fatal. Just butt ugly, that's all."

"Thank *God.*" Our attention is diverted by a howl of indignation from the teeter-totters. By the time Lexi speaks again, her voice is back to normal. "And it's good about the not contagious part too because eventually, you know, I would have wondered."

I snort. "Eventually, as in maybe a minute from now."

This time when Lexi laughs, it's for real. Something bursts in me and I start laughing too. But seconds later my laughter morphs to tears.

"Hey." She touches my arm. "It's okay, Sloane. Really."

"It's *not* okay." My shoulders are shaking, I'm sobbing so hard. "I'm turning into a *freak.*"

"You are *not* a freak."

"Says somebody who has all her hair." I've never been a crier or a whiner, but I've cried more lately than I've cried in my entire life. Once again, I'm a mess of snot and tears and swollen eyes. I'm so embarrassed I want to slide under the picnic table and die. I wipe my face with the sleeve of my hoodie.

"Ew, gross. That hoodie might be ugly but that's no way to treat it." Lexi digs into her purse and pulls out a tissue.

By the time I wipe my face enough to see clearly, Lexi is surfing on her phone. "I'm sure there are treatments," she says. "Things you can do."

For the second time today, I pluck the phone from

her hand, push end, and toss it down. "I've done a ton of research, I've lurked on chat rooms, and I've seen two doctors." I outline what the specialist told me earlier, ending with, "There are a couple of different kinds of alopecia and they aren't sure what kind I have yet, so it's a waiting game and there are no guarantees." Especially if it's universalis like the doctor thinks. But Lexi doesn't need to know that right now.

"You could always shave your head completely. Embrace your baldness."

"Are you *nuts*? I don't want people staring."

"Then you'll need a wig."

"Says Kim. We went to this store and she ordered me one. But you should have seen them. They were so fake I almost threw up in my mouth. Can you imagine what Breanne would say if I showed up wearing one?"

"Forget that dumb-ass. Think about yourself."

"I am. The wigs were way too hot. They just weren't me. Kim bought me this ball cap with attached hair too."

Lexi wrinkles her nose. "That sounds even worse."

"Actually, it wasn't so bad. At least it didn't make me look like I'm ready for a walker. I don't know if I'll wear it, but I do know I'm getting my brows tattooed back on."

"Seriously?"

"Yeah, apparently they look so real it's hard to tell the difference. Kim gave me the name of someone. I called and made the appointment. I'm getting them done tomorrow morning at eleven. Right after my meeting with Isaac and Fisher."

"Are you sure you want to?"

I'm not sure of anything anymore. "I have to go

on-camera for the laughter flash mob. I can't do it looking like this."

"Could you skip the flash mob?"

"No. I'm leading it, remember? Besides, if I bail, that would lead to too many questions."

After a minute, she says, "I'll make sure Miles gets lots of B footage. With any luck, you'll only be on at the beginning."

"Just don't tell him!"

"I won't. I swear."

Across the playground, the mom zips up one of the kid's coats. They're getting ready to leave. I grab my bag and root around for the brow pencil Kim gave me. "But I absolutely have to go to math this afternoon and there is no way I want Breanne saying anything about my brows again, so I need you to fix them so they don't look like ... you know."

I scoot over until our knees are touching. "Don't do them as thick," I say when she picks up the pencil. "And maybe feather them if you can. Short little strokes. That's what Kim does."

I shut my eyes. I feel her wipe at the brows with the tip of her finger, and then I hear her pop the lid on the pencil. Her touch is light and tentative at first, but after a minute, both the pressure and speed increase. "There." I open my eyes to see her frowning at my forehead. "I think that's better."

"Do you have a mirror?"

She pulls a travel-sized mirror from her purse and flicks it open. It's so small I have to check one brow at a time. "Do they look okay?" It's hard to tell with these small mirrors.

"Yeah." She hesitates. "I did the best I could."

That's not reassuring. I check the right one again. "They're not too thick?"

"No. Trust me, Sloane, I think they look fine."

My shoulder blades tighten. I lower the mirror. "Don't you get it? Fine isn't *good* enough!"

Her head rears back. Colour floods her cheeks. Shame stabs me. "I'm sorry, Lexi. It's not—" I swallow hard, will myself not to cry again. "It's just—I never thought I'd be this way."

"Who does? Nobody expects to be bald."

"That's not what I mean. I never thought I'd care so much about how I look."

She stares at me, a knowing look in her brown eyes. I expect an "I told you so" but she shrugs and says, "So you're human. Don't beat yourself up about it."

But I am. This obsession over my appearance consumes me.

"Wearing mascara doesn't make you any less of a person," she adds.

No, but I'd somehow thought not wearing it made me more of one. My shame deepens. I turn away. "I don't want people to stare," I admit. "I hate the thought of going back to school and having other people thinking the same thing as Breanne." *Isaac thinking like Breanne.*

"I get that."

But she can't. Not really. And I can't expect her to. I put the brow pencil away and force myself to think of something else. What I'll say to Fisher tomorrow. How much more tape I need for the video. But a pair of crazy brown-gold eyes keeps floating across my mental hard drive, reminding me of the thing that scares me the most. "I'll never be able to date," I blurt out as we get down from the picnic table. "I'll never have a relationship."

Lexi stuffs the mirror into her purse. "There you go again, underestimating yourself."

"Oh *come on*. I know you're trying to make me feel better, but now *you're* being the dumb-ass. Who's gonna hook up with a girl who has no hair?" If she says another freak, I'll deck her.

"Having no hair isn't a deal breaker." She slings her purse over her shoulder. "Somebody who likes you is going to like you no matter what."

I pick up my bag. "Yeah, like Matt did."

"Let me rephrase that. Any *decent* guy who likes you is going to like you no matter what."

We start to walk. Just before we reach the gate that leads to the street, Lexi turns to me and says, "You're not only underestimating yourself, you're underestimating him too."

She means Isaac. But I refuse to go there. "I don't know what you're talking about."

"Oh my God, you're a shitty liar."

I open my mouth to protest but she holds up a hand to stop me. "You need to give him a chance. That's all I'm saying."

Silently I follow her. Lexi is wrong. To give Isaac a chance, I'd need to tell him. And that's something I'll never do.

Seventeen

"I'll write the narrative Sunday night after we shoot at the Embarcadero, and I'll do the final cut Monday and Tuesday so it'll be ready to go to Clear Eye Wednesday for sure," I tell Fisher Friday morning when we preview the footage in his classroom. "But those are the scenes I'm thinking of using and in roughly that order." I shut the laptop.

I was up until after midnight, shifting scenes, playing with concepts, getting part of a rough cut done. I'm second-guessing myself and part of it is the time crunch. I hate that the flash mob shoot is only three days before the submission deadline. Rushing makes me nuts.

Fisher's chair squeaks as he tilts back. He looks at Isaac. "What do you think about Sloane's decision?"

Beside me, Isaac shifts. He's still pissed that I bailed on viewing the footage at his place the other day. He hardly said hello when he walked into the classroom this morning. It probably didn't help that I got to school early and was cueing everything up when he arrived. "I think it's a good one," he says.

Voices float in from the hall. When I glance at the clock,

the hair fringe on the ball cap I'm wearing gently slaps my neck. Kim and Ella both swore they couldn't tell any difference when I put it on this morning, but it feels weird to suddenly have thicker hair.

"You look like you, only better," Ella had said. Then she'd turned to Kim and asked, "Can I get one?"

Looking "like me, only better" is a necessary evil since there's no way I can avoid going on-camera. And the thinner my hair gets, the more the fedora slips. The ball cap fits better. Plus, as Kim pointed out, I need to get used to it—and get others used to seeing me in it—before Sunday's shoot. Today I've pulled out all the stops: new clothes, new hat, makeup.

Fisher turns his attention back to me. "Sloane, I realize this video is important to you and you have a large vested interest because of the possible scholarship, but this is a *joint* project. Isaac needs two arts credits and I expect him to do more than simply hold the camera."

"He is. The laughter flash mob was his idea and he's done pretty much all the publicity for it." Isaac nods. "Plus, he's gotten really creative with the footage, taking shots I never would have suggested."

"You noticed." He sounds surprised.

"Yes."

"But Isaac also needs to demonstrate an ability to tell a story through the video," Fisher says.

"We plan to weave the Embarcadero footage through what we already have," Isaac explains. "That was my idea too and Sloane seems happy with it." When he glances at me for confirmation, it's my turn to nod. "And we'll be doing that part of the editing together," Isaac shoots me another look. "Right?"

Crap. "Right." But not in his basement.

"We could also write the narrative together," he says.

Oh no. I went through that with Matt and Breanne and it was a disaster. Isaac is way more easygoing, but still. This is supposed to be *my* video. "I'm not sure that would work."

"Frankly, neither am I." Fisher's chair emits another squeak as he shifts again. "Clear Eye will be judging voice as part of their scholarship criteria, and for that reason, it's important that Sloane's voice comes through." He looks at Isaac. "But I cannot, in all fairness, let you off the hook on this. So I'd like you to do the final rough edit together, weaving in the Embarcadero footage. After that, I'd like you to dub two copies, with each of you doing your own narratives. It'll make the marking process fairer."

After murmuring our agreement, Fisher gives us a few suggestions on the kinds of shots we should try for at the laughter flash mob—both close-up shots from Isaac and wide shots from Miles, who's running backup.

By the time we leave the classroom, the halls are full of students hurrying to second block. I pick up the pace; I'm meeting Lexi at the front entrance in about two minutes.

"Watch it!" Isaac grabs my shoulder and steers me around a band geek who almost decks me with his saxophone.

I go to shrug him off but I'm pinned on that side by three freshmen giggling over something on an iPhone.

"Isaac!" A familiar voice calls out. "Wait up!"

Breanne. I stiffen. Isaac's grip on my shoulder tightens. She's with Matt and the Bathroom Brigade.

Great. An ice pick of panic stabs the back of my throat. I try to ease myself out of Isaac's clutch but he won't let me go. My body tingles at the feel of his leg pressing into me.

Ignoring it, I plaster a smile on my face and pretend not to see Kohl Girl mouth "tranny" at me.

A toxic cloud of sweet perfume fills the air when Breanne stops in front of us. "Perfect timing!" She flips a chunk of blonde hair over her black tank, gives me a critical once-over, and then beams at Isaac like he's a demigod or something. Matt glares at Isaac's hand on my shoulder. My smile deepens. *Bite me, Matthew.*

"We're organizing rides for Sunday's flash mob but it turns out we're short of cars 'cause Matt has his in the shop and everybody else is full so we were hoping we could go in your van."

"Sorry," Isaac says. "I only have three seat belts and I'm taking Sloane, Lexi, and Mandee."

What? News to me.

Matt looks clearly relieved. "I told you."

I open my mouth; Isaac pinches my shoulder. Kohl Girl giggles, and whispers something to the girl beside her.

"We'll figure something else out," Matt says. "Come on, Bree." He reaches for her hand. "Let's go."

She pouts. "But we *can't* figure anything else out. We've already tried."

"There's always public transit," Isaac suggests.

Breanne recoils like he slapped her. "I *don't do* public transit. It smells."

I stifle a laugh. Given the amount of perfume she wears, I'm amazed she can smell anything.

"Oh well." She shrugs a perfectly tanned shoulder. "If we can't get a ride, we won't be able to go, and if we don't go, that means most of my friends will bail ..." The Bathroom Brigade nods like choreographed groupies. Breanne flashes a piranha-like smile in my direction. "And that will suck for you guys because hardly anybody will show up then."

Breanne's ego is so big it deserves its own zip code. Still. Nerves flutter in my stomach. I know a warning when I hear one. I understand the power she has over the girls who follow in her wake. "You can take my seat." I talk over Isaac who starts to say something. "Lexi's too." Misery flashes in Matt's eyes. *Library stall*, I remind myself. "I insist. We've got an alternate organized." I turn to Isaac. "You need to take them," I say. "Please."

His eyes lock with mine and I can tell he wants to argue, but something stops him. "Sure," he finally says to Breanne. "No problem."

"Excellent!" She throws her arms around his neck and kisses his cheek. I almost pass out from her noxious perfume.

Matt yanks Breanne back. "That's great." His tone is so flat you'd think his grandma just died. "Let's go tell everybody." He steers her away. Like dutiful foot soldiers, the Bathroom Brigade falls into step behind them.

I slide out from Isaac's arm. "Thanks."

"You're welcome." He gives me a lopsided grin. "Anything to avoid me, right."

I clear my throat. "I don't know what you're talking about." I start to walk.

"Yeah, you do. Lately you're doing everything you can to steer clear of me."

So he's noticed? "You flatter yourself, Voice Man." I stop at the water fountain. "I would've gone in your van except Breanne's a bitch and I don't trust her." For once, I'm telling the truth. I shift my bag and lean down for a drink.

He props his arm against a nearby locker and studies

me. He's way too close. And he's staring too hard. My scalp prickles. *He can't see. The ball cap covers everything.*

"That may be true about Breanne but my instincts are saying you don't want to be alone with me."

My heart starts to thrum. "Your instincts suck." I straighten.

He leans close. My throat constricts when his dreadlocks graze my cheek. "Then why'd you lie about going for tests at the hospital the other day?" he whispers.

My heart slams to a halt. *Crap.* We're so close I can practically count the gold flecks in his eyes. "I don't know what you're talking about."

"I waited. I saw you leave five minutes after me."

My shoulder blades tighten. I hadn't counted on that.

"So you either had no tests at all or the tests were over so fast, I could have waited and we could have previewed the footage together." He pauses. He's waiting for me to respond. When I'm silent, he adds, "Either way, I think you did it on purpose because you didn't want to be alone with me."

Suddenly breathless, I spin away from the water fountain. "Think whatever you want."

He falls into step beside me. "I'm just trying to figure you out, that's all."

"I am not a puzzle. There's nothing *to* figure out." I quicken my pace. I need to get to Lexi. I need to get away from him. "Other than the video. That's the only thing we need to worry about." *Liar, liar, pants on fire.*

He grins. "I'm not worried, sunshine, but I am curious."

"Curiosity killed the cat."

"And cats have nine lives."

"I don't play cat-and-mouse games," I counter, relieved

that I've diverted his attention from my lie. "You should know that by now."

"Too late. Game on." He winks. "You've been warned."

My heart flips. I turn the corner to the entrance. Lexi is there, waiting for me. Thank *God*.

"Cat got your tongue?" he calls after me.

I don't turn around. But over my head, I give him the finger.

His laughter follows me down the hall.

—

"Seriously, Isaac sees me as conquest," I whisper to Lexi when we walk through the door of Salon Aya forty minutes later. "I'm the only girl who doesn't drool when he comes within a hundred feet."

Tinkling New Age music plays from hidden speakers. A calming floral smell hangs in the air. I tap my fingers impatiently against the blonde wood counter. This is the place Kim recommended, and I know she was in touch with the owner by email, but she's been so preoccupied with a fundraiser at Ella's school that I've had to make the arrangements myself, so I'm not entirely sure what I'm getting into. After a minute, when no one comes, we sit.

"You're wrong. He likes you. A doorknob could see it."

I roll my eyes. "And you should know."

"I *am* an expert on human nature."

"Right. That's why you and Miles keep breaking up and getting back together."

Ignoring the jab, Lexi gets up and helps herself to some filtered water. A striking orange and blue Japanese screen separates the waiting room from a long hall and presumably the tattoo room. My uncertainty roars back. I was up half the night worrying. What if this is a mistake?

I can remove makeup. Take off a wig. But tattoos are forever. I chew the corner of my lip. I sound like a freaking commercial. Except it's my life. And getting brow tattoos is a permanent step into a girlie world I've always avoided.

Tranny.

It's not a mistake. It's the only right decision. I won't let people judge me by my looks. And without brows, they will. Lexi sits back down. "I was the only one out of all your friends who warned you about Matt, remember?"

I don't want to talk about Matt. Taking a brochure from the side table, I change the subject. "Did you know you could get your eyelashes permed?"

She grimaces. "I wonder how safe *that* is."

"Very," says a woman who steps out from behind the screen. She's wearing a long, beige lab coat over tan pants and she has a file folder—also beige—tucked under her arm. She smiles at me. "Hi, Sloane. I'm Bo. I'm ready for you if you want to come back."

"This is Lexi. I was hoping she could come in too." Lexi was more than happy to skip second block. *Who needs planning,* she'd said. And then she'd added, *Besides, somebody has to make sure those needles are clean.*

"I prefer not to have anyone there while I'm working, but you can come back while I do the outline and freezing," she tells Lexi as she leads us down the hall.

Bo has a slim build, delicate face, and the curliest lashes I've ever seen. I wonder if she perms them. "Kim emailed one of your school photos and I blew it up so I could see the natural shape of your brows," she says. "I assume you want to go back to that?"

"Yes."

"Good. That'll help me draw them on." She stops at an open door and gestures us inside.

It's a tiny space, more examining room than spa. Tiled floor, bright lights. A white cabinet. She points to a large reclining chair, the kind found in a dental office. "That's your chair," she says.

I sit. Lexi stares at the rolling tray of equipment. "So you, like, use sterile stuff, right?"

"Of course. And I wear gloves and use disposable needle tips. There's nothing to worry about."

"I don't see a tattoo gun."

"I apply the pigment manually with a hand-held needle," Bo explains. She pulls something from my file, clips it to the wall, switches on a light. An ache goes through me. It's a picture of my old eyebrows. "The hand-held is more precise, less painful, and generally results in almost no after-effects."

She retrieves a brow pencil from the tray, pulls out a stool, and scoots over to me. "I'm going to draw one in to make sure you're happy with the shape." She reclines my chair. "If you're not, say so, because it's easier to make changes now."

It's like being at the dentist, the way she hovers at my head. Only I can keep my mouth shut and it's not painful—yet.

"There." She returns my chair to the upright position and hands me a mirror. "See what you think."

Something about it is off. "Maybe a little thicker?" I lower the mirror so Lexi can take a look.

"I think the arch should move a little to the right," she says.

The two of them study me like I'm an exhibit in a museum.

"Let me do the left one." Bo lowers my chair and goes to work again. After a few minutes, she asks, "Is that better?"

The change is subtle but noticeable. "Yes."

Bo tweaks the first brow to match the second, smears numbing cream on my brow area, and then we discuss pigments. I have naturally dark brows but Bo says I need to go a shade lighter. "Too dark will be too harsh with your pale skin. Trust me."

Lexi just shrugs.

"You can always go darker when you come back for the touch-up," Bo adds. "But you can't go the other way and lighten up."

"Okay."

As Lexi follows Bo back to the waiting room, I hear her say, "The Mayo Clinic says you can get an allergic reaction to tattoos years after you get them. Has that happened to any of your clients?"

Bo's answer is muffled. One thing's for sure: Lexi wouldn't have left me here if she had concerns. She told me that on the way over, when she googled to see if Salon Aya had any health violations lodged against them.

"You have a good friend there," Bo says when she comes back.

"She worries a lot."

"There's nothing wrong with that. Or with asking lots of questions." She bends over me. "I'm going to check to see if the numbing cream is working. Shut your eyes for me, please." A few seconds later, I feel a slight prick on my forehead. "Can you feel that?"

"A little."

"How much does it hurt, on a scale of one to ten?"

I've never been good at the pain scale thing. I open my eyes. "It doesn't really hurt. It's more like a jab."

She smiles. "Then I think we're ready." She lowers my chair, pulls the equipment tray over, and puts on a set of goggles, and then a pair of gloves.

Here we go. Sweat blooms on my palms. I wipe them on my jeans.

She unwraps something. I assume it's the needle but I don't look. Instead I clutch the side of the chair and stare at the ceiling. "This is the disinfectant." She wipes my forehead with a wet cotton swab. "You'll feel a slight vibration and maybe a little pain when I touch your brow. Let me know if it's too much."

My heart trips into my throat. "Okay."

"Some clients are more relaxed if they shut their eyes."

She thinks I can relax? Is she *kidding*? But I'm not going to watch so I shut my eyes.

Her lab coat rustles as she leans close. "Here we go."

I brace myself. A soft, whirring sound fills the air. And then I feel it. A prick followed by a slight burn. It's bearable. Like being poked with a really sharp brow pencil. I let my breath out. I didn't realize I was holding it.

"You doing okay?" she asks after a minute.

"Mm-hmm." The area she's done stings like water on a bad sunburn but I don't tell her. I just want to get this over with.

"Your alopecia diagnosis must have come as a bit of a shock."

"Yeah."

"I have a number of clients with it and I know it's a difficult condition to deal with," she says. "I admire you for being proactive and not letting it stop you."

I'm not being proactive, I'm being protective. I never realized how easy it was to hide behind being normal until normal was gone.

"There are other things we can do for you besides brow tattoos," she says. "Make sure you take a brochure when you leave."

I don't want anything else. I change the subject. "Have you known Kim long?"

"Sixteen years." Her hand moves a little to the right. "We trained at the same school but only became friends when we started volunteering together."

"Volunteering? For what?"

Her hand presses against my right nostril. "There's a non-profit group in town that provides clothing to women who are applying for jobs but don't have the resources to dress appropriately."

I can hardly breathe but I manage to say, "I've heard of them."

"They wanted professionals to help with hair and makeup, so we started going in. Then a shelter called. And another non-profit." She shifts her hand, freeing my nostril. I take a grateful breath. "Word got around that we could make women feel better and also hide bruises." She pokes me with the needle.

I gasp. "Ouch!"

She pulls away. "Sorry. I'm near the frown line and it can be painful. Do you want to take a break?"

"No, keep going. I'll be okay." I'm no baby, but that hurt.

"Kim didn't say much about it." Didn't say anything. Bo stabs me again. The pain is so intense I grit my teeth and clutch the edge of the chair.

"She doesn't do much anymore. Not since she got roughed up by that client's boyfriend when she was pregnant with Ella."

I gasp.

"Sorry." She lifts the needle. "Maybe I should give you more numbing cream?"

"No, I'm—" *Shocked.* Kim got roughed up? And I didn't know? "I'm fine."

She goes back to work. "Yeah, it was a long time ago now, but an angry boyfriend didn't like how well Kim covered up the results of his beating, and he found the shelter, and the next time your mom left, he was waiting for her. Thank God someone saw and called for help."

I seem to remember something about Kim going to emergency when she was pregnant with Ella. Dad told me she fell. She had her arm in a sling at her baby shower; I remember that.

Bo lifts her head. I open my eyes. "One down and one more to go," she says.

I brace myself while she goes to work on my left brow. This side hurts even more. My left eye waters; a headache starts at the base of my scull. I fist the chair and try to make sense of what I've learned. How could I not know something this important?

"We still call Kim once in a while," Bo says. "Especially when we get bruises we can't cover with over-the-counter makeup."

Gross. I don't want to think about the why of that.

"Kim can hide bruises and scars better than anyone. But you know that, right?"

No, this is all news to me, but I want her to keep talking so I mumble, "Mm-hmm."

"But since Kim promised your dad she wouldn't go to any of the shelters alone, Martin almost always takes her."

Martin. I remember the look on Kim's face when she spoke to him on the phone. The intimacy in her voice when she said "darling." She's having an affair with another volunteer.

"Martin's good with a makeup brush and so's his partner, Brian, but—"

I suck in a quick breath.

Bo thinks she's hurt me again. "Sorry," she says.

Martin's gay. And unless he plays both sides, he's not messing with Kim. More to the point, she's not messing with him. My stomach sinks. And I was so quick to assume she was.

The needle whirs against my brow line. "But neither guy holds a candle to your mom when it comes to camouflage and hiding things."

No kidding. What else is Kim hiding?

"And besides that, the shelters are really strict about men on the premises. Even if they're gay."

Why didn't Kim tell me? About Martin? The women she's helped? Why would she keep something like that private?

Makeup saves lives too, Sloane.

She did tell me, in a roundabout way. But did she expect me to read her mind?

Kim isn't having an affair. Nor is she the shallow bimbo brain I thought she was. I made an assumption. A judgment.

Judgments can bite you in the ass. Lexi has told me that more than once.

No kidding. I've been so worried about others' judgments I've paid no attention to my own. My headache intensifies. Kim let me think the worst.

It pisses me off. And it hurts.

After a while, Bo pulls back and studies me, her impossibly curly lashes blinking as she looks from one brow to another. She smiles. "I think my work here is done." She switches off the spotlight, removes her gloves and goggles, and returns my chair to its upright position. "Have a look."

Heart hammering, I take the mirror she hands me. *What if I hate it? What if she has ruined me?*

I stare at my reflection. Fear dusts my mouth; I cannot swallow. I bring the mirror closer. "They look real." I reach up to touch them but she stops me.

"No. Your hands may not be clean."

"The colour is perfect." I glance from one to the other. "Just dark enough."

"They won't stay quite that dark," she says. "The colour will soften to its final shade in the next week."

I tilt my head. I can't believe what I'm seeing. "It's like I have individual brow hairs or something."

"It's called feathering. It's my specialty."

"Kim was right. You *are* a magician."

She smiles. "We're all magicians, honey." She puts the mirror away and grabs a white tube from the nearby tray. "Your mom's a magician at hiding bruises and I'm a magician at making brows."

She dots my forehead with cool gel. "This will speed

healing and keep the brows moist. It'll also help with any swelling or irritation."

I wipe my suddenly clammy hands on my new jeans. "Swelling?" I can't afford to swell; I have the laughter flash mob to do.

"It shouldn't be too bad. The needle is much gentler than the tattoo gun. But if it swells, use ice. Disinfect and moisturize several times a day too." She covers each brow with a strip of gauze. "Take these off as soon as you get home. Avoid the sun, try not to scratch, and don't pick at any scabs that form."

Scabs? My unease edges closer to panic. I should have asked Kim more questions. Why didn't Kim tell me?

Bo hands me a small, clear bag. "Here's a sheet with after-care instructions as well as some antiseptic wipes and a little moisturizer to get you started."

"Thanks." I stand. I expect to be light-headed, but except for tingling where my new brows are and the stupid headache that won't leave, I feel fine.

"If you have any questions, call." We walk down the hall. "Or check with your mom. She's familiar with the procedure."

"Sure." Butterflies dance in my stomach as I go into the waiting room. What will Lexi think?

Bo gently pulls back one gauze strip so Lexi can take a look. She stares at me for a minute. "Whoa! They're, like, totally natural."

"They turned out pretty well," Bo says.

I dig for my wallet. "How much do I owe you?"

"Kim took care of it." As Bo steers us to the front door, Lexi's narrow-eyed gaze burns into me. What's she thinking? Does she really like them?

"Don't forget to book your follow-up appointment," Bo reminds me. "Maybe in a couple of weeks, once you've finished the video and handed it off, and things settle down for you."

My hand freezes on the door. "You know about that?"

"Of course." She smiles again. "Your mom told me. She's pretty proud of you."

If that's the case, Kim hides it well. My cheeks burn. Like she hides a lot of other things.

Eighteen

The next morning, my forehead is a red hot mess.

"Bo said I might get a little swelling," I tell Kim when I march into the kitchen and confront her at the counter minutes after I get up. "This isn't a *little*. This is a *lot*. I may as well be wearing *those* on my forehead." I point to the strawberries she's rinsing.

She glances at my forehead. "Ice will help."

My vision blurs. I blink back my tears. "What am I supposed to do? Walk around all day with an ice pack on my face?"

Dad looks up from his paper. "It's not that bad."

I catch my reflection in the patio door. Swollen brows. Bald spots. Nasty-assed green pyjamas I should have thrown out last year. Trembling, I turn on him. "Would *you* go out of the house like this?"

He simply looks at me.

Ella jams the last spoonful of cereal into her mouth, puts the bowl in the sink, and slinks out of the kitchen. I turn hot with humiliation. I'm being irrational but I can't help it. I'm sick of looking like a freak. Sick of having to deal. I want my life back. I want to be normal.

Fury building, I switch back to Kim. "The laughter flash mob is *tomorrow*. Why didn't you talk me out of this? Why didn't you tell me this would happen? Did you have to keep this a secret too?"

"Wait a sec—"

I interrupt her. My anger has a life of its own. "You always said I was ugly, Kim. Well, now I am. How does it feel to have an ugly-ass freak for a stepdaughter?"

"I never said you were ugly."

"Plain, then. What's the difference? You've never liked me. You've always tried to fix me!"

Her lower lip trembles. "That's not true. I've tried to help you because I care."

"Yeah, right," I mutter.

"That's enough!" Dad interrupts. "Don't throw accusations around, Sloane. I understand you're upset. I know you're hurting. But you made the decision to get your brows tattooed and you need to take responsibility for it." He slaps his paper down. "It wasn't up to Kim to talk you in or out of it."

The fury drains out of me like air leaving a balloon. He's right. It's not Kim's fault. I wish I could blame her—I wish I could blame someone—but I can't. Suddenly cold, I sink into a kitchen chair. "I'm sorry." I hug my knees to my chest. My words sound hollow, meaningless. "I am."

"At least it's Saturday and you don't have school," Dad adds.

My anger sparks back to life. "What about the *rest* of the year? What am I supposed to do about that?"

"One day at a time, Sloane." He picks up his dishes, puts them on the counter. "I'll take Ella to dance this morning," he tells Kim as he gives her a kiss. "If you don't mind holding down the fort here." The two of them exchange a look before he leaves the room. A look that would translate on film to: if you'll stay and deal with The Freakish One.

"Ice packs will be a big help." Kim blots the strawberries and puts them in the fridge. "You should be fine tomorrow."

"But what if there's scabbing? Bo said that sometimes happens too." What a holy hell of a disaster. I can't stop the flash mob. I can't undo the tattoos. But I *can't* go out with scabs on my face.

"Not always," Kim says. "Lots of women don't scab up."

"Not everyone swells either!"

"If you're worried, I'll buy you some medicated ointment and you can apply that. If you do scab, they'll be very, very tiny and I can cover them with makeup for a few hours, even though you're really supposed to keep the area clean."

Mumbling my thanks, I head for the shower. After I ragged on her, Kim is still willing to help me. I should be grateful. Instead I feel small.

—

"Bo told me about Martin," I say to Kim later that morning. Sunshine streams through the kitchen window. A grey sparrow pecks at the birdseed in the feeder on the deck.

"Huh." Ice clatters as she removes a handful from the bin in the freezer and fills a small plastic sandwich bag.

I've spent the last hour with an ice pack on my forehead watching sitcom reruns and trying not to think about tomorrow. But the ice pack has thawed, and while it refreezes, I'll need to resort to baggies with ice.

"And about what you do at the shelter sometimes," I add.

Kim doesn't respond. She zips the bag shut, opens a drawer, and pulls out a tea towel.

"Why didn't you tell me?"

"It's a private thing. We're not supposed to talk about the women."

"But in general terms. You could have told me."

She folds the ice pack into the towel. "I do it for me and I do it for them. I don't do it for anybody else."

She still hasn't answered my question. I stare at her, looking for answers, trying to make sense of it. Of her. But Kim's veneer is in place, flawless, perfect, giving nothing away. Not long ago I would have taken her rebuff personally. But Kim's enigmatic nature isn't about me. It's her deal. Still, one thing bugs me.

"That night Martin called, why didn't you explain what was going on?"

"It didn't seem important."

"Not important? But I was implying—" I stop. *Something ugly.* "I just don't get it."

A cloud passes across her green eyes. I've touched a nerve. And, I suddenly realize, I've used her phrase: I just don't get it. *You have every opportunity to do something with your appearance and you don't. I just don't get it.*

I brace myself, expecting to have my own words—*you don't have to get it; it's my life*—tossed back at me.

Instead she hands me the ice pack and asks, "Would it have made a difference, Sloane?"

Probably not. I would have found fault with her anyway.

Because, as far as I'm concerned, Kim never could do anything right. I've found fault with her for years. I hold the ice to my flaming cheeks and wander back to the TV room. And that says more about me than it does about her.

—

Sunday, I wake up before dawn. This time tomorrow, the laughter flash mob will be over; I'll be working on my video for Clear Eye. But my excitement is tempered by dread. What will I see in the mirror today?

I lie there for a while listening to the birds and watching the sky get lighter. It's going to be a beautiful day, perfect for shooting. Finally, when I can't stand the suspense anymore, I get up and pad to the mirror.

My knees start to tremble. The redness and swelling is gone. But my right brow is starting to scab. "Kim promised she could do something about that," I say into the silence. "She promised."

And she does. Before I leave, she performs magic with concealer and suggests wearing the ball cap with the fringe, which I'd planned to wear anyway. Pulled low on my forehead, my brows are barely noticeable.

I get to the Embarcadero early. I buy a coffee, walk the perimeter of the Ferry Terminal Plaza dodging the pigeons and mentally rehearsing what I need to do. This has to go well. It has to! After my coffee's done, I stop pacing and calm myself by staring out across the water to the Bay Bridge and the rolling hills of East Bay. Lexi and Miles arrive just as the Sausalito ferry is pulling into the dock. Isaac and the others appear a few minutes later.

"So three minutes before the clock in the tower strikes eleven-thirty, Lexi and I will walk over to the centre of the plaza, whip out our phones, and start laughing," I tell Isaac. He's leaning on the railing staring across the Bay at a cluster of navy ships anchored offshore for Fleet Week. Two seagulls soar above the water; they look like tiny white tissues floating in the blue sky.

"We've programmed in a short laugh track to help us get started," I add. "You remember, right?"

"Yep, for sure." But he doesn't turn, doesn't move, doesn't reach down and take the camera out of its bag. He seems mesmerized by the birds, the sun turning the tips of the waves silver.

My palms are sweating; I rub them against my jeans. This shoot is critical. The footage we've gathered so far is fine but fine doesn't get scholarships. And I want this scholarship almost as much as I want my hair back.

"As soon as we start laughing, that's your cue to start your camera. And Miles will start his. Everybody else will join in after that." I've managed to waylay most people as they've arrived to give them instructions.

"Sounds good." His dreadlocks bounce as he taps out a beat on the railing.

Nerves thrumming, I add, "Don't you think it's time to get the camera set up?" I check my phone. I synchronized it to the clock tower when I arrived. Three minutes and fifty-four seconds until we start.

He turns, rests back on his elbows. "Relax. We have hours yet." The glint in his eye tells me everything I need to know.

"Quit messing with me."

He spreads his hands in fake innocence. "Who, me?"

"Don't."

He smiles. "But you're fun to mess with."

My girl parts clench. *Don't go there.* "Everything rests on this shoot," I remind him. For Isaac, it's about getting his two arts credits. For me, it's no longer only a dream, it's also an escape. Film school would be my "get out of jail free" card—a place where nobody knows me, where I can hide behind the mask I've created and work at an art form I love.

I glance around the plaza. My fear that people wouldn't show up was unfounded. A dozen kids from the strings class are sprawled on the concrete benches framing the perimeter. Eight or nine rugby players circle a ring of cheerleaders. On the other side of the plaza, the drama geeks are listening to a bluegrass fiddler. My gaze lands on a familiar group. My stomach knots. Breanne. Matt. Kohl Girl. And their friends. Quickly I avert my gaze. The hair fringe on the ball cap gently slaps my neck, a reassuring reminder that I'm faked up, made up, and ready to go. Between the eyebrows, the hat, and the new clothes, I hardly recognize myself.

"I've told everybody not to go past those doors over there." I point to the musician. "And to stay this side of that green umbrella." I gesture to the vendor selling fruit and nuts a dozen feet away, down from the ticket booth for the ferry. "It'll make shooting easier if everybody stays in this general area."

A bead of sweat trickles down my back. The sun is hot; it's a perfect day for a flash mob. But I'm sweating in the jacket Lexi loaned me. Hell, I'd be sweating if it was snowing. "I hope people remember to stagger their start. I want the laughter to go in waves."

"You're going to have to go with whatever happens,"

Isaac says. "We can mess around with it later. Let it flow organically."

Organically? Does he think we're talking apples here? I bite my tongue. The miniscule part of me that's not a control freak knows he's right. "Yeah, I know."

"It'll be great," he says. "A couple of the guys told me they brought clown noses and Mike said he'll walk on his hands to get the crowd laughing."

For everybody else, this is fun. For me, this is big-time serious. All eyes will be watching me. And if there's an art to getting stared at, I've never mastered it. "When the clock rings out eleven thirty, Lexi and I will hold up our fingers in the *shush* signal and everybody will stop laughing," I remind him. "I want that sudden stop. We talked about it, remember?"

"Yep, I remember. And I coordinated the time on our phones so we'll be in synch."

Special emphasis on "in synch." A tiny smile just for me. Flirty eyes. I look away.

He slings the camera bag over his shoulder. "I'll go get set up."

Finally. My breath slows. I check the time. Two minutes, nineteen seconds.

As Isaac wanders off, Ella, Beth, and a girl I assume is Felicity run up. "Sloane, Sloane! We're here and we're ready to go!" I spot Kim a dozen feet behind them. "What do you want us to do?" Excitedly she claps her hands. "Tell us. Just tell us."

"Go stand by those two people over there." I point to Mandee who is hanging out with a chubby guy in baggy checkered shorts. Apparently Isaac's known him since grade nine and promised him a sack of beer if he'd stick with Mandee at the flash mob. "That's my friend, Mandee. She's nice." If Sack Boy bales, the three of them can keep her company.

Giggling, they bounce away.

"You okay?" Kim asks. She's wearing a white sun hat the size of a small car and leopard sandals that are practically stilts.

"Fine."

"Anything I can do?"

Move on. Stay out of sight. But I can't be mean. Kim spent almost an hour doing my makeup this morning, and she didn't make one single comment about how I looked. Not one. "I'm good." Breanne is staring at us. Sweat beads the top of my lip. *Oh crap.*

"I can hold your jacket if you want to take it off," Kim offers.

"It's okay." I survey the crowd. People are too spread out. I need to get them in closer. Plus, Miles isn't in position. "I have to go."

Before I can move, Kim grabs me. "Blot." She presses a tissue into my hand. "Never let them see you sweat."

I shove it into my pocket and check my phone. My heart stutters. One minute, twelve seconds.

I sprint-walk to Lexi. "We're at the one-minute mark. Get Miles to stand by the trash bin. Tell the strings guys to get off the benches and have the jocks move in closer. I'll round up the drama geeks and then we need to get into position."

Breathe, I remind myself as I hurry through the crowd, asking people to move in closer. *Breathe.*

"Where are *we* supposed to stand?"

Crap. The noxious fume of rancid perfume almost chokes me. *Not now.* I turn, and come face to face with a sequined pink tank and an acre of boobage. Breanne.

"Everybody else has been told where to stand but we haven't." She frowns. "Are you ignoring us?"

Yes, you and the Bathroom Brigade. "Nope. Just been kinda busy." I flash a crocodile smile and wave in the direction of the green umbrella where Matt and Kohl Girl are hanging out. "Where you are is great."

Her frown turns into a scowl. "I don't want to be that far away. I want to be *on*-camera, not behind it."

Perspiration pools under my armpits. I glance at my phone; my stomach does a backflip. Forty-nine seconds. "Don't worry. People will be recording it on their phones and stuff."

"I didn't come here to be on somebody's *phone*. I came here to be on the actual camera."

Bite me. Thirty-seven. My scalp prickles under my ball cap. *Damn,* it's hot. Kim was right. I probably should have taken off my jacket. "You'll be in it, I promise."

Breanne's eyes narrow to nasty little slits. "And your promises mean so much."

Wha—? *My promises?* "Stand wherever you want. But pick a spot. We're starting in—" I glance at my phone. *Oh God, oh God.* "About thirty seconds."

Her lip curls. "This whole thing is dumb. It's never gonna work." Breanne stalks off.

I don't need her vote of confidence. *Breathe.* I check to see that Isaac is in place. He gives me the thumbs-up sign. *Breathe.*

Lexi is back. "You good?" Her voice seems to be coming from the far end of a tunnel yet other sounds seem crushingly loud: a barking dog, a ferry whistle, a crying child. My senses are razor sharp; my body is wired. I smell the vinegar on someone's fries. Sea spray off the ocean.

"Fifteen seconds," Lexi murmurs. She reaches into her pocket for her phone. "Get ready."

My breath stalls. What the *hell* am I doing? I stare unseeing into the crowd. I'm vaguely aware that Matt and Kohl Girl aren't by the umbrella anymore, but I can't see them. I can't see anyone. I'm blind with panic and fear and adrenalin. Why did I think this was a good idea?

My phone hits eleven twenty-seven.

Blood rushes into my head. *It's time.* Silver stars swim across my line of sight. *Don't faint.* I blink them away, take a breath. And then I see him. Isaac. He is gazing at me, steady and true. He nods, and lifts the camera to his shoulder. "Now," I tell Lexi, kicking into autopilot. I hit play on my phone. The laugh track spills out.

Lexi freezes. She stares at me like I've turned into a five-headed monster. I know exactly what she's thinking because I'm thinking it too: What if this doesn't work? What if we fall flat on our collective asses in front of everybody?

Then an unmistakable girlish shriek rings out behind us. *Ella.*

I start to giggle. So does Lexi. Two women walking by arm-in-arm give us snotty "are you for real" looks, which makes us laugh harder.

Seconds later, the drama geeks burst into obviously fake, over-the-top laughter. A couple kids make stupid, exaggerated faces. One girl titters. Another whoops. A guy with a wispy goatee doubles over like someone has rammed his gut with a pitchfork. Then he starts snort-honking like a maimed giraffe. The jocks laugh at *him.* Then the cheerleaders start. And the drama geeks. Kim.

And like the wave I wanted, laughter ripples through the

crowd. Confused passersby stop to watch. One guy pulls out his phone to take a picture.

Thank you, God. My relief is a physical thing, flowing through my body like blood flowing through my veins. I'm euphoric, light-headed with joy.

More students materialize, moving in from the periphery, crowding the plaza. Dozens of people surround me, laughing, holding up their phones, recording every minute. And Isaac is there too. The camera follows me as I move through the crowd with Lexi, but I'm okay with it.

Anything for the video.

A kid in a green T-shirt pulls out a red clown nose and puts it on. One of his buddies yanks it away. The hand walker lifts his legs in the air and does his thing. A little boy laughs. His younger sister clutches her mother's leg and turns away, unsure.

Perfect, just perfect. I hope Isaac got it.

I spin away, glimpse Mandee and Sack Boy. Breanne and Matt. Ella and Kim. Two drama geeks. They're laughing. Everybody is. And so am I. For real this time. Because I'm stoked. The flash mob has worked. A little longer and I'll have the footage I need.

The jocks start to play-punch. A few kids throw themselves on the ground and roar with laughter. The clown nose goes flying. There's a scramble of bodies. A lunge for control.

Laughing. Pushing. Shoving.

Behind me, someone pulls the hat from my head.

And the bottom drops out of my world.

Nineteen

No.

Heart hammering.

Sweat dripping.

I cannot breathe.

Eyes staring. Mouths gaping. Laughter dies.

And something breaks open inside of me. *Everybody knows.*

Ella freezes. Lexi looks aghast. Breanne smirks. *Look,* she says to Kohl Girl. I can read her mouth. *Gross.*

And Isaac is there, getting it all on-camera.

Isaac.

Stabs of laughter. Pockets of silence. Familiar faces. Phones in the air. A hot, tight band squeezes my chest. There's a minute till the end. *What do I do now?*

Appalled, I whirl around, thinking of escape, looking for my hat. It's on the ground. I lean down to grab it at the same time Lexi does. I want to run, but I have no legs. No courage. Nowhere to go. The band in my chest tightens. Besides, running won't change this.

"Laugh," Lexi hisses. She slaps the hat back on my head.

I can tell it's crooked and I want to straighten it, but even though Lexi is laughing, her eyes issue a warning. "Laugh like it was planned," she mutters. "Like you don't care."

But I do care. Right now, I care more about my looks than a million stupid videos combined. The realization hollows me out. I've tried to pretend otherwise, but I can't pretend anymore.

I've always wanted to be pretty. Always. But I never thought I could be so I didn't try. Because I am my mother's daughter. Because I didn't think I had a choice. Because I didn't like Kim.

I search for her in the crowd. Her hat is sideways, at a ridiculous angle. Holding my gaze, she flips Ella's hat backwards in a crazy tilt. Her eyes bore into me. *Keep going.* I know what she is thinking. *Never let them see you sweat.*

A lump the size of a cable car jams my throat. *I've tried to help you because I care.* Kim is on my side. I don't know if she always has been, but she is right now. Lexi jiggles my arm. I manage a stab of laughter. It's the most miserable sound I've ever heard. Like an elephant dying.

I need to get out of here.

Mechanically I follow Lexi as she spins through the crowd. Laughter rises and falls around us, mocking, grating, slicing at my nerves. I can't look at the camera; I can't look at anyone. I stare out across the Bay. I want to jump off the end of the pier and sink to the inky black of the ocean floor.

Everybody knows. I'll never be able to leave the fucking house again.

I glance at my phone. Thirty seconds to go. I see Kim and Ella. Lexi and Miles. Matt who studies me with a question in his eyes. And Breanne who stares at me with judgment in hers.

There's Mandee, giggling with Mr. Promised Six Pack. And Isaac. The laughter catches in my throat. Still behind the camera. Still filming.

He knows. At least he'll stop flirting with me now. That'll be a relief. Only I don't feel relieved. I feel like I've eaten poisonous crab meat.

Or that I'd like to.

Ring, clock, ring.

I let my gaze hopscotch through the crowd as though the entire thing were planned. A joke to keep everybody laughing. I see the jocks, still goofing off. Another drama geek walking on his hands. The cheerleaders are playing with the clown nose now. Maybe they didn't see? Maybe not everybody did?

You won't know till you see the playback. A sick, sinking feeling twists my gut. Like I want to watch it? Like I can? The footage could be ruined. For sure my life is.

After the longest minute in the history of civilization, the clock in the tower finally strikes eleven thirty.

Though I'm tempted to pull a Cinderella and run, I force myself to follow Lexi's lead, raise my finger, and give the signal to stop. And miraculously people do.

A few bystanders start to clap. A little boy yells, "Again."

"I'm outta here," I tell Lexi, gazing uneasily into the crowd. Kim is rounding up the girls. Isaac is packing up the camera. My stomach jackknifes. He's looking right at me. I grab Lexi's arm. "Let's go."

"I want to find Miles," she says. "Hold on."

"No!" I see Isaac—walking towards me. "You go," I drop her arm. "I'm leaving right now."

I hurry over to Kim. "Can I get a ride with you guys?"

"Of course." She straightens my hat, quickly tucking the fake hair into place. Tears press behind my lids. It's the kind of thing Mom would do. "Smile," she whispers.

"Everybody *saw*." My voice quivers. Behind us, the girls are in a huddle, no doubt discussing me. "They all *know*."

"You don't know that." She tucks my arm through hers. "Get a grip, Sloane. You can't afford to fall apart now."

Kim's bluntness saves me. I've always hated it, always taken it as a personal attack, but her no-bullshit attitude is who she is. For the first time, I'm grateful. Pity would do me in. We start to walk. In spite of the heat, my body is like a block of ice; my movements are leaden.

"Sloane!" Isaac calls. "Wait up."

I freeze. Kim presses a warning into my arm. "Keep moving. We're three minutes to the car."

"I need to talk to you," Isaac says.

I glance over my shoulder. "Not now." I sorta, kinda smile. "I've gotta go."

"But—"

"Not right now," Kim repeats with a smile. "She'll catch you later."

"I—" He stops, scratches his head, studies me for a minute. "Sure." His smile is forced; it doesn't reach his eyes. "Later."

My heart falls to Middle-earth. I turn away. I feel him staring after me, his gaze burning a hole through my jean jacket, through my T-shirt, through flesh and bone and sinew that protects my heart. I know that look. Pity and disgust. I'd recognize that particular combination anywhere.

—

"Quit surfing!" Lexi grabs my phone and shoves it down the side of the sectional where I can't reach it. Not that I need to. The images of me already on Facebook are burned into my brain.

"I wasn't surfing. I was reading my texts." Text singular. From Miles. Telling me he got some fabulouso B footage. No mention of what I've dubbed my Gross Reveal.

"*And* surfing."

We're sprawled in the TV room at Dad and Kim's. A dozen feet behind us is the formal dining room, and just beyond that is the kitchen. The fridge opens and closes; someone drops a piece of cutlery on the floor. Kim and the girls are assembling nachos. It's clearly Kim's consolation prize. *Reveal yourself as a freak and I will feed you junk.*

My cell phone buzzes, signalling a text. "That might be Mom. I need to look." I texted Mom the minute we got to Kim's car.

Lexi gives me a look of disbelief as she digs out the phone to check. "It's Isaac. He says: *Miles gave me the B footage. We need to do final edit before dubbing copies + we need to talk.*"

He's the last person I want to talk to. I hold out my hand. "Lemme have it."

"No."

"I need to answer him."

Her chin juts out. "You are *not* getting this phone while I am in this house. Tell me what to say and I'll text him."

"Tell him we'll do our own edits. Tell him to burn all the footage to a disc and leave it in my mailbox. Tomorrow is fine." I can't watch the footage right now. "Give him this address too. I don't think he has it."

While Lexi answers, I burrow deeper into the corner of

the sectional. Giggles come from the kitchen behind me. At least someone is still laughing.

And then it hits me. A lot of people are still laughing. For real this time, and at my expense.

Two images have hit Facebook so far—one of me just after the cap flew off my head (looking like I'd been electrocuted) and the other with my cap back on but a sideways fringe of hair where it's not supposed to be (looking like my BFF just died).

And then there are the wall posts, many of them courtesy of the Bathroom Brigade:

Bad hair day 4 Kendrick.

LOL!! When you can't keep ur hat on!!

No, when you can't keep ur hair on!!

Hair of the dog: woof woof.

???? Let yr hair down or whaaa?????

Talk about humiliating. I will never live this down.

"Done." Lexi shoves the phone back down the side of the couch.

"This day was a total disaster. I'll never be able to leave the house again."

"You have to stop thinking about it, Sloane. Seriously!" She sounds matter-of-fact but sympathy flashes in her dark brown eyes. "Yeah, it sucks and some people are being ass-hats but your video is due at Clear Eye in a couple of days. You need to focus on that. You can't afford to be preoccupied."

I lower my voice so the others can't hear. "I'm not even sure I want to do it anymore." It's not that I don't *want* to. It's that I don't think I *can*. "I can't watch that footage." I'd be living it all over again.

Lexi scoots close. "You have to watch it. You have to do the video." Her voice is low and urgent. "I can't believe you'd give up your dream."

Tears cloud my vision. I'm not giving up my dream. Film school is still on the top of my list, but maybe I should forget the Clear Eye scholarship for this year. Maybe I should try next year. Maybe by then, I'll have my hair back.

"You've wanted to go to film school since grade five. That's not going to change. Whether you have hair or not. Whether you grow a third arm or a second head."

Blinking back my tears, I manage a tiny snicker. "Do I get hair on my second head?"

"I'm serious, Sloane." But she smiles just a little. "You've never been a quitter. Don't start now."

She's right. Miserable and bald is bad. Miserable, bald, and a quitter is worse.

"What was it you told me when you were doing the final edit on the shoe video? That you needed to box up your feelings and serve the film?"

"That was different. Breanne was being a douche."

"It's not so different. She still is. So box up your feelings and serve this film. When you see yourself, pretend you're watching somebody else."

I don't know if I can do that. But I can edit and splice and write narrative. I'm good at that. And right now I need something I'm good at. I need to focus on film school. I need a reminder that I am more than the hair on my head. "Fine, I'll do it. But I'd like you to hand it in for me. There's no way I'm going back to school."

Ella materializes in front of us, her two friends trailing behind. "Why not?" she asks.

Kim steps into view. "Here are your nachos, girls." She places a long, wooden tray onto the ottoman in front of us. Five plates are piled with nacho chips, onions, salsa, and browned cheese. Real cheese, it looks like. My mouth starts to water; it smells so good.

"You can eat them here or in your bedroom." Kim points to a stack of napkins on the edge of the tray. "Just make sure you use those."

"Why aren't you going back to school?" Ella demands. She picks up a plate and almost dumps the nachos onto her lap when she tries to sit down.

Kim grabs the plate just in time. "Sit first," she says. Once she's settled, Kim gives her the plate along with some napkins.

I glance at Lexi. *Bedroom*, I mouth. She nods.

"Why not?" Ella demands.

"I don't need the hassle," I say.

"Because of your baldness, right?"

Felicity lets out a nervous giggle. Beth glares at her.

But Ella is undeterred. "Right?" She stuffs a handful of cheese-crusted chips into her mouth.

Totally. "Maybe in part." Felicity and Beth are taking their time choosing their plates; Lexi and I have no choice but to wait.

"So what if people think you're bald? You always say appearances don't matter."

I clench my teeth. Busted by a ten-year-old. "Yeah, well, I lied. I guess they do."

"So it's okay to be dumb as long as you look good?" Ella asks as Felicity chooses her plate.

"No! That's not what I meant."

Ella looks truly perplexed. "Then what *did* you mean?"

Beth finally chooses her nachos. Lexi and I grab the remaining two plates. Kim says, "Sloane was confusing appearance with beauty, girls."

I almost drop my plate of nachos. I was?

Lexi hands me some napkins.

"Appearance is superficial but beauty goes deep," Kim says. "Beauty is the way we live our life, how we dress, even how we do our jobs. Beauty is an art. And with so much ugliness in the world, beauty is never wrong."

Even when we feel rotten? Isn't it hypocritical to put on our best face with tattooed brows and makeup and hats?

"Beauty," Kim adds, staring right at me, "is doing the best we can with whatever situation we find ourselves in."

Even a bad situation, she means. I avert my gaze. Once upon a time I pretended I didn't care what I looked like. When people judged me for it, I made it their problem. I slide another look at her. Or I got angry. But I was such a fake. Covering up my sense of lack with defensiveness.

"Thanks for the nachos," Lexi says as she turns to go.

A sick, sinking feeling swamps me. "Yeah, thanks." I'm not defensive anymore. And the only person I'm angry with is me. Now I know what it's really like to care about my looks. And to truly not measure up.

===

When the doorbell rings later that night, I almost slosh root beer onto my lap. I know it's him. So strong is his presence, he may as well be standing in the TV room with me. "I'm not home," I hiss at Dad. Thank goodness you can't see into the house from the front door.

"It's probably the Girl Scouts selling cookies." Dad stands and arches his back. "I'll go see."

It's not the Scouts. It's Isaac. I know it. I grab the remote and push the pause button. "If it's the mint kind, buy two boxes. But if it's for me, I am *not* home." Dad and I are watching Anthony Bourdain eat cobra heart in Vietnam. Kim and Ella have gone for a walk. It could be a million other Sunday nights in my life. Except, it's not.

"Seriously," I whisper at him as he ambles away. "*Not* here."

Seconds later when the front door opens, I hear that unmistakable baritone. Voice Man. Heart thrumming, I straighten the cotton scarf on my head. Just in case Dad is stupid enough to let him in. But when Dad says, "She's out for a walk with her sister. Can I help?" I turn limp with relief. *Thank you, God.*

A few minutes later, he comes back into the TV room with the camcorder and a small bag. "So that's Isaac."

"Yeah." Why is he smiling? "That's Isaac."

He puts the bag on the couch between us. "Everything you need is in here. He says he took copies for himself and gave you the originals."

"Thanks." I pick up the remote.

Dad crosses one leg over the other. "We can watch TV another time if you want to go and get started."

"No, I want to watch the show." And another and another and another. Until the nasty Gross Reveal (now on YouTube, thanks to Breanne, I am sure) is erased from memory. I push play. Bourdain's about to eat fried tarantulas.

But Dad is looking at me, not the TV. "I know this is hard for you, Sloane, but you can't hide forever."

Why not? "Yeah, I know."

"Running away won't help."

It wouldn't hurt. "I'm not running anywhere."

"You know what I mean." He rubs his chin. He seems to be searching for words. "The sooner you come to terms with things, the easier it'll be."

Blah, blah, psycho blah. "Right." I boost the volume.

Dad takes the remote from my hand and stops the show again. "I'm serious."

Reluctantly, I turn to face him. "I hear you, Dad. I do. But cut me some slack. It *just* happened." My lower lip starts to tremble. "I need time." Like a year. Or three. "Tomorrow is Columbus Day so I'm off school, but Tuesday first thing, I need you to call and make arrangements so I can work at home for a while."

Dad picks up his glass, stares into it like it holds the answer to life's mysteries. Or at the very least, the answer to his messed-up daughter. "I'm not sure, Sloane. I need to think about that."

"What's to think about?" My anger rises along with my voice. "It's not like things will change by Tuesday."

He rubs his face again. "The thing is, Sloane, if you want others to accept your hair loss, you need to accept it yourself."

I groan. "Dad! If I needed a shrink, I'd get one, okay?"

"Sorry." He grins. "I've been watching too much Dr. Drew on my layovers." After a minute, his face turns serious. "But it's true, Sloane. The most important relationship we'll ever have is with ourselves."

I raise a tattooed brow. "So, if I accept myself, can I stay home from school Tuesday?"

He grins again. "I'll sleep on it."

═

Monday morning I dawdle: showering, checking my texts (Mom still hasn't replied), and assembling an extra-large plate of nachos and cheese—with olives this time—when I realize I'm alone in the house and Kim isn't around to suggest one junk food pig-out a week is enough. I eat them barefooted, standing on the back deck. I don't even sweep up the crumbs. I let the birds have them instead.

Kim would be horrified. It is my little rebellion.

When I can't put off the inevitable, I take my coffee to the bedroom where I lock the door and retrieve the bag Isaac dropped off. Along with the camcorder, I'm surprised to find two discs—disc one and disc two. Maybe Isaac put the B footage on a separate disc.

I pop disc one into my laptop. Isaac has dubbed everything we shot, right from the beginning. It gives me a chance to immerse myself in the guts of the thing before my guts are turned inside out at the end. By the time the flash mob footage appears onscreen, I am thinking solely of the film.

Or so I tell myself.

The truth is the first time I appear, I jerk like someone poked me with a hot stick.

Breathe. Box up your feelings and serve the film.

I watch myself laugh. It's hard to believe that person is me. I look so different with the hat, the perfectly arched brows, the thick concealer, the lined lips. Such a try-hard. Like a member of the Bathroom Brigade.

When the jocks start to play-punch and a few kids throw themselves on the ground, I drop my pen and grip the sides of my chair. *It's coming.* I stare at the screen. The clown nose goes flying. My heart starts to gallop.

And the hat is pulled from my head.

I don't see who did it, I just see their hand. A guy I think. But it doesn't matter.

There is a sense of otherness as I watch the emotions flash across the face of the person on the screen. Horror. Panic. Fear. My heart slows; I loosen my grip on the chair. I glance at her head and see three round patches of pink scalp where her hair should be. *How sad,* I think. *How very, very sad.*

But that is not me. I watch the figure on the screen turn and grab her hat. The chair presses into my shoulder blades as I lean back. The real me is bigger, fuller, wider. The real me cannot be captured on film or frozen in time or diminished.

The real me isn't about hair or makeup or anything else.

Impassively, I hit rewind and watch the flash mob footage again. I look at the crowd this time, or as much of it as Isaac managed to capture. *Think laughter. Serve the film.*

I study faces, looking for reactions to my disaster. Some people seem oblivious. Others are clearly shocked. Gaping mouths. Embarrassed laughter. The same reactions I saw yesterday only now I'm viewing it from an outsider's point of view. Through the eyes of the film.

It's laughter at someone else's expense. It's what Isaac and I saw at the zoo when that little girl dropped her ice cream and her brother laughed. It happens all the time. It's common. I can use it.

Miles's footage is also on the first disc. Like we asked him to, he focused mostly on the crowd. Lexi and I are in a few shots but not many. And my unveiling is absent. Instead,

Miles got creative with camera angles and close-ups with eyes and mouths. For a guy who doesn't take film, it's great stuff. It'll give the video the texture and the punch I want.

I don't need to include my reveal. I can insert the flash mob footage and still get something worthwhile.

But there is no escaping the truth. I am losing my hair. I will become bald. I can try to hide it but I cannot escape it. People will, inevitably, find out. Many already know. Many find it funny.

And that says a lot about my subject. Do I have the guts to include myself? How honest do I have the courage to be?

I'm not sure.

Privacy versus art. Humiliation versus honesty. What to do? Wrestling with the dilemma, I eject disc one and insert disc two. When the music swells, I jump. When my face appears onscreen, I freeze. Outtakes?

Blinking, I stare at the screen. When I realize what I'm seeing, I stop breathing. It's not outtakes. It's me. Blood roars in my head. Without my knowledge and in secret, Isaac has filmed me.

Me laughing with Lexi. Me staring into space, a tiny frown tugging at my old brows. Me with my lip puckered writing something on a piece of paper. Caught in a beam of light from the sun. Talking to Fisher. Hugging Jade. Touching Mandee.

It is me set to music: beautiful strings, a quiet flute, the soft swish of hi-hats. The melody rises and falls with the changing images of my face. It is the real me, seen through his eyes. The bigger, fuller, wider me.

Hot, salty tears drip down my face, pooling in the V of my T-shirt. A sob catches at the back of my throat.

And I am beautiful.

Twenty

By four o'clock Monday afternoon, I have a rough cut of what the video will look like, so when I start getting a headache from the intense concentration, I stop and play a few rounds of Go Fish with Ella. We're stretched out on her bed, cards scattered on her frilly pink duvet, when Dad calls.

"Sloane, telephone."

I don't move. "Go fish," I tell Ella.

She picks up a card. "You have a phone call," she repeats.

Anybody I want to talk to would call my cell. "Who is it?" I yell.

Dad appears in the doorway. "It's your mother."

Finally. I jump up so suddenly the cards go flying. "Hey!" Ella hollers.

"Thanks." I grab the receiver from Dad, hurry to my bedroom, and shut the door. "Mom!"

"Sloane, darling." Her voice is clear and strong; she sounds like she's down the block. "Your dad told me everything. I'm so sorry you had to go through that."

Her sympathy makes me feel little-girl weepy. I pull a

chair over to the open window and prop my feet on the ledge. The afternoon air flutters the curtain and skims my cheeks. "It was *the worst* experience of my life. I can't show my face at school ever again!" The confidence I felt after seeing Isaac's video has somehow left me, trickling away like air slowly leaking from a balloon. Now I feel as off-kilter and ugly as I did last week. Will this constant flip-flopping ever stop? Will I ever stop worrying?

"Dad and I talked about that, and we've agreed you can take a week off."

"A *week*? Seriously? That's not enough."

"It'll have to be," Mom says firmly. "A week is enough time for the whole issue to die down and for you to come to some sort of resolution."

I almost snort. "Mom! Everybody *saw.* They're not going to forget about it in a week." *Resolution.* This isn't a cold I need to get over.

Her voice softens. "I know, darling. I understand."

No, she doesn't.

"Honestly, Sloane, you're strong. You can do this. Appearances don't matter; I've always told you that."

"You were wrong, Mom. They do matter."

But she has turned her attention elsewhere. I hear her talking to someone. When she returns, she says, "Your father told me you had your brows tattooed."

"Yeah, and they were a hellish mess for the first day but ice helped and then Kim—" I stop. Kim's always been a hot button for Mom.

"But then Kim?" she prompts.

"Put some concealer on and covered up the scabs and they looked okay."

"I saw them. Ella took a picture of the flash mob with her phone and sent it to me."

I close my eyes as if that will help push the vision away. "So you saw my hat fly off."

"No, she took a picture of you and Lexi at the beginning so I didn't see it. Hold on." I hear her murmuring to a third party. After a minute, she says, "I wish you hadn't done that."

At first I think she's talking to the other person, but then I realize she's talking to me. "Done what? The flash mob?"

"No, silly. That was a wonderful idea. The brow tattoos. I hardly think they were necessary."

"But—"

"And all that makeup?" Her laugh is strained. "I barely recognized you."

I take a deep breath before saying, "It's just makeup, Mom. What does it matter?"

"It's not you, Sloane. It gives people the wrong idea of who you are."

Suddenly needing air, I jerk my feet off the window ledge and stick my head out the window. "Who am I, Mom? *Really*?"

"You're a smart, bright, caring, creative woman who will go far in life."

"And how does makeup change that?"

She pauses. I picture her, hunched over the phone, chin on her hand, and frowning. "Makeup is fine. I'm not opposed."

Right.

"In moderation. But too much gives people the wrong idea."

"And what do I care about what other people think? Haven't you always told me that's a waste of energy?"

She sighs. "I didn't phone to argue with you, Sloane. I'm just saying I don't like to see you covering up who you are."

Mom's message is one I've taken to heart since that disastrous makeup session with Kim when I was a little girl. *Will I spend my time being who I am or pretending to be someone I'm not?* But maybe it's not an either-or scenario. "Maybe I can do both."

Her laugh is genuine this time. "That's not possible."

"Why not? Wearing makeup doesn't make me any less smart or creative or caring. I'm still me. With eye shadow or not." With hair or without. I have to believe that. I *need* to believe that.

"I suppose you can always get them removed."

At first I don't get it, but when I realize what she's suggesting, my stomach sinks. I jump up and start pacing. "I'm keeping the brows, Mom. I might even get a tattoo on my arm. A dragonfly," I add recklessly, remembering those crazy, meddling moms at the coffee shop. The ones who didn't care if their daughters were tattooed.

"But we're not a tattoo family."

Mom's definition of family has always been us two. Even Ella, as much as Mom loves her, is outside our unit. I'm not sure the unit of two works for me anymore. "You may not be a tattoo *person*, Mom, or a makeup person, but I might be." My voice is thick with tears. "And I can still be your daughter."

"Sloanie, of course you're my daughter. I didn't mean to upset you. I'm sorry. You know I love you. I wish I were there to give you a hug. We'll talk more when I get home, okay? Only four more weeks to go, and we can be together and hash things out and get a plan."

"Sure." But I already have a plan. And it's a plan Mom won't like. After saying goodbye, I go into the bathroom to splash water on my face. As I'm towelling off, I'm struck by a thought that makes me freeze.

Mom is judgmental. She likes me to think she's all accepting and open-minded but she's as judgmental as anyone else. I should know. Because for a long time, her judgments were mine.

—

Lexi comes over for dinner later that night. After eating roast chicken with Dad, Ella, and Kim, we help ourselves to warm apple crisp (hers with ice cream, mine without) and retreat to my bedroom. I'm booting up the computer to show her the final cut of the video when she says, "You heard about Georgina, right?"

"No. What about her?"

She pulls up the vanity stool and sits down. "It's all over Facebook."

Facebook, ugh. "I haven't been on there since Friday." And I don't plan to be anytime soon. I open the menu.

"She got ripped and puked all over the table at this pizza joint last night," Lexi says around a mouthful of crunchy oats. "Somebody took a picture and it's gone viral."

"It sucks to be her." I click on the video file.

"At least they're not talking about you."

Not today. But when I show up at school, they'll be all over me like a bad rash. Just the thought makes me queasy. I boost the volume. "Watch."

My narrative spools out into the bedroom. Having seen it a billion times, I watch almost impassively although the sight of Jade gives me a little heart clutch. When the laughter flash mob appears and I lose my hat, Lexi's eyes widen but she doesn't say anything. After the music fades, she turns to me, brown eyes shining and says, "It's brilliant! I was shocked to see you kept it, but it works."

It more than works. It takes the video to a whole new level.

"Very impressive." Her open admiration makes me want to squirm. Instead I manage to smile and say, "Thanks."

"I can't believe you kept it."

"Yeah, well. Serve the film, right? And the film needed it. I couldn't do a half-assed job. I want that scholarship way too much for that. " Besides, it's way easier showing my bald self to strangers than friends. And maybe it'll give me courage for step two—going back to school. *Maybe.* "Just don't tell anyone, okay? I've asked Fisher to keep quiet about the content too."

"For sure." She dips her spoon into the apple crisp. "I think it's better than the shoe video."

I almost choke on a chunk of apple. "I hope so."

"Bet it was easier doing this one without Breanne's input."

"And without Isaac too. I am so relieved Fisher insisted we each do our own." I poke at the crunchy topping. "There's no way in hell I could've sat down with him after—after what happened."

"He called me," Lexi says.

My breath seizes. Which is totally and completely lame. "How did he get your number?"

"He Facebooked me first. When I didn't answer, he called a pile of other people." She licks ice cream from her spoon. "Eventually he called Miles who gave it to him."

I shove an overly large chunk of dessert into my mouth.

"He wants to talk to you but you won't return his calls or his texts and he's frustrated."

Chew. Swallow. Breathe. Don't think of his *footage.* Seeing myself through Isaac's eyes gave me the courage I needed for the video, but it also left me incredibly uneasy. "I'm sorry but I don't want to talk to him."

"All he wants is five minutes."

I wouldn't know what to say. Right now I don't even know what to *think* of that footage. Ignoring her, I set my bowl down and reach for the large envelope with Mr. Fisher's name on the outside. "Everything's in here. The video, the completed application form, my letter. Fisher needs it by noon tomorrow."

"I'll get it to him first thing," Lexi promises.

I've done the best I can. I put the envelope in her open hand. "Thanks. I appreciate it." I feel lighter already. "Now all I have to do is get through the next two weeks until they announce the scholarship winners."

"What about the camera? Shouldn't I return that too?"

Unease ripples down my spine. Earlier today, Leslie called with an update on Jade. I need to go to the hospital and see her. "I need to do something with it first. I'll see if I can get Kim to drop it off when I'm done." My relationship with Kim feels different now. Since the Gross Reveal at the laughter flash mob when she stood by me and turned her hat sideways and walked me out with my arm through hers, things are somehow easier between us. Or maybe it's me. Maybe I feel easier and freer because Kim felt like a real mom to me that day, supportive and strong.

Lexi tucks the envelope under her arm. "I hope you get the scholarship, Sloane. I really, really do."

"I hope so too." It'll give me something positive to focus on. It'll remind me of who I am on the inside. What I value most. "If I don't get it, I'll try again. I don't care what my parents say. One way or another, I'm going to film school."

She turns to go. "I hope you do. Maybe then you'll stop being so down on yourself."

"For that, I need my hair," I joke. I don't know if it's true. Mostly I'm just trying to be funny.

I expect her to fire back a smart-ass remark, but instead she says, "Maybe. Maybe not."

Irritation prickles the back of my neck. "What's that supposed to mean?"

Lexi glances at the thin paisley scarf I'm wearing before looking into my eyes. "You were down on yourself before you lost your hair, Sloane. You never think you're good enough. That's why you're running from Isaac. That's why you ended up dating a loser like Matt. I kinda doubt if getting your hair back will make any difference."

=

Lexi's words eat at me. Tuesday morning, she texts to say she handed the envelope to Fisher; I text a simple thanks back. She asks how I'm doing but I don't answer.

How *dare* she say what she said? I'm not *running* from anyone. I'm *choosing* not to see Isaac. And confidence? I have plenty of confidence. Or I did until I lost my hair. At least that's what I tell myself. Besides, how would Lexi feel if she lost *her* hair? She might feel strong when she's by herself but still find it hard to face other people too. That afternoon, when I go to the hospital and take the elevator up to Jade's floor, I'm still obsessing over her words.

In the lounge, three nurses stand by the coffee machine helping themselves to fresh cups. After saying hi, I stash my jacket, scarf, and video camera in the locker and pull out my gear, shuffling through the stack of books while they add sugar and cream to their coffee.

I am dawdling. I don't want to take off my hat in front of them. I don't want them to see.

Pretending I have a lash in my eye (the irony doesn't escape me; my lashes are thinning at an alarming rate), I lean into the mirror and check out my new brows. The scabs are gone; the colour is fading slightly. They look good. Normal, almost.

Finally, the nurses leave. I pick up my Miss Cookie wig and take off my hat. My reflection stares back—beautiful brows; sad eyes; a patchy, disgusting mess of pink skin and dark hair.

Every day I lose more hair. Panic squeezes my gut with each lost strand, and I find them everywhere: on my pillow, in the shower, clinging to my hoodie. I should be used to seeing them by now. But I am not. I am not used to any of this. I wonder if I ever will be.

Carefully, as if being gentle will make a difference, I twist up my remaining strands and tuck them under the wig cap. Of course I'd feel better if my hair came back. At the thought of Lexi's words, my anger flares to life. *Of course* I would!

But underneath my anger, a small, hard kernel of truth pokes into my soul and won't leave me alone.

In one way, Lexi is right.

I straighten the wig, adjust one of the fake cookies, and reach for my tube of lip gloss. Until I started losing my hair, I thought I was confident. More than confident. In a lot of ways, I felt I was better than other people. Certainly better than Breanne and her crowd. Better than Kim for sure. Sometimes better than Lexi with her obsession about clothes. Colour floods my cheeks. And often better than Mandee because Mandee is slow and I never am.

But it was false confidence. I was judging others and finding them wanting so I could cover my own fear of not measuring up. And I put a lot of the blame on Kim. The colour spreads to the tips of my ears, races down my neck. What an ugly way to be.

For the next hour, I read to the children who have asked for stories; I tell jokes, and laugh when jokes are told to me. After I put the books away and retrieve the video camera, I check in with Leslie at the nurses' station.

"She knows you're coming," she tells me, her normally cheerful face solemn. "But don't stay long; she doesn't have the energy."

Jade is failing. As I walk down the hall to her room, my stomach falls a little more with each step. Though Leslie didn't come right out and say so, the fact that she called me yesterday is enough. I know they don't expect her to make it.

When I pause in Jade's doorway, my heart does a nasty tango. I've never been around someone who is dying; I don't know what to expect.

The lights are low. Soft music plays from an unseen radio. A purple and pink balloon bouquet floats high in the far corner where Jade can see it. Her parents are there; one sits on the bed, the other on a chair. They aren't crying or anything, just talking softly. My heart slows. Maybe this won't be so bad. Denver looks up and beckons me forward.

"Look who's here to see you," Latanna says when I reach the foot of the bed.

Jade's eyes flutter open, two huge ebony discs in a sharp, gaunt face. "Miss Cookie! I wanted to see your video." Her voice is a barely-there whisper; her words are slurred.

"I know!" My voice, in contrast, almost booms into the room. I dial back my enthusiasm. "Nurse Leslie called so I brought in the camera and we can watch it together." I lift the camera to show her.

"I wanted to be there," Jade says as her mother moves her pillow and rearranges her IV before shifting her to a sitting position. "But I fell asleep."

The drugs make her pronounce it *assheeep*. "Well, Miss Jade, the next time I do a flash mob, you aren't allowed to fall asleep, and you have to be there, okay?"

"'K." Her hospital gown shifts, revealing razor-sharp collar bones. *Oh man.* If Jade loses any more weight, she'll disappear. Averting my gaze, I fiddle with the camera. "Here you go," I say after a minute. "Watch."

Other than a slight smile when the guy walks on his hands, Jade has almost no reaction. *She's only five,* I remind myself. Even if she were healthy and not medicated, she probably wouldn't understand much of what I'm saying. When it ends, she's silent. Her eyelids are so low I wonder if she's dozed off, but then she whispers, "Where's the bad guy?"

Denver and Latanna share a look; Latanna's eyes fill with tears. Oh crap. What have I done? "The bad guy?" I ask.

"Everybody has a bad guy. Every movie has to have a bad guy too."

"Not this one. There isn't any bad guy."

She wrinkles her nose. "That's dumb."

I laugh. "It's not that kind of movie."

"Huh." She shuts her eyes for a minute and this time I'm sure she's dozed off but they fly open again. "My bad guy is cancer," she whispers.

"I know."

"He's not gonna win 'cause the bad guy never wins, you know that, right?"

A lump the size of Nob Hill threatens to cut off my air supply. "Right," I manage. "Bad guys never win."

"Sometimes it looks like they do, but in the end, the good guy always does." She yawns. "I'm tired."

"I know." Legs trembling, I stand. I feel awkward and uncertain. I want to lean down and kiss her forehead but I've never kissed Jade before and though it would probably be okay, it feels too personal and ... too final. I squeeze her fingers instead. "See you later, alligator."

She smiles and I glimpse the real Jade, the bigger, wider, whole version of the sick little girl lying on the bed. I feel at once both weepy and awed. "In a while, crocodile." She shuts her eyes.

Latanna walks me to the door. "Thank you for coming. I know it meant a lot to her and I'm sure it wasn't an easy thing for you to do."

I nod; I don't trust myself to speak. By the time I get into the hall, my eyes are blurred. I'm sure Leslie expects me to stop by the desk and tell her how it went but I don't want to talk. I want to get out of my wig, grab my stuff, and go home.

I want to hold close my memories of Jade and the courage with which she has embraced her life. I want to think about what truly matters and let go of the things that don't.

I want to be alone.

I'll spring for a cab instead of taking the bus, I decide. I can't handle crowds right now. Head down and eyes brimming, I bolt around the corner to the nurses' lounge. And plow into someone coming towards me.

"Sorry," I mumble, stepping sideways. "Excuse me."

A hand reaches out to stop me. "Not so fast."

My head snaps up. Oh my God. Not him. Not *now*.

"We need to talk," Isaac says.

Twenty-One

I make Isaac wait downstairs in the lobby. He makes me promise I will, in fact, come out that way when I'm ready to go, that I won't ditch out another door. The thought crosses my mind, albeit only for a second or two.

You are running from Isaac.

In the lounge, I put away my Miss Cookie wig and take my time layering up in my jacket, scarf, and hat. So maybe Lexi was a little bit right about that too, I silently admit as I reapply lip gloss. But I'm not running today. After seeing Jade I don't have the energy. And I know Isaac. He won't leave me alone until I listen to what he has to say.

When I get off the elevator, he is standing a few feet away, waiting. Those crazy tawny eyes lock with mine. My mouth goes dry. *He sees me. The real me.*

It's a crazy scary thought.

I can't look away. I stare back, thinking of all the labels I have attached to him: Voice Man. Flirt. Mr. Unreliable. Maybe it's time to do an edit. Maybe it's time to reframe this picture.

Dreads swinging, he swoops forward and takes my

elbow, steering me away from the crowd. He reminds me of a panther, black clothes, slick movements, silent intensity.

And panthers are dangerous.

"We need to talk."

"You already said that." He's still holding my elbow and it's making my heart stutter. I ease myself away. He yanks me back.

I stiffen. "I'm not a dog that'll bolt if you let go."

"I don't trust you."

I roll my eyes. "Nice." I brace myself for the chill as he propels me out the main entrance, but the cool air feels good against my flushed cheeks. We turn towards the parking lot. His long leg presses into me; I have to practically run to keep up.

"This gives new meaning to being joined at the hip," I mutter. He doesn't respond, doesn't even crack a smile. After a minute, I relax—as much as I can, considering he's wearing some kind of musky spice cologne that makes me want to both jump him and run away. Honestly, how can *one* guy mess with my head *so much*?

The van comes into view. "I thought we could talk in there," he says.

"We don't need to sit inside. We can talk here." He has parked two spots down from the ticket machine, which isn't ideal in terms of privacy but an audience should keep things superficial. I'm counting on it.

"It's cold." He shoves the key into the driver's door.

He is right. A cold front moved down from Canada over the weekend. "It's not that cold." I lean against the van. It's like an ice cube. I am being a dolt. And I don't know why.

You are running from Isaac. Silently, I address the Lexi in my head. *I'm not running. I am standing still, listening.*

He slams the door. "Fine, we'll talk here." He turns to me. We're so close our breath clouds puff out, mingle, and slowly dissolve in the cool air between us. *What a great tight shot,* I think, ignoring the flutter of desire that ripples through me. I can see it now: soft edges, a slow dissolve. It's sexy as hell.

I expect Isaac to say something but he's looking over my shoulder at the machine. He's waiting for a guy in a blue windbreaker to take his ticket and leave. As soon as he walks off, a woman in stilettos tap-taps her way to the machine.

Silence yawns between us. I shift from one foot to another. At this rate, we could be here an hour. Finally, when the breath thing and the stillness get to be too much, I say, "Thanks for the, um, video you did." *Why did you do it?* "It was good." *Lame, Sloane. Totally lame.* "I mean ... I don't mean of me. Not exactly." *Yes, I mean me exactly.* "But, um, the music. The music was really, really nice." *Nice. What a stupid, empty word.*

"You're welcome." But he's not looking at me. He's still watching the machine.

What does it mean? I want to ask. *How am I supposed to feel? Did you show it to anybody else?* The questions bounce around and around my head. I'm about to pick one when Isaac looks at me and says, "When were you going to tell me?"

He expected me to *tell him?* "Tell you?" My tone is level; I manage not to snap. But my anger starts to simmer.

"Yeah, tell me. Did you think I wouldn't understand? Did you think I'd go around telling everybody else you have cancer?"

He thinks I have cancer. My knees start to tremble. It's a good thing the van is holding me up. *Cancer*. I almost start to laugh. How insane is that? But my relief is immediately tempered by a sobering thought: cancer is easy to understand. It's acceptable. Alopecia isn't.

"I don't have cancer," I tell him as a man and two young kids walk up to the ticket machine. "I have alopecia."

He looks blankly at me. The word means nothing to him.

"It's a hair loss disease." I remember Lexi and Ella. "And it's not life threatening or contagious or anything like that."

"Oh for shit's sake." He slumps against the van. "Is that all?"

I stiffen. "What do you mean, *is that all*?" One of the kids shoots me a nervous look. I lower my voice. "That's enough."

"But it'll grow back, right?"

Here goes. "Maybe. Maybe not. This could be forever." As I say the words, that hard pit of despair lodged in my chest softens a little. It's still there, it'll probably be there as long as my hair isn't, but resistance and denial only makes it worse. I know that now.

Isaac stares at me, his gaze steady and true. "Okay."

The trembling in my knees spreads up my thighs, into my arms. "*Okay?* You know what? I hate the word *okay*. *Nothing* about this is okay."

"Whoa." He holds up a hand. The man at the machine grabs his two kids and hurries them away. "It's just hair," he says.

My hands form fists. I clench my teeth. For a minute I can't speak. But then all the pain and anguish and fear and disgust I've fought to suppress over the last few weeks explodes out of me. "*Just?*" He sounds like my mother and

I hate it. It's all I can do not to pummel his chest in fury. "Hair isn't just decorative; it actually fulfills a role. *And* it's part of our identity. *And* the average woman spends two and a half years of her *life* dealing with it. Did you know that?"

He almost smiles. "So think of all the time you'll save."

My breath hitches. "I can't believe you just said that."

"Come on, Sloane, lighten up."

Trust Isaac to minimize this. "Lighten *up*?"

"Yeah, lighten up. Just when I was starting to think we were possible, I figured out something was wrong. I thought you were sick. I spent all of last week thinking you had cancer. I felt like shit. I felt like we never even had a freaking chance."

Starting to think we were possible? "A chance?"

"Yes, a chance." Exasperation darkens his eyes. "I like you, Sloane. I thought you got that by now."

"You like all the girls and besides—"

"No." He interrupts. "I might flirt with all the girls but you're the one I want."

... the one I want.

A car starts up a dozen rows away. A gull caws in the sky above us. A single hair falls from my head; I'm sure I feel it hit my shoulders. My senses are magnified a thousand times over. How could I not see what Lexi saw? How could I miss it? Even after the video, I didn't get it. Clearly I only see what I want to see.

"And now you tell me you don't have cancer. You aren't going to die." I swear his lower lip is trembling. "You can walk and talk. You can see and hear." I know he's thinking of his little brother. "You aren't *sick* sick."

Not like Jade. And for that, I am extremely, profoundly, ridiculously grateful.

His amber eyes are smoky serious as he laces his fingers through mine. My heart jackhammers in my chest. Isaac and me. We are possible. We do have a chance. I've always felt it. And I've always tried to deny it.

But guys like Isaac? Girls like me? I crash back to reality. Not happening. "I'll be bald, Isaac. Next week. The week after. Soon."

"So. It's not like this will affect how you are in the world."

How can he say that? "Are you *kidding?*"

A muscle twitches in his jaw. "No, I'm not kidding." He glares at me. "It's just freaking hair," he repeats.

Adrenalin surges through me. I drop his hand. Hair matters. Without it, people make judgments. "You don't get it."

"Like hell I don't."

"Right. I'd like to see you lose yours."

"Shave my head."

I snort. "Right."

"I'm serious. Let's do it. Right now."

"You can't shave your head. What about all those PR shots of you around town? With your dreads."

His face is thunderous, splotched with angry colour. "Fuck the photos."

Breath leaves me in a giant whoosh. He *is* serious.

He yanks open the van door. "Let's go. Your place or mine?"

—

Big disasters can start small. It's true. A little hole can sink a big ship. A lone cell can lead to cancer. One lost hair can start a catastrophe that changes your life forever.

And a single slip can reveal a truth you'd rather hide.

But just as laughter can hide pain, disaster can hide opportunities. Not everybody on the *Titanic* died. Not all diseases kill you.

And not every guy who flirts or every girl who wears makeup is shallow.

"It's here somewhere." I'm on my knees digging through the bathroom cupboard for the electric razor Mom uses. She wouldn't have taken it to Africa. No way.

"A straight edge is supposed to be better." Isaac steps over to the claw foot tub and brushes against me; I jump like I've gotten a shock. Maybe coming to the house on Jackson wasn't such a good idea. "There's a pink one here." He has found the disposable I left in the shower caddy before I went to Dad and Kim's. Not even two weeks ago. It feels longer.

"We don't need it." My fingers fold around the plastic case. "I found her electric." I straighten and almost bump into him. We do a nervous two-step and resume our side-by-side position in front of the mirror.

"They say it's better if you do it in the shower." His lips curve; his gold eyes issue a dare. "The hot water opens your pores and follicles and relaxes your scalp muscles."

"I'm already relaxed."

He laughs. "Right."

Palms sweating, I unzip the case and place the razor beside the scissors. I thought it would be good, coming here. I didn't want to go to Isaac's and meet his family. Not now. And I didn't want to go to Dad and Kim's. I wanted privacy.

But this is beyond private, this is intimate. The cramped bathroom, the frilly bathrobe on the back of the door, what we're about to do.

And Isaac. The heat from his body, the scent of his skin, his very essence; it fills this tiny space. Head down, I fiddle with the stuff on the counter: scissors, razor, cream. But really, I am peering out from under the brim of my fedora, studying us in the mirror.

We are side by side, inches away, close. My stomach goes into free fall. And we're going to get closer. *It's impossible to shave your own head,* Isaac told me on the way over. *We need to do each other.*

I look up and stare him straight in the eye. "Are you sure?"

He nods.

If he raised his arm, I would tuck in under his shoulder like a puzzle piece. I would fit. My mouth is suddenly, inexplicably, dry. "This isn't something you can take back. You've got your DJ gigs to think about, those commercials you do. People will talk."

"So what? We'll tell them we did it for Cops for Cancer. And anyway, I don't care what people say."

He doesn't. That is one of Isaac's charms. One of his strengths. A strength he can teach me.

"They're going to say it's a pity move on your part."

He winks. "I feel a lot of things for you, sunshine, but pity isn't one of them."

There's something about his lopsided grin that reaches into my chest and squeezes tight. "I'm not your sunshine." But inside I am melting.

He holds out his hand. "Shut up and hand me the scissors."

"Are you *positive?*" I need to give him one last out.

"Positive."

The sound of snipping fills the bathroom as he hacks at his dreads. He is losing his hair for me. I watch them fall into the sink. *For me.* When the sink begins to fill, I grab the garbage can and toss them away. They are springy beneath my fingers.

"How long have you had them?"

He cuts at a chunk above his ear. "Since my granny died."

"Oh, Isaac." My voice catches. A lump of emotion threatens to swallow me whole.

"She's gone." His eyes meet mine in the mirror. "But you're right here." And my heart turns over.

With his dreads cut away, Isaac's face and the shape of his head become more pronounced. He has gorgeous ears, I realize. Flat pinkish brown shells against creamy brown skin.

"I can't reach the back," he says after a minute. "I need your help."

He sits on the edge of the tub. Pretending I do this all the time, I pick up the scissors and slowly cut away the last few dreads. I love the feel of his hair under my fingers, but I'm also trying to postpone the inevitable. I don't want it to be my turn. "Done." I drop the last dread into the trash.

"Now get the razor."

"Can't you do that yourself?"

"Like I said, it would be easier if you did it."

Hand shaking, I plug in the razor and start at the back, shaving away strips of stubble and bits of dreads. He has a great-looking head, I realize, as his scalp goes from bristly to smooth under my fingers. Perfectly proportioned.

When it's time to do the front, he spins around and

opens his legs. I step between them. Our gazes lock; a shiver races down my spine. My breasts are almost in his face. Skin tingling, I step back. "I need room to see."

The corner of his mouth lifts. "Sure you do."

I work quickly now, hot and bothered and crazy dizzy from the chemistry between us. "Done." Resisting the urge to brush him off, I hand him a towel. "Take a look."

He stands and turns to the mirror, angling his head from one side to the other. "Cool." A slow smile spreads across his face. "Very, very cool." He looks at me. "Now you."

My pulse jumps. "You probably won't need the scissors." I can't meet his gaze. "I don't have a lot of hair left. The razor's probably good enough." My voice is molasses thick; I can hardly breathe.

I don't want to take my hat off in front of him. I really, really don't. I'd rather take off my clothes.

My face flames. Okay, maybe not. But still. I don't want him to see. Not again. Not up close. My heart thunders in my rib cage. It's so loud I'm sure he can hear it. I stare at his T-shirt.

"Sloane?"

"Yeah?" A small clump of hair clings to his shoulder; I brush it away.

"Are you sure about this because it's not something you can take back and people will talk and they'll probably say it's a pity move on your part, you know, because of me and stuff."

A tiny giggle bubbles out of me. Ella will freak. Kim will probably disapprove. Dad won't say much. Mom will say it's just hair. In the end, though, it's up to me to figure out how to deal with this stupid disease. Or not deal with it. Some people will support whatever decisions I make and other people won't. "Shut up, Voice Man. We'll tell them we did it for Cops for Cancer, remember?"

"Right." He touches the curve of my cheek with his thumb. "Cops for Cancer." His hand drops to my waist; he inches me close. My breath stutters at the feel of his body against mine.

And then he kisses me.

His mouth is warm and searching, tender but surprisingly firm, a contradiction just like Isaac himself. I kiss him back, drowning in the scent of his soap and cologne, the faint taste of mint in his mouth. When he reaches up to touch my head, I stiffen and pull away. "No."

"Yes." Before I can move, he kisses me again and this kiss is so consuming my knees buckle and I can't think of anything but him. At some point, somehow, my hat comes off. It doesn't matter; I don't care.

When Isaac finally lifts his head, we're both breathing hard and my stomach is knotted with nerves and desire.

"After that, there's only one thing left to do," he says, his voice a low rumble.

Yes. No. "I don't sleep with guys after the first shave." I'm almost out of breath.

He laughs and drops his arm. The spell is broken.

Come back, I want to say, feeling almost bereft. *Don't look at my head, just come back and let me kiss you again. Let me forget what you're about to do.*

"In that case." He picks up the razor and lifts a brow. Who knew bald guys were so damned hot? "Will it be toilet or tub?"

Squaring my shoulders, I sit on the edge of the bath and

lower my head. I feel both brave and foolish. This is right. This is good. But what if I have an ugly head? What if I look worse than I do now?

Isaac fiddles with the razor. He has the most competent hands of any guy I've seen. Long, tapered fingers; neat, square nails; a sprinkling of black hair on the backs of his knuckles. My heart skips a beat. The hands of a lover.

"Ready?"

"Ready."

He turns on the razor; a soft hum fills the room. The buzz of cold metal hits my scalp. I jump. "You okay?"

"I'm fine," I lie.

My hair starts to fall. I don't notice at first. I'm too focused on the foreign feel of hard steel against cold skin, the rush of wind hitting bare scalp. But after a minute, I realize what I'm seeing and as the dark strands fall to the floor, my tears start. I make no move to brush them away; I let them drop: tiny, salty circles plopping onto the fabric of my jeans, bearing witness to my final sacrifice.

After a while, my hair stops falling but Isaac keeps going, skimming my scalp with the razor, following its path with his fingers, gentle and steady and sure. And then he puts the razor down, picks up the cream, and begins to rub it into my head.

My nerve endings come alive. I take a breath and shut my eyes. It's the most intimate feeling: smooth, warm fingers covered in cool cream gliding over hot skin. Naked skin. Goosebumps pepper my arms as he takes the straight edge to my scalp. It is exquisite torture. It reminds me of our kiss. Of how we were together. How we might be next time. And then he stops.

"You might want to rub some of that off." He hands me a towel.

"Thanks." I dab my head, drop the towel into the tub. He is waiting for me to get up and look in the mirror but I am scared. I feel so exposed.

He pulls me to my feet. My throat threatens to close. I squeeze my hands together, nails pressing into skin, and I stare at the floor. What if this was a mistake? What if Isaac has second thoughts when he sees me without hair?

He lifts my chin so I'm forced to look right at him. "You're beautiful," he says. The heat in his eyes scorches me. "You really are."

I manage a wobbly smile. "You are such a flirt, Voice Man."

He turns me to the mirror. "Look," he says. "It's true." He stands behind me, cradling me with his arms, resting his chin on top of my head. I stare at our image in the mirror. There is no separation; we are one. One body, one smooth, sleek, bald head. Shades of pink and cream and gold and brown. But one.

Overcome with emotion, but not wanting to cry, I shut my eyes. When I open them Isaac is still there, still holding me, still gazing at me with unflappable confidence. And with fire.

He is the sexiest guy I have ever seen. With hair or without. And he likes me. It's still hard to believe. "Thank you." The words are so hollow, but they're all I have. And anyway, no words could ever convey how much this means to me. "Really."

He trails a kiss along my scalp to my ear. I start to tremble.

"About that sleeping together on the first shave thing," he whispers. "Just how set are you on that?"

It is a good thing he is holding me, otherwise I would be a puddle on the floor. "Set."

He groans softly. "I was afraid of that."

I turn and face him. "But hair grows fast." Gently I run two fingers over his clean, sleek scalp. His Adam's apple bobs; I feel a tiny thrill at my power. "I'm pretty sure we'll need to shave again soon."

He smiles slowly, lazily. The gold flecks in his eyes flash. "Maybe next time we can do it in the shower."

"Don't get ahead of yourself, Voice Man."

He laughs.

And right now, with so many unknowns ahead of me, that crazy laugh, and the hope it gives me, is the only thing that matters.

Acknowledgements

Books are generally written in solitude but I'm lucky to have a great deal of support in the wings. Deepest thanks to Fay Melling, Carmen Rogers and Jessa McGregor for sharing their stories and answering so many questions. A big shout out to EC Sheedy, Bonnie Edwards, Vanessa Grant, Gail Whitiker, Alice Valdal and Rachel Goldsworthy for brainstorming help when I was sure I'd dropped the ball. Thanks to Barry, Zachary and Tlell for the love, the laughter, and the clearheaded feedback; I couldn't do this without you guys in my corner. Finally, thanks to my editor, Lynne Missen. Working with you is a privilege and every book you touch is better for it.